AF594689

THE REMEMBERING

SUSAN
SINNOTT

Vagrant
PRESS

Copyright © 2022, Susan Sinnott
Cover artwork: *Blue Reverie* © Carolyne Honey Harrison

All rights reserved. No part of this book may be reproduced, stored in a retrieval system or transmitted in any form or by any means without the prior written permission from the publisher, or, in the case of photocopying or other reprographic copying, permission from Access Copyright, 1 Yonge Street, Suite 1900, Toronto, Ontario M5E 1E5.

Vagrant Press is an imprint of
Nimbus Publishing Limited
3660 Strawberry Hill Street, Halifax, NS, B3K 5A9
(902) 455-4286 nimbus.ca

Printed and bound in Canada
NB1611
Editors: Emily MacKinnon and Claire Bennet
Design: Jenn Embree

The poem on page 232 is "Erosion" by E. J. Pratt.

This story is a work of fiction. Names characters, incidents, and places, including organizations and institutions, are used fictitiously.

Library and Archives Canada Cataloguing in Publication
Title: The remembering / Susan Sinnott.
Names: Sinnott, Susan, author.
Identifiers: Canadiana (print) 20220235910 | Canadiana (ebook) 20220235937 | ISBN 9781774711002 (softcover) | ISBN 9781774711019 (EPUB)
Classification: LCC PS8637.I635 R46 2022 | DDC C813/.6—dc23

Nimbus Publishing acknowledges the financial support for its publishing activities from the Government of Canada, the Canada Council for the Arts, and from the Province of Nova Scotia. We are pleased to work in partnership with the Province of Nova Scotia to develop and promote our creative industries for the benefit of all Nova Scotians.

In memory of Rene, Ken, and Nana

CONTENT NOTE

Please be aware that there are scenes in this book that deal with a past sexual assault. Take care as you read.

PART ONE

CHAPTER ONE

1993

LIZ

IT WAS RAINING THE MONDAY I FOUND OUT ABOUT EVE. Bad news always arrived with bad weather. The traffic hissed and growled—everyone driving too fast as if trying to reach Friday sooner.

I checked on Eve and Michel's house each day after they went to Mexico, and there was nothing untoward until the Monday afternoon, a full week before they were due home. The house was a blur through the deluge, but I could see a light on in the kitchen and I stood on the brakes in a panic and parked too far from the curb with the tail sticking out, in a way you would have condemned. I saw movement through the living room window and realized it was Michel, walking up and down, talking on the phone. I rang the bell and waited, rang again. I had lifted my hand to knock when he opened the door.

"Oh," he said. "We..." Michel glanced back over his shoulder then stood looking at me, without his usual smile. Finally, he opened the door fully and stepped aside. "We're...early."

"Sorry. Just making sure.... I'll come back."

"No! No, Liz. Please. Come in."

I squeezed past two suitcases in the hall, stepped over a carry-on bag, and stopped dead in the doorway of the living room when I saw Eve, crouched on the edge of the nearest chair—that antique Victorian chair which was so uncomfortable they joked about only offering it to unwanted visitors. Jacket and purse lay at her feet. She was curled up in a ball, hugging herself, thumbs scraping over and back, over and back on her shoulders. She did not look up or say hello.

"Eve! Whatever's the matter?"

Silence.

I walked over and knelt beside her, wobbling a little when I put weight on that knee, shifting off the sore spot. I put an arm round her but there was no response; Eve still coiled up tight, taking quick shallow breaths.

"What happened?"

Silence.

I looked over at Michel, but he was watching Eve with his lips squeezed together and such a look of pain on his face that fear billowed up inside of me. Someone was hurt, sick, dead? Eve started rocking back and forth and I was rocked with her, sideways, awkward on my knees. She took a breath and tried to say something but couldn't get it out and rocked faster, shaking her head.

"I can't hear, dear."

Silence.

"Say that again. Please."

The rocking sped up, and the quivering and keening. Was she sick? No. Somebody else? No. Was there an accident? Her body spasmed and her voice came out in a croak, hard and bitter: "It was no accident."

Oh, god. Mugged? A holdup? For god's sake…talk to me… not leaving until you tell me…. Possibilities screamed round my brain. What, what, what?

I stroked her hair, tucked a wisp behind her ear, and whispered, "Tell me."

Then there was a tiny pause, a void, like a deep cut that stays blanched for a second in shock before pinpricks of red appear and coalesce and the blood gathers itself together and gushes out.

"Eve. Were you raped?"

Eve was nodding into my shoulder, sobbing and nodding. "They hurt me, Mom."

They. I realized I was holding my breath and my vision had blurred, black specks everywhere. My little girl. My Eve. The sweetest natured, the most vulnerable of them all. How could this happen? How could Michel let this happen? I looked up at him and saw he was waiting for this question, looking agonized. I managed not to say it, burying my face in Eve's shoulder and hugging her with both arms, hugging whatever I could reach. What seemed like ages later I said she had to see her doctor.

"I saw one. In Mexico., after it happened. Three days ago."

"You need to see your own doctor."

"No."

"I've made an appointment," Michel said. "Last in the day."

"No."

I said she needed to check. Blood tests. Antibiotics worked best if taken right away.

"I'll get the blood work. But the doctor's not touching me. Nobody's touching me."

Eve's troubles tormented me all night. Gone was the torpor of the past months. A spiderweb had been on the ceiling forever: one long thread from the round base of the light fixture out to some spidery landmark my eyes couldn't see, remnants of cross threads floating from it, slack and lazy. I only noticed it lying down. That night I heaved myself out of bed, fetched a broom from the kitchen, and swept it away.

Since the funeral, my three daughters had tried to help. Ginny knew what was needed, but she was always a few steps ahead of what I was ready to try.

"Mom, I'll come and help you go through Dad's things." Bracing.

"That'll be nice, dear. Later." A smile and a pat on the arm to soften the offence, but it was an effort to do even that.

And again, just last week, she had arrived at my door. "Got some boxes and bags, all ready to roll."

"Not yet, Ginny. Not today. Come and have a cup of tea instead." My panacea, that tea: something to keep visitors off my back, an excuse, an escape. It used to be a reward.

Caroline—Carlie—was away for months at a time doing her anthropology thing, in a desert or a rainforest or the Outer Something Islands, some faraway place where letters she sent didn't arrive until after she came home. Remember how you had maps of her latest adventure spread everywhere, marked with crosses and circles, annotations in the corners? Born academics, the pair of you. After you'd gone, Carlie's being home was a welcome distraction, shaking me out of my folds and creases, filling the silence with her recordings of local languages or strange musical instruments or bird squawks, saying, *Imagine hearing this at dawn.* But then she was off again, and I was just as glad to sink back into my rumpled humdrum life.

It was Eve who hit the spot. My baby. I would wander round the house unaware of time then realize I was hungry and there would be a yellow Post-It on the fridge with Eve's handwriting saying, *chili blue container, beef stew round green.* Eve being in the house filled the emptiness without imposing expectations or triggering anything seismic. She would sit in the corner of the couch, not saying a word, legs tucked up under her in a way that would have Ginny growling about damage to her knee joints. Just having her there was soothing.

I always said the girls fit their careers perfectly, all three, but privately I thought Eve and clinical psychology were the best fit of all. She was such a good listener, a born listener. All through high school she would be hidden away in whatever private spot she could find in the house while some girl poured out her woes into Eve's ear. Now and then I would ask about it.

"Margie alright?"

"She'll be fine."

"That tall guy with the loud voice?"

"Mmmm."

"Hope you gave her good advice."

"God, Mom, I just listened. Margie saying it out loud, laying it all out, just made her see things better, that's all. She'll make up her own mind."

I could never have said that as a teenager. I would have been bursting with bad advice, full of silly romantic ideas. Where did all that wisdom come from?

Remember when Eve first came home from Montréal with her doctorate? She joined a loose partnership with those other two psychologists, sharing rent and utilities. Not sure you ever saw her workplace—you were in hospital for our guided tour. It was in one of those big old houses on LeMarchant Road, converted into clinics and offices, on the side overlooking the harbour. Eve didn't want "intimidating." Her own squatty brown office was on the ground floor at the end of a dingy linoleum corridor, but she had painted the insides in soft greens and creams with a touch of amber, saying unpretentious did not have to be ugly. It was like being inside a daffodil.

Eve went back to work as planned the Monday after they came home, but when I let myself into their house late that afternoon, she was sitting on the porch floor, half out of her jacket, blank-eyed and limp. I aimed my voice somewhere between sympathy and cheerfulness, saying, "Rough time?" She drifted into the living room and curled up on the couch with an arm over her face and I sat opposite, wondering what to say.

"A client's going to tell me she was…was…what happened to me." Her voice was muffled and I had to lean close to hear. "Must get used to saying the word, de-sensitize myself." But she didn't say it. She was concerned that the young woman was working up the courage to tell her everything—the next visit or the one after. Eve sat up then and I was shocked at her hollow cheeks, the strain lines by her mouth and the shadowed eyes. "I can't do it, Mom, can't help her. All day replays of… of Mexico have been going through my head, over and over." She was afraid she would not be able to hang onto herself if the client really did tell her about being…again, the avoidance of that word. She sagged back on the couch.

This was not the real Eve, so helpless and hopeless. I tried to keep my voice brisk, but it wanted to wobble. Who was the best person to take over for her? Eve would only consider one therapist, and she'd have a waiting list a mile long. That was the trouble. And there were other clients with similar issues…so hard to gain someone's trust…put them back months….

All I could offer was my presence and a sympathetic silence. We stayed there quietly and I must have nodded off because I awoke with a start. "Oh, my. It's almost dinnertime. Brought some chicken breasts for your supper…in the porch all this time…should have put them in the fridge." I headed for the door saying I would take off now—Michel would be home soon—but Eve straightened up immediately and asked me to stay and eat with them. Please?

So I stayed, and Michel and I organized the food and carried on a laboured conversation about Bill Clinton's planned health reforms while Eve stared at her plate. "Your mom's chicken is excellent, dearest," Michel said. "Try some before it goes cold."

No response.

I cleared my throat in a pointed way and Eve flinched and looked up, eyes startled, and I gentled my voice. "Yes, eat some dinner, dear."

But Eve could not eat, whispered *Excuse me* and headed upstairs and did not come back. And that was just the first time.

I started wearing noisier shoes around their house so Eve would hear me on the hardwood floors. She reminded me of Rusty—a horse on Fred Morgan's farm when I was little—only without the kicking part. He would lash out at anyone who came up behind. You had to introduce yourself to Rusty—walk round in front in a big circle and talk softly, with your palm out flat. Some of the boys would try sneaking up to see how close they could get but Rusty would roll his eyes and dance sideways and his kicking muscles would bunch up ready.

"What's going on with Eve and Michel?"

We were having takeout pizza for Saturday lunch at Ginny's, two weeks after the return from Mexico, one week after Carlie's arrival from Senegal. Eve and Michel had pulled out, saying Eve had a migraine.

Lunch had been...boisterous. Young Jeremy was grounded and not taking his punishment graciously, shouting at his father, "But I *promised* them! You're making me break a promise!"

Carlie asked what he'd done, and Ginny paused in the middle of telling her daughter to go clean up her room, saying, "You don't want to know. He was bored. He had twenty minutes between events with nothing to do so...." She glared at Carlie then laughed in an unconvincing way. "Well, like his aunt, when he's bored, he gets creative."

"So now it's my fault?"

I did not trust the grin on Carlie's face and said, "Carlie, be soothing."

Ginny refilled our cups and Carlie made purring noises. Remember all the coffee she would drink whenever she was first home? Always complaining about the stuff they drank in Senegal: some kind of instant flooded with milk.

"So. Eve and Michel." Ginny put her cup down in a solid, definitive way and I temporized—whatever did she mean?

"We aren't stupid, Mom. They hardly look at each other anymore and Eve sits in that awful chair by the door. They used to sit next to each other on the couch and—"

"They don't touch at all," Caroline said. "Used to be always standing close, sitting close, smiling sloppy smiles at each other. Nauseating, really."

Ginny shot Carlie an irritated look. "They talk to us, but not to each other."

"It's like bouncing things off a satellite: you to me to Ginny to me to you to me." Carlie was pointing her finger to demonstrate, said she suspected Eve and Michel didn't talk at all when nobody else was around.

"And we know that *you* know what's going on," said Ginny. She and Carlie turned their thousand-kilowatt stares on me and waited. I said Eve would not have told me either if I had not arrived just as they got home and Ginny pounced on that, saying yes, it happened in Cancún, didn't it? I noticed my hands clutching each other and stilled them, spread them on my knees, loosened the knuckles.

After a moment Carlie said quietly, "Was Eve attacked?"

Ginny looked shocked and opened her mouth but closed it again.

Carlie just kept looking at me, and when I didn't answer and the silence had gone on for ages she said, "Mom. Was Eve raped?"

Ginny hissed air in through her teeth, but Carlie said it was the only thing she could think of that fit all known facts and observations.

I still did not answer, but by then I didn't need to.

Later, they wanted to know what was done to track down the men. Michel had said resort security and local police lost interest as soon as they found out the men were foreigners, speaking German, though Eve wasn't even sure it was actual German. Dutch maybe? And she had not seen their faces. They were told there were multiple flights to and from Europe every day and it was impossible to find them. They checked the hotel register, of course, but the only German-speaking guests were a group of seniors. And anyone could access the beach from along the shore. Anyone.

The girls told Eve they had guessed. That you couldn't keep something awful like that a secret from family, and Carlie threw in the castration she would carry out on those creeps, given the chance. They said they loved her and if there was anything they could do they would do it. Eve smiled a stiff smile and let them hug her, but when Ginny told her sister she was still the same person, Eve turned away and started talking about her car needing new summer tires.

Nothing more was said except once, weeks later, by Carlie, who said there had been enough pussyfooting and was Eve aware of the risk of false negatives with those urine pregnancy tests? Maybe she should take another one to be sure. (You know Carlie.) Then Eve was all upset and said yes, of course she was aware, and she knew they were trying to help but she wished they wouldn't.

I gave Eve a hug as I left one day and realized it had been a long time since the last one. She seemed to melt away at hug times, busy fetching my coat or having her arms full of laundry. How bony she had become round the shoulders. "You should take up yoga again, dear." I said, "You're losing your shape." It was not obvious because she was always covered up that summer: pants rather than dresses in spite of all the hot weather, shirts with long sleeves—still elegant and fashionable but.... And even you would have noticed her new haircut, George, with bangs and hair hanging loose over half her face. And her face had those hollows and shadows you get when you haven't slept. Eve admitted to being up in the night, said she had moved into the other room so she would not keep Michel awake with her thrashing around. *No point in both of us being zombies the next day.*

They were all striking, our girls, but Eve was beautiful. Now I wondered if part of that beauty had been her serenity, and would she ever get it back? Ever since Mexico, Michel had looked sideways at Eve with such a look of yearning on his face. It made me think of those novels by Thomas Hardy—I always thought of those as the "if only" books. If only that letter had not gone under the mat; if only the dog had not chased all the sheep off that cliff. If only Mexico hadn't happened. Eve hardly looked at Michel, or at any of us for that matter. She seemed to look beyond people, through them. You had to say her name to make sure she had heard and if you touched her arm or spoke loudly to bring her back, she startled and stepped away. So I began tacking her name onto the front of every sentence.

Eve announced she would be closing her practice for eight months, the time left on the current lease. (She hoped she would need less time, but she did not want her clients to hang around waiting.) I offered to help pay the office rent but neither Eve nor Michel would hear of it.

After that, Eve barely left the house. We persuaded her to go to a surprise birthday party in September for an old school friend, but she came home without going in because the only parking space was a block away, under some trees where the street light was out. In her own house she stayed in her room more and more. On bad days she ate nothing, said nothing, did nothing.

For weeks I went over every other day, afraid that if I didn't, Eve would make even less of an effort, then afraid that maybe I was fussing. Michel thought it helped, so I kept going. I worried about Eve's deteriorating health, physical and mental, and that the gap between Eve and Michel was growing wider. Once I asked if those *female things* were back to normal and Eve stopped in the middle of shaking out a sweatshirt of Michel's, rested it back down on the laundry basket, and said, "Mom, nothing is back to normal."

I wish you were here, George. I know you'd leave all this to me, but your just being here....

Ginny phoned me twice in one day, insisting I do it, saying Eve would not listen to a sister, and really there was nobody else. So I dropped in before supper, before Michel was home. There was Eve, standing in a pool of sunlight, ironing her beige pants with long, slow sweeps. It was a good day, a good time.

"Eve, it might be an idea to see your doctor, get some help to pull you out of this hole you're in." So many hours of thought to produce such a weak, banal statement!

"I'm fine."

"You're not fine. You know you're not fine. What would you tell a patient who presented this way?"

"Client, not patient."

"And that's a perfect example of avoidance behaviour if ever I heard one. Client indeed. You're feeling awful and you're getting worse. Everyone can see it but you." I recommended she go see her Dr. Clarke, who already knew what had happened so would not need an explanation. "Just tell her you aren't managing."

"I am managing, Mom. Leave me alone."

I kept insisting. She was collapsing inside and ignoring it. It was time she did something. I half expected her to march out of the room, but the iron just thumped harder and moved faster, until Eve said in a sharp voice, "Mom! Mind your own business."

"I'll set Ginny on you if you're not careful." I tried a smile, but Eve was not in the mood for cute comments and glared at me with a tight face. But at least she was still there. I would have followed her right into that bedroom if she had taken off. Eve's eyes were disappearing inside the scowl, but I barrelled on, saying psychologists were allowed to have problems too.

"Thank you, Nurse, for the psych lecture."

I offered to make an appointment.

"I can make my own appointments, Mom. When I want them." But ten days later Eve said I would be pleased to know she had talked to Dr. Clarke. "And don't say another word."

CHAPTER TWO

1993

LIZ

THEN CAME THE DAY EVE FOUND OUT SHE WAS PREGNANT.

She was frantic, blundering up and down the living room, still with her jacket on, banging into the corner of the chair, knocking a book off the end table, not noticing. "They won't take it out. She says it's too late to take it out. Says I have to go to term and have that, that…thing, to let it be born in the normal way then give it up for adoption." Eve collapsed onto the big chair, head and arms dropping back into it. Then moments later she bounced out again and charged off down the room. "As if anybody would possibly want it." That was a whisper. She stopped dead at the wall, looking surprised to see it there. "No, no, no. I have to get rid of it. Now. I won't walk round with that thing inside me, that lump of…of Them."

Michel was motionless in his chair, white-faced. I pushed myself up from the sofa and tried to slide the jacket off Eve's shoulders just to break the spell, but she shrugged it back up, hugged it round herself, kept moving. "Have to get rid of it." She charged out and I could hear her in the bathroom, rattling bottles in the medicine cabinet, so I rushed in after her, pulled Eve's arm away, and slammed the cabinet door, saying it was only two months, she could get through two months; she was strong. And after a moment Eve turned and walked back to the living room, saying there was nothing of any use in there anyway.

"Are you sure?" Michel's voice sounded squeezed. "About there being a…a baby?"

But Eve had seen it on an ultrasound, heard a heartbeat. Her voice was flat. She shuddered and went back to pacing but in a more steady, methodical way. "Dr. Clarke says there should be no problems after the birth; I won't need to do anything. Social workers at the hospital will sort out adoption arrangements. That kind of thing."

She stopped pacing suddenly; everything clenched tight, and she whispered something about people knowing. About it being nobody's business but hers. I glanced at Michel but he did not react. Then she said more clearly, "I can't have it here. A nurse in the delivery room will recognize me…somebody will. You know how it is in St. John's."

Michel stood up and moved towards her, but Eve set off walking again and he stopped abruptly with his hands out. "We can arrange to—for it all to happen in Montréal," he said. "Maybe Dr. Clarke can contact somebody there." He backed up to his chair and lowered himself down like an old man.

Whenever she was not active in the kitchen or out buying groceries, Eve disappeared into her room—still the spare room, not the one she used to share with Michel. I tried brief encounters through the door. *You okay? Yes. Need anything? No. You can't stay in there all day.* Silence. Once, I started telling her through the door about Jeremy's latest escapade, but when I paused at a place where you would expect a laugh, a comment, something—there was nothing. I left the story unfinished, stood in the kitchen for ages staring at the wall and went home without saying goodbye. Really, she had to start pulling herself together, but maybe that wouldn't happen until after the baby was gone.

Eve did not acknowledge the pregnancy in any way. She appeared to have gained a little weight but never did look pregnant, even at full term. She wore her longer jackets and looser tops, and may have bought pants a size larger, but made no other concession. She did make another appointment with Dr. Clarke. She did allow me to tell Ginny and Caroline, but said it was not up for discussion and we were absolutely not to tell anyone else.

Caroline wrote Ginny from West Africa, saying, *How could she not have known,* then complained about information overload when Ginny sent details.

Christmas felt artificial. Remember how you used to take the children into the woods every year? You would cut the best fir tree you could find close to a trail, towing it out on the sled if there was snow, drag-carrying it if not, which was messier—lumps of ice and moss and undergrowth all over the car and half the house. You always loved the tree business. That year I just arranged holly from the garden, poinsettias from the supermarket, and cards, of course, on every surface. I hardly sent any myself. Ginny's children kept the season from being derailed completely and the festivities were all held at their house.

I made Christmas puddings, a light Christmas cake and a rum-soaked dark one, just for something to occupy my hands. I froze the remnants, and we were still eating them in August. I spent a whole day measuring and chopping—such an unwieldy bowlful. My stirring arm ached for a week. My upper body strength was sadly lacking so I hunted down those weights, the little pink dumbbells that had caused such hilarity in the family. *You'll work up a real sweat with those, Mom.*

Everyone I knew disappeared round the bay or out of the province. My siblings had long since stopped visiting at Christmas—storms, cancelled flights, lost luggage, high-season prices. The last time we were all together was at your funeral, which was not...not the same. This Christmas, Michel flew home alone to visit his parents in Montréal, just for the weekend. The Simard family would have top-of-the-line cakes, no doubt, made to order and looking magnificent on those Limoges plates with the fancy silver cake forks, *Florentine, Elisabeth.* My cakes would taste better.

The baby was due on January nineteenth, so Eve planned to fly down soon after the New Year in case it came early. She said there was no reason for Michel to take so much time off work just to hang around, so he made a reservation for the fifteenth. It is dangerous to fly in the third trimester—the water can break with the change in pressure—which was why I, in my nursing hat, insisted on going with her. We took the only direct flight from St. John's at five o'clock on a black, dismal, freezing-fog morning. It was much colder in Montréal.

We rented an apartment near the Royal Victoria Hospital. We did not contact the Family Simard. There were a few pleasant days before the weather broke and we spent them checking out art galleries, sampling restaurants, and browsing stores we didn't have at home—like Simons and Eaton's and The Bay—having ourselves a little holiday. It would have been fun to shop for baby clothes. We took regular coffee-slash-rest breaks, but they were more for my benefit. Eve waved away my questions about her own possible aches with the usual *I'm fine.* But she talked more than she had in the previous six months, about art and books and French fashions, reminiscing about people and events from her student years.

She stopped on a corner near her old apartment block and exclaimed at a hole in the sidewalk, said it had to be the same hole the city dug years ago. They had put cones and orange mesh stuff round it and never come back. "It's still here. Four years later and it's still here!" There must have been a billion orange-and-white cones scattered across the city like Halloween streamers. An enterprising craft shop on St. Catherine had a display of imitation cone salt-and-pepper shakers. There was a Gallic shrug in that—some tongue-in-cheek Québécois making the most of it. Eve bought a set just for fun. Finally, she was doing something just for fun.

There was one incident outside the Musée des beaux-arts, when three men swooped past us into the entrance, all talking over each other and laughing in a male version of the Wallace supper table. Eve froze. Her face drained of colour and she swayed and clutched my arm, sagging against me so I had trouble keeping us both upright. The men were talking in something Germanic. My only exposure to German was from television, and I just had an impression of a growly language full of *schkug*, *floof*, and *hawk* noises—a masculine-sounding language, heavy on the palate. In Montréal, foreign languages roared round you all the time, so I hadn't noted those particular voices until Eve reacted. I recalled a burst of laughter then, amongst the words, the kind of overpowering laugh that drowns out everything else. Dominating.

We stood on the sidewalk for ages before Eve was able to move, with the wind dancing the end of her soft wool scarf across our two faces, and me being slowly compressed so my back started to complain, and my knees. The traffic hissed and growled, and that feeling of dread crept over me as it had on the day I found out. That was what Eve must feel with every flashback, only so much worse. Eventually we went back inside, and I called a cab, Eve's grip vice-like on my arm and her eyes still dilated, but by the time the cab came she had regained her colour and was steadier on her feet.

"Ready?" I said, but she did not respond.

There were no ill effects from the flight—no immediate ones, anyway—but the baby did come early. It arrived in a hurry at four in the afternoon on Sunday, the fourteenth of January, after Michel had changed his flight and while he was still pacing around the airport in Halifax, waiting for his connection.

Not an *It*, a *She.*

The birth was fast. The staff kept commenting on how easy it was, especially for a firstborn. *This one's in a hurry to get here.* After a while, a nurse laid a bundle in Eve's arms, with care but with that brisk manner that did not allow for argument. *Here you are. A little girl.* Then she busied herself at a cupboard across the room. Eve had her eyes closed and was taken unawares, and it all happened so fast there was no time to object. I was in the delivery room at Eve's request, standing by Eve's head out of the way, as instructed. I would have taken the baby, but the nurse was not looking my way, and maybe she would not have given her to me anyway; I was just an appendage here. So, there was Eve and the result of her rape—two victims, looking at each other. I moved closer, on alert, not knowing what would happen next.

And nothing happened. Nothing visible. The baby lay swaddled in hospital white, with faded pink giraffes striding stiff-legged up and down the folds. She was not crying and her eyes were wide open, unusual so soon after birth, and I could see the fixed blue stare taking everything in. Wallace eyes. There was a suggestion of pale, damp Wallace hair under the little hat and a bow-shaped mouth just like Eve's. She was Eve all over again. And Eve just looked down into the little face with the same unblinking stare. The usual competent bustle of clearing up after a delivery was going on around them: murmurs and water running and the squeaking of rubber soles, rubber wheels on gurneys, but there was a silence around mother and baby, a stillness. Then very slowly Eve touched a finger to the baby's cheek and smiled.

Heavens. Don't tell me....

Everything inside me clenched. "Don't get too attached if you're going to give her up." But there was no reply and the next minute an aide was whisking Eve out of the delivery room in a wheelchair and along miles of corridor, with me scampering along behind. I started to say, "Eve, don't..." but they were too far ahead and nobody was listening to me. *Not my business,* I told myself. *None of my business.* But new mothers are all hormones and emotions after a birth and Michel was not there to balance them. This was not a decision to be made in a hurry.

I sat back in a chair in the corner while the aide organized everything. The room was painted in pastel colours with animal decals on the far wall, but it was not like the room I remembered from my own deliveries: flowers everywhere, balloons tied to the bed rail, cards crammed onto the bedside table and along the narrow window ledges, falling off with the slightest draft. But finally, when I could see Eve without the aide bustling about, she was gazing at the baby with that look of total wonder and delight—the magical glow of new motherhood.

"She's a Wallace," Eve said. "She's family: like you and Carlie and Ginny. Like me. I can't just give her away." And looking down at the sleeping baby, I had to agree. She pulled at your heart. She deserved a life too, and love. Born of such an evil act but so innocent, so tranquil, with a face that was only of Eve. And out there in the world, who would adopt a child of rape? Would they tell prospective parents what she was? If some unknown, tentative parents out there changed their minds, would the baby end up as a ward of state, shuttled around from foster home to foster home?

Eventually I said, "But how will Michel feel?"

"He'll come around. Maybe he'll come around." Eve was looking beyond the room, eyes unfocused, but her jaw was focused. "Anyway, I'm keeping her."

My heart lurched. We took such care not to interfere in the girls' adult lives. *We'll be there for you always. You know that. But we won't butt in.*

"I just want to make sure you've considered every angle before you make a decision which..." I said each word with care, picking amongst thoughts for the best way to put it. "...which will have such a huge effect on your future and on Michel's."

"And on Rosie's."

Rosie? Oh. "When...when did you decide on a name?"

"As soon as I saw her in the delivery room." Eve was smiling. "She's so perfect, like a little rosebud, cheeks shading from cream to pink like petals, and as soft as petals. Rosie."

So that was that.

The baby deserved a home, yes, but I was thinking of Michel, that this would be the end. I tried to think *maybe.* Maybe it would not be the end. Maybe he would accept the baby. But my gut was dropping and dropping, leaving a negative space full of instinct that said *No.* Michel was someone who had to like a person, approve of them, before he could love them—head before heart. *A different man would have room in his heart.... Ben would have room.... Dear Ben.* It was a fleeting regret, banished immediately. Almost immediately. What to say? How to mitigate? I rejected my first few thoughts. "Maybe," I hesitated. "Maybe Michel will want to pick out a middle name?"

Silence.

"Maybe something French?"

Silence.

I tried to tread gently. "Michel needs to be involved too, Eve. You're...in this together. He should have a say in...should have a choice in your plans for the future. What will you say when he arrives?"

"I'll tell him what I told you, what I will tell the social worker. I'm keeping her."

I leaned forward in the chair and pleaded with her to give her husband more time and not to present an ultimatum the minute he walked in the door. They were a couple. Big decisions should be shared decisions. "Good god, Eve. You're a psychologist. You know better than that. Tell him you *want* to keep her. Give him time to get used to the idea."

I was getting angry, and that never worked with Eve.

I smoothed my voice, my thoughts. Somewhat. I said he would be expecting Eve to have given up the baby and would be looking forward to getting her back again. She had been locking herself away ever since she found out she was pregnant—ever since Mexico—and he would be hoping... My heart was dropping again.

"Eve, do you *want* him back?"

(It was a question that had to be asked, George. It had to be faced, and I was not sure if Eve had asked it herself.)

The silence that followed weighed me down. There was a slither of snow from a roof above and a *thump* as it landed somewhere below. A drip was gathering at the end of an icicle outside the window, and I watched as it slowly filled, lengthened....

"I don't know," Eve said eventually. "Yes." She turned to me, went up on one elbow and flopped back again. "I can't forget his face when he first found me—the disgust. Revulsion. Rejection. He turned his loathing on those men, but it was too late. He kept telling me how much he loved me. But I remember his first reaction. How he really felt."

I leaned over and gave her an awkward hug, entangled with bedding, saying how we don't always think straight when faced with something so unexpected, so awful—none of us do, and he would have been revolted by what had happened, not by Eve herself. Anyway, those kinds of reactions were just in the heat of the moment. Now he was back to the real Michel. I straightened and took a deep breath.

"You coped with the delivery so well. I was afraid it might trigger bad memories."

Eve said *No*. It had helped. She was pushing everything out. She had been in charge and was getting rid of... "Of them." Eve looked down at the infant asleep in the bassinet. "And now it's entirely my own decision to keep Rosie."

I looked at the baby, too, scooped her up, and held her close. Pure delight. If only Michel could feel like this. If only he and Eve could love each other enough to overcome...to become a family. What kind of home would they make for this child? I laid the baby down again and sank back in the chair. Eve's head was turned away a little and her eyes were closed, and I could not tell if she was sleeping or avoiding.

It was late by the time Michel appeared, pulling a black carry-on, pausing in the doorway of Eve's room with snow melting on his hair and shoulders. An aide hovered behind him, so enthusiastic, *Oh, monsieur, tous les deux sont trop belles, trop belles.* I had been dozing and the baby stirred in the bassinet, then was still again. A vase of pink and white roses glowed on the bedside table. I had found them in the hospital gift shop: pink for grace, happiness, gentleness, so the woman in the gift shop said; white for purity and innocence.

I was tucked away in the padded armchair in a shadowy corner. I had switched off the big fluorescent light, leaving a softer light shining on the pillows and bedding, picking out the two pink and white faces. Eve was awake and her face was...calm. Calmer than it had been for months. Michel came a few steps into the room looking only at Eve, then his eyes swung to the bassinet in the corner and he stopped dead. Eve said, "She's all Wallace, Michel. She's like Mom, my sisters, me. She's a beautiful, innocent little girl. I'd like to keep her." She reached her hand out towards him. "Will you...consider it?"

Michel said nothing, and the only movement in the room was a brief quiver of air through the ferns around the roses; the only sound was the aide's heel-thumps fading down the corridor. After a while Michel walked over to the bed and stood looking down at Eve, at her outstretched hand, and finally he took it, first with one hand then with both, and stood holding it.

"I was hoping we could start again. You and me. Try to get back what we had."

"Yes," she said with a tiny nod.

"I don't know if we can with..." He turned his shoulders toward the baby a little, without really looking at her.

"I don't think I can give her up." They stayed motionless, gazing at each other.

"So. I either learn to live with it, or...?" Michel let go of her hand and stepped back, looking around for somewhere to sit and saw me. "Oh!"

"I'm sorry. I should have...I didn't mean..." I heaved myself out of the chair, embarrassed and breathless and faint. I swayed and grabbed Michel's arm and it felt stiff and unhelpful, but he reached for me when I staggered a little as I made for the door—not a good time to be feeling dizzy. It was an effort to straighten up and look normal, to open the door with decision, to crisp up my voice. "I'll be back in the morning."

I had to lean against the wall in the hallway to regain my composure, to remember the apartment address so I could phone for a taxi. Michel would be staying—they accommodated husbands at the hospital for that first night.

Thoughts of what to do next churned through my head all night, but of course the decision was out of my hands. After breakfast I stood outside Eve's room, gathering my forces, and a nurse came out bustling and beaming, saying something about *la grand-mère* and that they were waiting for me. *They* were Eve and the baby. Michel was missing.

"He's gone to see his parents for an hour or so," Eve said. That was unfortunate. That was a disaster. The Simards would have their claws in him now. How I disliked that family, so arrogant and belittling. I had liked the father—there was something of Michel in his father—and I know you had some good conversations with him, George. But the mother was always so condescending, patronizing, as if she expected one of us to wipe a nose on a sleeve. And the uncles' wives were worse. At the wedding I was in constant fear of Carlie succumbing to her desire to shock, such as telling the Simards how impressed she was with their indoor plumbing, *although the Wallace outhouse is a real nice one.* I could see it happening. I kept reminding Carlie that this was Eve's special occasion, think of Eve, restrain yourself. And Carlie said of course she would, she was not a complete moron.

I suppose I ought to have been grateful the Family Simard accepted Eve herself, although why would they not? She was the kind of daughter-in-law anyone would be proud of. Before the wedding, I thought the family very kind in offering to help organize the ceremony in Montréal, *when M. Wallace is going through such trying times with his health.* Eve wanted the ceremony upalong because all their mutual friends were in Montréal or Ottawa or Toronto. It seemed appropriate. Later, I suspected that no way would the Simard family have stooped to attend the wedding of their only child in Newfoundland. And back then the Meech Lake Accord (discord, really) had added a layer of political antagonism between the two provinces, back at the time of the wedding. But still.

I should have been listening. "…and I may be discharged today, and we'll stay in the apartment until Michel can get tickets to take us home." Eve sounded pleased, and I felt encouraged for a moment, but concerned, too.

"Isn't that a bit soon? Is the baby nursing alright, latching on alright?" And getting home needed some planning. The apartment could accommodate all of us, but they probably wanted to be on their own, so, reluctantly… "I can try and fly out today? What do you think?"

Eve nodded. Well, of course she did. "Yes, Mom," she said. "You've been a marvel. I can't thank you enough. But there's nothing more you can do here. You go on home."

I sat for a moment, gathering my thoughts. The baby would need more than just diapers for the trip home. I headed straight to the nearest store that sold baby gear, cutting across to University Avenue from the Vic, then down the hill and along St. Catherine, enjoying the thrum of the city one last time. I bought basic supplies, all except the car seat. Michel could deal with the car seat. The cold made the bridge of my nose hurt, so it must have been at least ten below, but it was calm and bright and the sidewalks were clear of snow. The walk did me good. I took a taxi back up the hill with all my packages and unloaded them onto Eve's hospital bed. Michel was back, but on the phone with the airlines.

First was the bunting bag. I looked for an elegant French design—this was Québec after all—but the only ones around were in a shade they called *graphite*—the colour of a hard, black pencil. Why did people impose adult sophistication on infants? (And those unsuitably sexy clothes for little girls always upset me; let children be children.) There was a pretty diaper bag, the latest in disposable diapers, and five colourful onesies. I stuck to stripes and patterns and avoided comments like "Thing" and "Daddy's Girl." There were Fruit of the Loom undershirts, which took me back to my own babies. How reassuring to see some brands could survive a generation or two.

"I had to buy a blanket, Eve," I said. "Whoever buys a blanket?" Maudie would be round with a hand-knitted one the day after Eve arrived home. She always had one on the go; yellow or white to cover all contingencies. And that knob-knuckled lady up the street, Mrs. Ryan—she would up-needles the minute she heard the news.

There were no seats available until midnight, so I waited for hours at the airport on stand-by, pacing and circling then dropping exhausted into a seat, reading the same half page three times. I heaved myself up to get in line for a cup of restaurant tea where the water had never reached boiling point in its whole life, and the teabag was hidden behind the teapot and wouldn't come out of its paper casing, and the string was yanked into the water after the teabag like a mermaid's tail; who knew how many hands had touched that string. And by now the water was tepid and I had to beat the daylights out of the teabag with a little plastic stick to get any flavour at all.

Would they help each other? Would they learn to pull together again?

I stood at the sink in the ladies' room, irritated when I had to bounce my hands up and down to make the water come out. How would they manage? What could I do to help?

I phoned Ginny. Carlie was not due home until April, but I would have phoned Ginny first anyway. I also knew what the first words out of her mouth would be:

"So why aren't you staying?"

"I'm not needed now. And they'll have to sort this out themselves. It's awkward."

"You should stay, Mom. I'd stay."

Maybe, maybe not. But then Eve would have to waste energy resisting Ginny's bulldozer tactics. Eve needed to keep her mind clear to concentrate on being a mom and a wife, a wife and a mom. Both.

So, we stuck to practicalities on the phone in matter-of-fact voices, such as who Ginny knew with baby gear in their basements. Ginny had given her own stuff away, but she always knew somebody.

I felt overwhelmed suddenly, and asked Ginny to write and explain everything to Carlie, and Ginny said, "What will we tell everyone else?"

The truth, or as close as we could get: that the birth was a total surprise, that it explained some of Eve's previous health issues, that Eve was delighted and was receiving excellent maternity care, and that mother and baby were doing well. Need-to-know basis.

CHAPTER THREE

1994

LIZ

BY THE TIME EVE ARRIVED HOME FROM MONTRÉAL, GINNY had whipped up a pile of second-hand baby paraphernalia and had strong-armed a store into sending a new crib. Immediately. I kept away initially, to allow space and time for Eve and Michel to become a couple again—a couple with a baby—but every time I phoned there was background noise of at least one visitor in the house. Eve said they were dropping in all day and all night, so I broke down and visited too.

To say people were flabbergasted when Eve came home with a baby tucked under her arm was an understatement. The world and his wife kept coming by, bearing gifts and flooding the house with pink tissue paper and questions and advice.

"Why didn't you tell us?"

"My god, another Wallace clone!"

"She's just like Eve."

"No wonder you were looking peaky." That was old Mrs. Ryan up the road, who brought a beautiful peach-coloured blanket. It was followed, as expected, by others in salmon and rose and a sugar-pink confection with scalloped edges.

"Rosie Wallace. I like that. And no middle name." That was Maudie, my friend from way back. "That's what our Jane should have done. She never should have listened to the in-laws. They all wanted their name in there, from Great-Aunt Matilda down."

Another friend commented on Eve being a Wallace, not a Simard, and how confusing that modern style was when it came to the children. "Did you hear that, Maudie? Michel says it's illegal to change your name when you marry in Québec.

Good grief! Couldn't wait to get rid of mine—well, I ask you—Ramsbothom!"

The ladies played Pass the Parcel with the baby, and Rosie stared around in an interested way, causing comments about her advanced powers of observation and her placid nature. A plate of Nanaimo bars and shortbreads followed her, and Michel was only too delighted to be sent to the supermarket to replenish the cookies. Relief came in the form of two fierce snowstorms in late March and a sloppy, mean-minded April.

Carlie came home at the end of April and was at Eve's house when your brother visited. He's getting doddery, poor Colin. He wanted to pay his respects and brought a plastic cat thing for the baby, and it played a very harsh jangly tune over and over.

"Alright for him," Carlie said afterwards. "He just turned down his hearing aid."

I told her it was a nice thought, and the poor soul must have had to look in all kinds of shops he had never been into in his life.

The real problem was that Colin lacked awareness when it came to personal space on top of being deaf. He loomed. He practically stood on your toes. He hung over you and breathed used air in your face. I could picture it. Carlie said Eve kept ducking under his arm and moving away, and he kept following her until finally she said, "Uncle, you've got to give me more room. I don't like people standing so close."

He stepped back then, all flustered and getting red in the face and said, "Excuse me for living," and left. Poor Colin. I had him over for supper to make up for it, and Eve dropped by with a bottle of Bacardi.

Michel did his best. He seemed to be making an effort to accept the baby—even signed the birth certificate as the father, which was an enormous concession, a priceless gift. It must have gone against his every instinct as such a correct, law-abiding person.

I could see Eve trying to be more welcoming but it wasn't nearly enough. She regularly sat next to Michel on the couch now, in the pre-Mexico way, but usually with the baby in her arms so it hardly counted. She kissed him when he came home from work, but it was a hit-and-miss affair and, although it was probably more a consequence of the time of day rather than intention, she often went to the door carrying the baby. *How was your day?*

The smile that went with it was just over midway on the enthusiasm scale. I told myself to stop with all the measuring. When Michel came home they would start making supper together, discussing menus and shopping lists the way any such couple might, and I would leave at that point, on a positive note.

How Eve loved that baby: cuddling her, talking to her, singing, murmuring, living in a warm bubble of new motherhood, while Michel remained helplessly outside. He did try. He walked around with Rosie, rocking her, repeating her name, but there was always that little hesitation before the name, as if it were something unpronounceable and foreign. The baby looked insecure in his arms, the blanket sliding down and her head dropping a little, so she would startle sometimes and began to cry. I tried to help at first, arranging his arms better, aiming them in towards the baby, but there was a resistance in those arms—they did not curve round to fit, did not soften. Wooden. Wouldn't. And when she started to cry, Michel would put her down again or give her back to me, saying, *You do this better than me.*

Even after Michel became proficient, Rosie still fussed in his arms. I worried that some trace memory was being laid down, some fear or dislike of being held in a certain way or by a certain person. Who knew how a small baby interpreted sensations, or whether they left an echo if repeated often enough. Michel always referred to Rosie as The Baby and later he called her The Child. The only time he said her name was when he carried her in that scheduled, dutiful way, and it was happening less and less, so even that little connection was fading.

He tried to keep the rest of life flowing. Michel did all the shopping and some cooking. He was good around the house, knew where everything was kept. He and Eve had always shared the chores. You were still asking where to find garbage bags after forty years of marriage. You would peel vegetables if I put them in front of you along with the knife and the scraper and a sheet of newspaper, then you'd ask where the saucepan was and expect me to bring it.

Michel was efficient and considerate, and Eve was politely grateful. Their house was like the pressurized cabin of a plane coming down from high altitude just before your ears pop: the muffled routines, *please return your seat to the upright position,* the controlled tension. It was staring out of the plane window for distraction then realizing how very far from safety you were, so instead you stared at some building exploding on a screen across the aisle two rows ahead.

Once I said *Let it out girl, for god's sake,* and Eve turned to look at me then away again, still with that expressionless face and without a word. As relations deteriorated, they hid behind politeness, Eve and Michel—a plastic coating allowing them to slide round each other without catching; that soft-spoken, work-to-rule way of sharing space with someone you just don't know what to do with. It gave me a headache.

Gradually, over the weeks, Michel confided in me less and less, did not look for my support, and was no longer anxious that I should come for supper. Half the time he was not there himself. He worked late and went into the office on weekends and flew to Montréal once to drop in on his parents. He flew to Qatar for two weeks that June on a *fact-finding mission* for work and stayed an extra week to have a look around. Eve seemed more relaxed without him—I even heard her singing that Disney song along with the radio one day, "A Whole New World."

"So, how was Qatar?" I asked when Michel answered the phone once.

"Hot," he said. "Interesting, but hot."

"And will you be going back again?"

There was a pause before he said, "Probably," then after a longer pause he said, "Definitely."

Once, I dropped in on them on a weekend and as I walked up the drive I heard a door slam and Michel shouting, "… because you won't let me!" I had never heard Michel raise his voice. Ever. I turned tail and fled. I saw bitterness in his face now and then, which I had not seen before the baby, and irritation when he was asked to hold her for a moment and his dinner went cold—a small thing, but shocking in one so habitually calm. And Eve still recoiled sometimes if he moved too close, even after all this time.

"You're going to lose him if you don't make an effort to include him in things," I said. "You're not giving him a chance."

"I've lost him already," Eve said. "Or he's lost me."

We did not need an oracle to tell us what was coming, but it was still a shock when it happened, in the same way the moment you died was a shock. And all Michel said at the time was *I can't do this.* The deciding event was on a wet afternoon at the end of August and I suppose I was the instigator. I'd been sitting in the living room with Rosie on the floor next to me, while Eve was in the kitchen preparing supper. Rosie was sitting with a cushion behind her against the chair, other cushions spread around in case she tipped over, somebody's washed-out receiving blankets covering everything. Later I realized how like dunes those pillows looked.

Rosie was bringing her hands up to her mouth in a purposeful way, trying to swallow the dimples on her fat little knuckles. So there she sat, burbling to herself and chewing her fists, and I allowed myself to be the Doting Grandmother. I'd seen Arrowroot cookies in the supermarket the day before and memories of sticky smiling faces had flooded me, and on impulse I had thrown a package in the cart. I gave one to Rosie that wet afternoon and watched her squeeze lumps of dissolving Arrowroot in both hands and aim them at her mouth.

By the time Michel came home, clumps of damp crumbs were stuck all over Rosie's face and clothes and in her hair. Rosie looked up at Michel, so much higher off the ground than me, and lost her balance, keeled over then lost her cookie. Her mouth turned down in that tragic inverted-U shape, eyes flooding, and she gazed up at Michel with a heartbroken how-could-you-do-this expression. Michel stood staring down at her, mouth open, stricken. He looked at Eve as she came in from the kitchen and shook his head, looking almost in tears himself.

"Sand. Like you. Like you in the sand. In the dunes." And he walked out of the room, leaving Rosie crying amidst her crumbs.

He left to set up a new branch in Qatar three weeks later. The business plan was to stay for two months and reassess. When the time was almost over, I said, "Heard from Michel, dear?"

"Just briefly."

"When is he coming?"

Any day. Eve did not know exactly.

So perhaps I should not have been surprised when Michel arrived in a taxi while I was babysitting. He gave me a long, silent hug, a kiss on each cheek, and a sad look. He took a step back and was still for a moment then strode away to the bedroom saying, "Must rush. I only have a day, then I'm off to Chicago. I'm having dinner with the bosses tomorrow."

I was babysitting while Eve gave an education session for the staff at a nursing home on Dealing with Challenging Residents. That was one of a series—part of the requirements for maintaining her professional registration, along with all that reading of papers and submitting of summaries to prove she was still honing her psychological skills. Did Michel know she would be absent? A question not to be asked.

Rosie was down for her nap, but he didn't look for her, didn't inquire. There were muffled scrapes and thumps, drawers and doors, some running up and down stairs. In no time Michel had filled two suitcases and one of those huge, bloated sports bags with wheels at one end, bulging round the straps like a fat man on a stretcher, and he was rolling them out to the door and lifting them down the step. He had brought the sports bag in with him, empty. There was a lump in my chest, a straining at my ribs. I saw the taxi driver climb out of his cab and open up the back, then Michel was standing in front of me, looking down. He took hold of my hands, which I had been clutching together, pressed against my heart so it wouldn't jump out of my chest. He lifted them up, bent, and kissed them.

"Thank you, Liz. You're a wonderful person. Nobody could have had a better mother-in-law." He opened the front door and signalled to the driver then turned back. "I still love Eve. I'll probably always love Eve, the memory of her, how she was. But there's too much between us now, and I could never love that child. I'm sorry."

And that was the last time I saw him.

I went to the door when Eve came home. Eve looked at my face and said, "He's been, then?" She looked into the house over my shoulder. "And gone."

CHAPTER FOUR

1997

LIZ

IT SEEMED TO ME THAT LIFE AT GINNY'S WAS ORGANIZED chaos, full of noisy comings and goings and all the exuberance and laughter, outrage and sulks of a thirteen-year-old daughter and a fifteen-year-old son. Behind all that loud humanity, the radio played from dawn until dusk and was then replaced by television. Nobody listened. Their house had that anticipatory, low-level-storm feeling about it, where all possible disaster preparations have been made and, so far, everyone was surviving.

Eve's house was the calm before the storm. Since Eve had started working at the hospital last September, she had an official sitter, recommended by Ginny, but I still looked after Rosie now and then. Rosie-the-toddler was in constant motion and talked non-stop and Eve answered all her questions in her usual gentle way, but apart from that, her house was so quiet. Even the twosome's kitchen noises were ten times quieter than Ginny's household of four. CBC Radio was turned on for *The World at Six* (six thirty in Newfoundland), and then switched off. Except for a weekly dose of satire on *This Hour Has 22 Minutes*, Eve watched very little television. There was an underlying silence in her house, but it was not a peaceful silence. I missed that aura of calm that had surrounded her before Mexico, but perhaps it was just me who was imagining a difference, a watchfulness.

The months went by smoothly enough, and the occasions where Eve became edgy and distant usually only lasted a day or so. The family asked no questions and ignored the edginess with great care. But then came the break-in.

Easter was at the end of March in 1997, and the Wallace turkey dinner was at Ginny's house. All the family was present except Carlie, who would be back from Senegal *sometime in the next few of weeks*. Carlie was notorious for only letting us know her ETA at the last minute. During the festivities at Ginny's, two young men in hoodies helped themselves to Eve's brand new laptop, the flat-screen TV, and two twenties from the emergency fund in her kitchen drawer.

They probably would have taken more items except that Mrs. Noseworthy, two doors down, heard the crash when they kicked in the back door and called the police. There happened to be a roving police vehicle in the area that responded quickly, but as it pulled up at the front, the thieves left by the back, and neither loot nor thieves were ever seen again. Mrs. Noseworthy would have known exactly when Eve left the house and in which direction she drove, and probably the colour of her underwear, so of course she rang Ginny's house as we were eating. I wished she'd held off until we had finished.

Eve had a relapse. That's what I called it to myself. She sat huddled on the edge of that misery-chair, rocking herself and quivering. Hot sweet tea, brandy—all the traditional home treatments for shock—had no effect. Even Ginny's competent chatty bustle, so everyday-ordinary, did nothing to restore her. Rosie stood close, leaning against Eve in tears, saying, *Mommy, Mommy*, and I waited, hoping for some maternal instincts to spring into action. She did wrap her arms round the child but otherwise Eve seemed unaware. She had gone somewhere else in her head, alone.

Ginny and I moved her almost forcibly to my house along with a clingy little Rosie and a suitcase full of the three-year-old's necessities. Easter Sunday was not a good time for medical intervention of any type, so we set up Carlie's room for Eve. We got her into bed eventually—still with half her clothes on because she had stopped being almost catatonic as soon as Ginny tried to remove her jacket. Instead, she had curled up like a little hedgehog, holding tight to everything we touched.

Rosie needed cuddles from anyone with a free arm and finally fell asleep in the two of mine, in front of the television, and stayed asleep, luckily, when I tucked her up in bed.

Ginny took Eve to the Upton Clinic, and I took care of Rosie. The babysitter was in Florida for Easter. I had looked after Rosie multiple times for brief periods, but this was three days and three nights. It might not sound like much, and she was a good-natured, cheerful child (although she dissolved into tears whenever she thought of her mother), but it was exhausting. We played hide-and-seek for hours, me folding myself down behind chairs and in cupboards with difficulty, expecting Rosie to find me by the screams from my knees. We batted a wilted pink balloon around, left over from her birthday, and this also felt like hours, though, when I checked, it had been a mere fifteen minutes. We baked chocolate chip cookies and Rice Krispie treats and went for short walks, but it was suddenly winter again, and the dressing for the weather and undressing afterwards took more time than the actual walks. I made a tent of the kitchen table with a sheet thrown over it, and Rosie arranged her stuffed animals inside and could be heard bossing them about. She had endless questions, which I enjoyed answering because it saved me from wondering what I would do next. I ran out of ideas for activities an hour after breakfast on Day One and felt brain-wracked that whole three days. I did not remember being so challenged when the girls were little. I loved Rosie. I did not enjoy being sole charge, nursery-school caregiver at my age, even for my own delightful granddaughter. May I be forgiven. I did not have the stamina.

After the Upton Clinic, Eve stayed with me and everyone stepped carefully. Ginny had arranged for a new steel back door with massive deadbolts to be installed, but Eve wanted other locks changed too with deadbolts on everything and bars inside her basement windows. It is the feeling of violation rather than the loss of *things* that lingers after a burglary—the knowledge that strangers have been rooting around in one's personal space, the sense of being touched by something repulsive and not being able to wash it off. Eve's house may have been watched and that would make anyone jumpy. She did not move back in until all the security changes were in place, and I barely had time to clean up before Carlie arrived.

CARLIE

The first thing Carlie always noticed coming out of St. John's Airport was the wind. Cool and wild and fresh. It tasted clean and smelled clean, of rock and wet spruce and brine, not dusty and dry and pepper-sweet like the Harmattan. The Harmattan sucked the moisture out of one's skin, cracking lips, tickling throats—a desert wind, like a hairdryer on its hottest setting blowing in your face all day.

Liz was waiting in Arrivals, all smiles and outstretched arms. She still looked about fifty although she'd be sixty-seven in August. They say blonds don't wear well but Liz broke all the rules. There was a taut look about her that day, though, and shadows under her eyes, although she brushed it off when Carlie commented. Carlie swung her last bag off the carousel and no, she would not bother with a cart. She wore the backpack and trundled the rest.

"How is Eve? And Rosie?"

"Rosie is a delight," Liz said. "Talks a mile a minute. Mimics everyone, so you'll have to be careful what you say in front of her."

Carlie saluted with her free hand. "I hear and obey."

"Hah!" They were across the parking lot by this time, and her mother was asking Carlie to drive. That was new. Liz had never liked being a passenger in her own car. Carlie looked at her sideways, wondering, but her mother just said she was a bit tired.

"Yes, young Jeremy's got Rosie saying *fart* and *poop* every two minutes. Well, she's potty training so I guess that's on her mind." And the conversation flowed to Jeremy's latest antics and how he was driving his father to the brink, and how Ginny had to keep the peace all the time. Then it was all about Ginny's new nursing position in Rheumatology, *but Ginny will tell you about that,* and when her mom paused for breath, Carlie tried again.

"And Eve. How is Eve?"

"Well, you know about her full-time position at the hospital, working with people who've had strokes or head injuries or spinal cord injuries?"

"Yes, Liz, I know all about that," Carlie said, trying not to sound impatient. "But how's she doing?"

"Well..." Then Liz told her about a break-in and a psychiatric admission and about Eve and Rosie staying with Liz until two days ago, and Eve only going back to work yesterday. Oh god. Eve, of all people, did not need this.

⁂

It was a lot to absorb, fresh off the plane. Carlie always felt out of sync when she landed. Home had moved on without her. You could never go back to the exact place you left months ago; you had to do a hop, skip, and a jump to catch up to where it was now. Land journeys were so much easier, letting you adjust and move with the time change, the terrain, the cultures you passed through. A flight was a vacuum with coffee breaks.

Liz seemed to be holding up well, taking life as it came. She still talked to George's photograph, but just the way someone living on their own might address a remark to their cat or the plants or let go a curse in the middle of an empty room—a safety net maybe. In Liz's case it was more a hot water bottle for a sore heart.

Carlie had been reading about post-traumatic stress disorder, but mostly as it related to military service because that was all she could find in the spring of '97. There were more examples of PTSD in troops returning home directly by plane than in those going home slowly by boat, or with a three-day stopover in a relaxing place with a chance to talk and unwind with peers—peers who understood. Eve had taken the first possible flight out of Mexico and constructive conversation with Michel (or anybody) had probably never happened. But maybe rape stress was different from combat stress? Then again, maybe not. And she was a psychologist. Would Eve feel she had nothing to learn from some other therapist and should be able to cope on her own? Would she feel inadequate if she could not?

Ginny had told Carlie the break-in had stirred up everything from Mexico. Even with all the extra home security, Eve was hyper-aware of people hanging around or things being out of place. She checked every room and cupboard each time she entered the house, investigated every strange noise, closed drapes at the first sign of the light fading—three in the afternoon on a dull day. Ginny hoped this was just a temporary thing.

A week after Carlie arrived, Rosie was tucked away for the night in her new dinosaur pyjamas (Eve's attempt to wean her off princesses), and Carlie and Eve were sprawled in Eve's living room. At least, Carlie sprawled; Eve came as close as she ever did, curled up neatly on the couch. They started on Carlie's bottle from the duty-free shop, the conversation wafting gently this way and that, until Eve said, "So what next?" She'd been hoping Carlie would come home after finishing her doctoral work, but then she'd gone on to other studies, "And now it's been ten years. What's the plan?"

Carlie stretched and sighed, stared at the ceiling, and said she didn't know; she always kept her eye out for interesting job opportunities, but otherwise she was just going with the flow.

"I'm not bored yet, and I like Dakar. Two of my Montréal friends are still there, so I feel less of a Toubab," (*Toubab* being a derogatory term used in West Africa for a foreigner.) Also Carlie was comfortable thinking in French now, as it was widely used in Senegal. They lay chatting in French for a while, Eve saying they should do it more often; she was rusty. Then Eve sat up and said in a more purposeful voice, "But seriously, Carlie. What now?"

Carlie had trouble sorting out possibilities and concerns in her own mind, certainly not with sufficient clarity to explain to anyone else. She just mentioned the big NGO where she was employed, and that teaching summer school here helped with plane fares. Then she explained in detail about the small local association in Dakar where she volunteered. This she loved—loved helping communicate with bigger organizations, writing funding applications, teaching free classes in English and resume-writing—*capacity building*, in current jargon—so people could learn enough to become independent of international aid. Carlie thought, really hoped, that she could contribute.

"But enough of that. I need something to soak up this wine." So they raided the kitchen for cheese and crackers and chips and a bit of apple pie, and chatted about the plants on the window ledge and that African violets were native to East Africa, not Senegal, and when they were settled back on their couches again, Carlie said, "How's working in a rehab unit compared to private practice?"

There was a pause while they changed gears, then Eve said, "Interesting. Different." Between sips they chatted about neurological issues they both had come across in their different lines of work. Then Eve said, "And working in rehab is safe." There was a tightening around Eve's mouth and eyes when Carlie asked if any of Eve's old clients had surfaced, and Carlie hastily said *never mind* and *sorry*, but Eve simply said, "Yes," and put her glass on the coffee table. She sat there, looking at it.

The client Eve had been most worried about was suddenly right there in front of her in the mall one afternoon. When Eve asked how she was doing the client said, *Well, after you dumped me, I met this wonderful guy online who turned out to be not so wonderful and I ended up with a broken arm and hearing loss from a whack on the head. So then I prescribed a few therapies for myself and now I've been sent to an addictions counselling program. But the counsellor's not like you. I trusted you. I <u>trusted</u> you.* And she had walked away.

Eve picked up her glass, swirled the liquid around a few times, and put it down again. She had frozen, right there in the middle of the mall, hardly able to breathe. Mom was home with Rosie and had started to worry, so she phoned Ginny and Ginny went looking for Eve.

Eve could still see the look on that woman's face. Accusing.

And what could Carlie say to that? A hug was the only possibility. Liz always said a hug was the greatest communicator when words failed.

CHAPTER FIVE

1997

LIZ

I HAVE ALWAYS ASSOCIATED BAD EVENTS WITH BAD WEATHER. This time, however, misfortune came out of a clear blue sky.

Ginny had a two-day conference in Gander and she had invited me to go with her for the ride. *We should be out of the worst of the winter by then, Mom, and it'll be a change of scenery. You can take the car while I'm tied up and drive over to Gander Bay or something.* That was before the break-in. I would not have gone, leaving Eve alone, if Carlie had not come home and agreed to stay with her. They all insisted I go.

Ginny was driving too close to the truck in front and braking every time the truck braked. The jerks were giving me a headache. Now we were past the long stretch where vehicles turned off from Kenmount Road or nosed into it from the strip malls and fast-food places and all those car showrooms, past the open part with the fifty-kilometre speed limit (such a trap for the unwary), past the turn-off to Donovan's Industrial Park and the overpass. Then the car eased to a steady purr as the Trans-Canada opened out before us and we could both relax.

I admit I was glad of a change. I was so tired. I watched the grey-brown-olive world go by, leftover snow patches, pearly in the sun, and a huge blue sky. *Pachelbel's Canon* exuded serenity from the radio, and I closed my eyes and felt the tension drain out, let myself sink back into the curves of the seat. This was my old eight o'clock feeling—that final peace and quiet after hours of turmoil. There were times, years really, when surviving until eight o'clock had been my foremost goal. Snippets of memory crowded in: picking up nine bags of groceries after my day at the hospital, *If I can just make it home;* fumbling with the door key, trying not to put bags on the ground in case they spilled or got their bottoms dirty, and Carlie and Ginny having a spat as I walked in so I'd have to referee—"Help put these away, please"—and how loud and exaggerated they would be with their putting away: *if I can just get dinner on the table.* And all through the preparation of the meal the thought would reverberate: *If I can just make it to eight o'clock.*

You always liked stimulating conversation at dinner, and the girls loved it too. You said it was the best part of a meal. But the noise made my brain rattle, and you would still all be arguing as the girls helped me clear away, and I would have to dodge round someone standing in the middle of the floor emphasizing a point until finally I would chase you all out of the kitchen. Then. Then I would close the bedroom door and collapse onto the bed, which was the only part of the house that was entirely mine—half a bed, really—and I would let everything go. This was my *eight o'clock.* I would feel my muscles slacken and all thought drain out, taking with it every irritation or intention or remembrance of something unfinished until I was empty. Peace.

I recalled that delightful priest on the dialysis unit back in Toronto, decades ago. He missed a dialysis session more than once because *someone needed him,* and his system went haywire. He was carried in, almost too weak to struggle, shouting obscenities through gasps and wheezes—atrocious things he must have heard working around Toronto's back streets. Quite out of his mind. Father Cadogan was his name. After dialysis he was the loveliest, most serene person alive. *Eight o'clock* was my own mental dialysis. I thought of people facing crises after their eight o'clock limit, myself included, handling them badly, being obnoxious because they were past thinking clearly, having to live with the consequences. And everybody else having to live with the consequences. Carlie should have studied chemistry if she wanted to change the world. Anthropology just observed and analyzed. It didn't change anything.

The soothing music had stopped and now there was an adenoidal tenor scooping up to each note, whining about somebody being unfaithful. Well, it was no wonder if he caterwauled like that. I reached to turn the radio off and paused with my hand out and...didn't know how. There was an array of knobs and buttons, and quite suddenly I had no idea what they were, what they did, or what I was supposed to do with them. Out of the blue, there was an alien landscape in front of me and I did not recognize any of it. Part of my brain, the part still working, told me I had seen it all before—had understood it and used it before. Fright. Shock. I had never felt this blank, this empty, in my life.

"Not the best song ever," said Ginny, and her hand went to the bank of buttons and the music stopped and she said the news would be on soon. Then she was pulling out this little black rectangle, saying something about putting this tape away and getting out a different one, waving the box thing at me. "In the console here." She tapped the division between our two seats.

A tape. Yes, that was the name. I held it in my two hands, turning it over and over. Two circles inside, with shiny black tape going from one to the other. But what was it? Yes, it was a tape. I could see that, and Ginny had just said so. But what...?

"Never mind the tape, Mom. It's four thirty, coming up to news time," and Ginny's hand was up to the buttons again and a CBC voice started talking about Iraq. I let the tape slide onto the seat, leaned back, and closed my eyes. My head ached and I wanted to sleep, and out there was endless black emptiness. And fear.

"Car like your old one," said Ginny. I opened my eyes a fraction. A mud-splattered car was level with us on an off-ramp, leaving the highway. It was blue under the dirt like my old car. It had two names, but they were gone: not just on the tip of my tongue but lost in outer space. My current car also had two names. I tried and tried to remember, went through the alphabet to see if it triggered something, though I knew somehow it would not. These words were not in reach of any alphabet. Before, the name of a person had lurked close by, teasing, showing itself as soon as the person was gone—ta-da. Before, a forgotten word had left a shadow, a first letter or a number of syllables or a predominant sound. But these words were gone completely—no after-image, no echo. Obliterated: from the Latin for erase—O, zero, a hole, nothing.

"What are the names of those two parallel rivers in the Middle East?" Ginny had turned the news off again, must have been trying to start a conversation. "You know, in Iraq."

I could picture the map, see those two north-south rivers, knew the names, except that I no longer knew them. "I don't know." It was a huge effort to sound the words and they came out in a whisper.

"You're always so good at those geography things," Ginny was saying. "I think that's where Carlie gets it from. Remember how you used to reel off the names of bays around Newfoundland? Hare Bay, Ha Ha Bay, Pistolet Bay, Hermitage Bay—no, that one's farther south. How does it go again?" But those names were also lost. I had grown up with those names, knew them as well as my own. I was too exhausted to say anything, so I kept my eyes closed and even though there was terror out there, waiting, I went to sleep.

When I woke, the clock on the dashboard said five thirty. I had slept for an hour and my headache was gone. My old car was a Toyota, a Toyota Corolla, and my new one...I recited the alphabet again until I reached H—it was a Hyundai, and as soon as I remembered the first part the second part came too, the Elantra. I tried to remember the names of the rivers. They were still gone, but back on the tip of my tongue and a few moments later they floated off: the Tigris and Euphrates.

It was during dinner at the hotel in Gander that the names of the bays returned, all of them: Halls Bay, Green Bay, Confusion Bay, Baie Verte, White Bay, Canada Bay, Hare Bay, Ha Ha Bay...I could go right round the island this time, which was a relief. But not a relief. Those little episodes of muddle and forgetting over the last few years...I could not write them off now as the temporary effects of stress. They were early warning signs I had ignored.

I had to be there for Eve. Had to. God, I could not let Eve find out. Don't get excited. It was getting excited that brought this on. I could not be a drag on them all.

Eve.

A Home: sitting in a circle with dribbly old women, soggy mashed potatoes out of a packet, Pampers.

"What's wrong, Mom? You're white as a sheet." Ginny was frowning at me.

I could not bring myself to talk about it, even though Ginny was the logical person to tell: Ginny the nurse, our first-born, Ginny who could keep a secret. My own father lived eight years after being diagnosed with transient ischemic attacks, or mini strokes, watching himself losing his mind, marble by marble. Was my brain going to disintegrate like that? No. I was too young, too healthy. Dementia? I could not take it in.

Ginny was still asking questions, looking concerned, but I just owned up to a bit of a headache and said I needed to lie down. I lay in the hotel bed with my eyes closed, wondering if doctors knew more these days. I could still remember something of my nursing explanation because I'd seen it in action in my father: *Vascular dementia is a decline in short-term memory because of cerebral vascular disease, where blood vessels in the brain are damaged and brain tissue injured, preventing essential oxygen and nutrients from reaching brain cells.* I was rusty about medical advances since retirement but perhaps treatment was more effective now?

I saw my family doctor as soon as I was home. *Tell me exactly*, he said. And I did, precisely, accurately, until I reached my Newfoundland bays and began to recite them. Then I was afraid. Afraid I would forget halfway, even though this was the reason I had come. I stopped after Confusion Bay—*can't stop there*—and jerked out one more name: Baie Verte. "You don't want to hear all that," I said, forcing a smile. The start of a trend. *Were there any physical signs?* Just the headache and that overwhelming fatigue. *Could I lift my arms?* Arms? I had trouble raising my eyelids. But yes, I could lift my arms. The symptoms were all mental. The doctor sent me for tests and started medications. He said yes, transient ischemic attacks were better controlled these days because modern medications were better at controlling contributing factors like cholesterol and blood flow, and not to worry.

Not to Worry.

George, what am I going to do?

Over time, I looked things up, talked to hospital people I knew (always inquiring on behalf of someone else), and I read, listened to broadcasts, attended talks. I had not realized how widespread a problem dementia had become—an unpleasant sequel to people living longer, perhaps. Each item about dementia seemed to contradict the one before, and the one hard and fast rule seemed to be that there was no rule. Sixty to eighty percent of dementia cases were Alzheimer's according to some authorities, with accumulation of a toxic protein, a totally different chemistry from TIAs, and a seemingly unstoppable slide into cabbage-hood over a period of about eight years. Researchers were hopeful of a cure one day. Cabbage-hood, when reached, was much the same in all types of dementia.

So if I had to have dementia, I preferred the vascular kind, the mini strokes, because the prognosis was a little more optimistic. Articles differed hugely on the anticipated lifespan with this type, from four years post diagnosis, five years, eight years, to the one I favoured which said it was unpredictable but could be anywhere between two to twenty years. That last number I could handle, as long as…well, I didn't want to think about what type of cabbage I would be.

I just wanted to see Rosie into adulthood. To see, and understand what I saw. I wanted to see her cope with learning about her parentage and still keep her self-respect and become whatever she wanted to become. I wanted Eve to start living a normal life again, maybe find someone else. I wanted her to regain her serenity and I must not let my mental state get in the way. And Ginny (and her husband, Anthony, and the children of course) and Carlie—I wanted them all to be happy. Don't go thinking I didn't care as much about them. It was just that Eve and Rosie were so much more vulnerable, and the outcome so much more uncertain.

Bottom line: give yourself the best chance, Liz Wallace: stick to a healthy diet, moderate exercise, lots of sleep—it seemed there was a correlation between dementia and lack of sleep—and stress management. (Hah! to that last one.) Keep these stroke things few and far between.

And at first, it did seem as if the medications were working, because nothing of note happened for weeks, months, except for not recognizing people and forgetting a word here and there. And people's names. (But I was always bad at names.) And I hemmed and hawed more than usual.

Then it happened again. At the gas station.

I had not slept well for several nights, for no particular reason. In the morning I stopped for gas. I popped the gas tank lid, unscrewed the cap and let it dangle, lifted the nozzle from the pump…and didn't know where to put it. There was a hole here somewhere for the gas, but I could not find it. How ridiculous. I stared at the pump for a moment, put the nozzle back in the stand and started again: Press the button for Regular, never mind the pay-at-the-pump instructions, pick up the nozzle and put it…where? I looked all over the gas pump. There was no hole. I went through the routine again. I sneaked a look at the pump next door, but the woman had just finished, was hanging up the hose and getting back in her car. The car drew away and I walked over, being casual, and checked out the other pump. Maybe the hole was more obvious on this one, but it wasn't. I turned to walk back to my own vehicle and the lid of the gas tank was sticking out from the side of the car. For heaven's sake, you put the gas in the car, dummy, not back in the pump. The whole routine came back to me, and I finished pumping the gas in the usual way and went inside to pay.

The woman behind the counter kept glancing at me, not with that take-the-money-and-move-on face but with a noticing face and a soft, sympathetic look in her eyes. Well, the little bell from the pump must have dinged a bunch of times while I was fiddling about. But this person had someone at home with dementia. She knew.

How could I sleep better when I already avoided caffeine except at breakfast and never watched horror movies at bedtime (and that included the news). I wished I could switch off my brain at night and switch it on in the day when I needed it. At least this episode was less extreme than the one on the way to Gander, and briefer. I was more aware of the normal world ticking around me: the wind catching a car door across the way and slamming it on the front corner of the driver's jacket; the hair of the woman at the next pump, immobile in spite of the gusts, and my being glad it was blowing the mousse-spray-glue smell the other way; the black and white number *three* above my pump. There was a bigger border of remembrance this time around a smaller black hole, the hole that had swallowed the central issue of where to put the gas—the hole in the hole. But what about those moments of dizziness that happened every few days? Were they super-mini strokes? Should I stop every time, rest for half an hour or something? Was that hypochondria or common sense?

The doctor changed one of my medications for a stronger one, *to stop those old platelets from clumping*. I started watching my diet more. The meals themselves would pass muster, but not all that tea and toast in between, and cookies. I had not realized there was so much caffeine in chocolate. I could do with dropping a few pounds, too. I could try walking more often, but who wanted to go for a walk when the wind chill was a minus in double figures and strong enough to blow your ears off? The thought of a gym made me cringe: Soviet Bloc industrial machines in bleak factory rows, workers sneaking looks to see if the comrade next door is up to scratch, having to fight with those malevolent robot arms in the weight room. No. I was using the weights at home—when I remembered—and I would rather walk through the university tunnels while the weather was bad, although I had better not tell Eve. There had been warnings about walking in the tunnels alone; girls had been attacked. But an old woman like me would be safe. I was sixty-seven for heaven's sake (which was still too young to have dementia).

CHAPTER SIX

1997

LIZ

ALL THREE GRANDCHILDREN WERE GROWING LIKE WEEDS, the same as any other children, but I could not help worrying a little more about Rosie, and the thing that worried me the most was her father fixation. We had all been so careful not to draw attention to her lack of father. I think the effort must have irradiated the atmosphere and been absorbed through her skin.

I acted as backup mom as best I could and Ginny tried to include Rosie in her family's outings, but her own children were not of an age to want a three-year-old around all the time. Apart from becoming very quiet and watchful when Eve was having a bad day, and keeping tight hold of Brown Bear (as opposed to all the other bears and beasts at the end of her bed) until things normalized, Rosie partook of her preschool and dancing classes with gusto. She showed no signs of insecurity, or whatever an only child of a single, very-slightly-unstable parent might be expected to show—except for her persistence in including a father in her concept of family.

Carlie made a point of taking Rosie places when she was home. She picked her up from Child's Play one day and said Rosie had bounced out full of vim and vigour, wearing the Union Jack T-shirt Carlie had brought her from Heathrow and clutching a week's worth of crumpled art. They had an Appreciation and Admiration session at my kitchen table. Rosie's castle was a lop-sided pile of Popsicle sticks heavily glued onto green construction paper. There was a paper tree with painted apples, a hemiplegic butterfly with yellow tissue-paper wings, which Carlie flit-fluttered round the kitchen then stuck on the fridge with magnets. Last of all, there was a black crayon drawing of a careful square house with stick figures lined up in front. Your house? Yes. And who are the people? Me and Mommy and Daddy. And Carlie admired the picture at great length but said her daddy didn't live here.

"Daddy lives here." Rosie was definite about that.

"Just you and Mommy live in your house. Maybe draw another house for Daddy?"

"Rachel says everybody has a daddy even if you can't see him."

"Absolutely. But you can't see your daddy because he lives in a different house—maybe over here?"

"No. He's at my house." Rosie's voice was rising, and her bottom lip was getting that front-end-loader look, so Carlie suggested a glass of milk and Rosie said *No* because the situation obviously demanded a No to any suggestion.

"So how about ice cream?" said Carlie, headfirst in the freezer. "Butterscotch Ripple?"

Silence. "N...okay."

"Magic word?"

Silence. "Please."

Carlie changed the topic to the frothy pink tutu Rosie was wearing on top of royal blue tights and her red, white, and blue shirt. Did she pick out her clothes in the morning?

No reply.

Did she wear it for ballet class?

Small nod.

It was no use trying to persuade Rosie there was no Daddy in her life. Carlie thought it was probably like believing in Santa Claus. Rosie would stop when she was ready to not-believe, and not one moment before.

Was that where it all started, with some well-intentioned remark by this Rachel person? However it began, the father thing followed Rosie into grade school.

"Mommy's sending my best picture to Daddy," she announced one day.

It put a knot in my heart, knowing items Rosie had laboured over were really going nowhere. "That's nice, dear." I managed a smile.

There was one particular kindergarten letter—just *Dear Dabby, Love Rosie*—which I took and put with Eve's wedding album. Rosie churned out pictures for all and sundry, not giving them a thought afterwards, in that way of small children living in the moment.

In the run-up to Father's Day in grade two, Rosie asked why Daddy never said he liked her pictures the way everyone else did, even the special one she had done for Christmas—the one with streamers stuck on in different colours. There was quite the meltdown over that and even my gingerbread cookies were no help.

Eve tried to explain how Michel had a new life now, completely separate from theirs, and he was very busy. What was he busy doing? Well…he might be writing reports at his desk like Mommy did the other night, or planning things and phoning people and travelling to other places to talk to people—clients. What was a client?

Rosie stood at the end of the couch where Eve was sitting, tracing the corded edge of the arm with one finger, over and back, over and back. I thought of fetching a facecloth to wipe her hands but any remnants of the crayons she had been using would be part of the fabric already—just as traces of burgundy nail polish, from the day before Ginny's wedding, could still be seen on the green stone tiles in my porch (if you knew where to look) and the painted-over grooves in the wall up the stairs marking scrapes from long-ago buckles on school bags. They were as much reminders of home and family as photographs, only more personal, like inside jokes. It was something trophy-homes were missing, the same way Botox erased people's laugh lines.

So, what did Daddy's clients talk about? Why didn't Mommy know? What was *separated*? What was a lawyer? Rosie stood right in front of Eve now, leaning in, knees pressing against her mother's legs. "If the lawyer isn't separated from Michel like you are, can we give the lawyer my picture to send?" Then the age-old prevarication: *We'll see.*

After the card-making in school came Rosie's friend Eryn's card-laden birthday, then her Aunty Ginny's, then my own. (Seventy-one!) There was a story to write for school called *My Family*. Eryn received a late birthday present from her father who had also *left,* and she brought the doll to show Rosie. Eryn's father talked to her on the phone, and she told Rosie all about it. Every month. So, over the next few weeks the scene was replayed with varying levels of hurt and despair.

Then came one particular card she wanted to send—blue, maybe, with glitter. This one. Please. Please. She sat on the floor and collapsed forward with her head down between her knees, arms withdrawn somewhere underneath, hair spread out like a pall, and stayed there totally still: such limber joints and such inflexible purpose. Finally, Eve decided Michel was the only one who could cut this umbilical cord. "Rosie, why don't we send this picture for Michel's birthday in September, and we'll take it to the lawyer's office, you and me both, in plenty of time for it to arrive on the right day." The smile through the tears could light rainbows.

Rosie chose her favourite pink dress to wear for the visit to the lawyer with sparkly shoes and a princess purse to put the card in, which she clutched to her chest with both hands. I remembered the one previous visit Rosie had made to that office, when she was three or four years old and unaware of the seriousness of the meeting in the inner sanctum. All she talked about after that event was the leather sofa in the waiting room, which stuck to the back of her legs and made a Band-Aid-peeling noise every time Rosie stood up—every thirty seconds, according to Eve—and her legs left foggy patches on the seat just like when you breathed on the window, and she had to sit down quickly before they faded. This time, after the letter was delivered into the lawyer's hand, she left the purse behind on that very same sofa, so they had to go all the way back to retrieve it.

And why did I remember those details so clearly when that same day I forgot the recipe for my apricot cake, which I had made a thousand times. Left out the eggs so the cake came out more like a biscuit—burnt too, and I didn't even smell the burning until I opened the oven door—but they say the sense of smell is the first thing to go with dementia.

Eve said she expected Michel's reply would be sent to herself through the lawyer, requesting no more cards, which she would then explain to Rosie. Show and tell. Instead, a reply came to the house four weeks after Michel's birthday, addressed to Miss Rose Wallace. Rosie was ecstatic. The mailman brought it right to the house? Even though they were all separated? I said we should wait until Mommy came home before she opened it, and Rosie was so focused on the envelope over that interminable hour that I half expected it to burst into flame.

Rosie met Eve at the door and when The Moment came, she opened the envelope so, so carefully with Eve's letter opener. Eve had to help because the envelope was of high-grade paper and hard to cut. It held a card of the same thick paper in the same cream colour with a gold rose embossed on the outside and, inside, the words Thank You in gold script. Below them, in regular black ink and careful, disconnected letters, were the words

Thank you, Rose, for the beautiful card.

From Michel

Rosie turned it all ways, peering at it. She ran her finger over the grooves on the back of the rose and Eve explained about embossing, how the shape was made to stand out on the front to look pretty, how it was a rose because she was a rose too and wasn't that nice? I expected her to rush about showing it to the whole world, but it went back in the envelope and onto the table by her bed, although for a while she informed every person she met that her name was Miss Rose Wallace. After a time, the envelope grew quite grubby and needed minor repairs with Scotch tape. Much later, the card with its envelope went onto the shelf beside her favourite books. I wondered when Rosie would notice the lack of xoxo and when she would analyze that lack.

The fallout from this event was Rosie's painful attention to the mail delivery. She inspected it all as soon as she came home from school and read out the name on each envelope. This was not a cutting of the umbilical cord; it was slow starvation.

"I don't think there will be anything else for you, Rosie." Then mopping up fat tears I added, "At least until Christmas."

But maybe that was worse.

"Probably not at Christmas either."

And there was nothing at Christmas, or on her birthday, and the school year was almost over before Rosie stopped checking.

CHAPTER SEVEN

2002

LIZ

OVER THE YEARS I HAD BECOME ACCUSTOMED TO THE IDEA of mental decline—more or less. I was five years post diagnosis at the end of April in 2002, and I remembered my father as being much more impaired at the same stage. The girls knew by then of course. It must have become obvious. Ginny sat me down and asked me about it eye-to-eye one day.

So there I was, sliding gently down my un-learning curve, with occasional nosedives. Mostly I just laughed it off, said I'd lost my memory and found a forgettery. A mini stroke was a physical diagnosis after all, and in some way acceptable. What I could not accept was being slow on the uptake, and it had happened so gradually that people must have assumed I was born that way, which eroded my sense of worth. What an appalling thing. I had thought I was so non-judgemental and open-minded about mental abilities, mental health, and here I was, persuading myself that this was physical, because it was easier to live with.

This re-evaluation was part of growing old too—having time to think and understand. Zora Neale Hurston wrote there are "years that ask questions and years that answer." Now was the time for answers. Retirement had not felt like old age at first—more like my eight o'clock time—and I loved it. There was time to relax, time to think. I was lucky with my health and had chosen retirement—it had not been forced upon me like it was on poor Maudie. But then you got sick and then my brain fell apart.

Nursing was all Doing. Not doing felt lazy. Not much time to wonder if there was a better way. Somebody has a law about that.

Parkinson? Peter? Anyway, I had been proud of being quick-witted growing up. I was good at the snappy one-liners and was on the debating team one year. Now it took so long for the threads of an argument to come together in my head that the conversation moved on without me. I could tolerate my forgettery, but I did hate being slow. If I were asked a long, rambling question I would forget the beginning before they reached the end. There were times when my mind was altogether absent: facts right there in my head would vanish as I started to speak so I lost my train of thought, or I would forget a key word and leave a silence while I scrambled for an alternative. I saw eyes drift away, bodies turn, and the conversation would continue around me but not with me. I wanted to shout *I still have a brain! Just give me more time.*

Doctor Fletcher ordered a brain scan that April and sounded pleased that the lesions were scattered. The dead bits in my brain were Scattered. At first I thought only that it sounded like a large number of lesions, sounded awful, and I wished I had asked how many. You didn't scatter six or seven, did you? You scattered dozens. I checked the dictionary: scattering seeds sounded scary but books on a table were not so bad. Then I heard on the radio of someone aged forty with early-onset dementia who had lost her driver's licence due to frontal lobe lesions. She had trouble with *executive tasks*. Focused, not scattered. Stirred, not shaken. But I felt shaken.

This was so much worse than those first few weeks in Paris—the year you were at the Sorbonne on sabbatical. Eve was at that international school, and I was hiccupping through my high school French, trying to make myself understood at the boulangerie and the épicerie and being tolerated by all. The French were not always patient with people who mangled their language.

I remember how chic all the women looked, how impressed I was. Madame Veronique in the next apartment was always made up so beautifully, even when she put the cat out first thing, before she was dressed, before her coffee. Even then she wore her taupe eye shadow, pale at the nose side and darkening as it arched outwards, and the perfect eyeliner, so symmetrical and precise, no blobs in her mascara, the just-right shading with the blush and such perfect hair. I tried, but those paint things made my eyes itch, so I gave them all to Carlie. I did begin wearing earrings again, which involved some painful self-mutilation to reopen the piercings from twenty years before. I did start paying more attention to clothes and learned something of that European, put-together look.

Eve was always good at that. But then so was Carlie, and she was only in France with us for six weeks in the summer. Perhaps what Carlie had by the ton was daring: that flowing orange silk shirt with the top button somewhere down near her navel, which she wore with a stern grey skirt you might see on a nun and spiky heels that made her look six feet tall. And she didn't care, bless her. Walked like a model and made people turn and stare. Even in Paris. We had words over that shirt. *Mom, I'm old enough to vote.*

Why was I thinking about Paris, for heaven's sake, and fashion? Nobody bothered about looks at my age, although the girls would have noticed if I stopped taking care of myself. You wouldn't worry—always said it was the insides that mattered. Do you worry about me now, George?

Remember the day Caroline came home from…from somewhere far away. It was after your cancer diagnosis but before my brain thingies. Or before I was aware of my brain thingies.

She arrived quite out of the blue, rang the doorbell because she wanted it to be a total surprise, and you answered. I was upstairs and I could hear you being delighted and excited: *Well I never* and *What a surprise* and *Well, don't just stand there on the doorstep.* And there were bumping noises of bags on the tiles that should have warned me.

You called up, "Liz, come and see who's here." And I came round the bend in the stairs and saw a person standing there in the hall, looking up at me with an expectant face, waiting, and I went down two steps before I realized who it was. Two whole steps.

My own daughter. And Caroline looked surprised, disappointed, hurt, all in that tiny second, and I ran down and flung my arms round her and tried to make up for it, but the memory of that hurt has been in my heart ever since. Two whole steps.

CARLIE

Carlie also remembered the hesitation that day because it was so out of character. She had felt a momentary flash of surprise, but what lingered was unease. It made her more aware of other little lapses, more frequent and more noticeable than when she had been home last summer. The eventual public acknowledgement of dementia was no surprise at all.

Her mother became more emotional, with spurts of irritability or tears. Sometimes she would stand staring at the dials on the dishwasher or washing machine, then finally nod and turn it on. Once she walked away and when Carlie asked if there was anything wrong, she said *no* with an airy wave of the hand; she had decided to do it later. She paused in doorways, saying, *Now what did I come through here for*? Forgot the salt in the potatoes or salted them twice, punctuated conversations with *umm* and *er* and *oh, I forget*, and repeated things day after day. She had a sticker on the back of a cupboard door in the kitchen with the names of all the neighbours—people she had known forever. She had notebooks and ballpoints in every room. *My aide-memoires*, she would say in a grand voice. The saddest part was her awareness of it all. Now and then she would announce, "I'll say sorry now for the next hundred silly things I do, or forget to do, because I can't keep saying sorry every time."

All Carlie could think of was to give a big hug and to say that Liz had always been absent-minded, and it was part of her charm. ("How many times did we have Pancake Tuesday on Wednesday, because you'd forgotten about it until we came home from school?") Liz needed lots of hugs these days.

Eve and Ginny were monitoring everything and so far the unravelling was slow. Ginny approved the medications and rationed the week's pills into one of those Monday-through-Sunday containers. How long could Mom live alone? How could Carlie do her share when the time came? Money for home care she supposed, while she was away.

Carlie checked her mom's driving before she left in that summer of 2002, asking for a ride rather than borrowing the car. Liz was seventy-two. She gripped the steering wheel with both hands and checked the mirrors multiple times like a teenager doing her test. She asked Carlie to turn off the radio, saying she could drive and talk, or drive and listen, or drive and find her way, but not all at the same time. Overall, she was good with the mechanics of driving. She had not lost the basic instincts and was extremely aware of the need to be diligent. There were worse drivers on the road.

CHAPTER EIGHT

2002

LIZ

I SUSPECTED CARLIE WAS TESTING MY DRIVING THAT LAST afternoon, she was watching me so carefully. I had a mind to ask her what grade she had given me. She would be going back on Monday, back to…wherever. She would not be home until spring, and I would miss her—for her own sake of course, but also for the fact that she disguised your absence. Other than that, time slid by quite gently without any major Brain Things happening. Christmas had come and gone and I was getting quite complacent. I should have known it was time for another catastrophe.

I had been feeling optimistic about Eve ever since Rosie started school full time and as always, when the worries about one daughter's problems began to fade, a crisis would arise with another. There had been months between those episodes of Eve retreating to her room and hiding from everything, leaving poor little Rosie to tiptoe around with troubled eyes and her mouth turned down, saying, *Is Mommy mad at me?* By the time Rosie was in grade three, Eve was regularly lunching out with co-workers, even hosting a small baby shower for one and quite a large retirement party for another. She was invited to join a book group but declined because of possible disturbing subject matter: *The Lovely Bones, Atonement, The Crimson Petal and the White.* Each year at recruitment time she considered rejoining her old choir, but that was demanding in a different way: full choir every Wednesday, sopranos every other Tuesday, more rehearsals before a performance. Tiring, but there was also pressure, commitment. But Ginny's daughter was keen to babysit, so finally Eve enrolled and found the singing wonderfully relaxing.

How tense I had become myself, always braced for the next emergency. This new calm felt like a warm bath. Luxury. Rosie turned nine in January 2003 and seemed so grown up, taking grade three in her stride. When I picked her up on Tuesdays after dance class, she was full of bubbles, doing little pirouettes as she gathered her belongings, scattering thoughts as she thought them. *Did you know…? …and Billy forgot his lunch so I gave him half my sandwich and my apple. Eryn's new dress… The teacher said…* She was so like Carlie growing up. Even now I might be in the kitchen and Carlie would start telling me something as she came down the stairs, before she even reached the room.

Carlie. Ever my greatest worry, especially in her teens. But she was like a cat, always landing on her feet, and I had learned not to wonder what she might be doing on the other side of the world. Ginny was stability incarnate, though there had been rough times after Anthony's company folded. But now, three years on and him in a new job, the bags under Ginny's eyes had shrunk to normal busy-working-mother size.

Maybe the mini strokes would stop now that I was less stressed. I opened a bottle of wine and made a toast to Peace and Quiet. It's just one glass, George. Don't fuss.

All through March there was a satisfying balance of family events and outside invitations sprinkled through the lazy calm of books and TV movies, of random documentaries and daily cooking shows, of *The West Wing* and detective stories where I kept my eyes closed through the nasty bits. There was a certain satisfaction in not having to fight for the zapper. I spread out on the sofa under my favourite throw, enjoying the rattle of sleet on the windows or the rumble of ploughs, because I did not have to put my nose outside the door. Someone came and cleared the drive when it snowed and the fact that I was last on his list never mattered because I had no desire to go anywhere. For the first time in years there was no pressure and I felt content. Apart from your absence, this was retirement at its best.

Then came Senegal.

It was three in the afternoon one blustery uninviting Thursday in the middle of March when I was roused from my semi-comatose state by the doorbell. One very long ring. I had to untangle myself from the throw and rescue my glasses and lay my book face down because I could not find the bookmark, all before I set off for the door. Alright, alright, I'm coming. And there, leaning against the doorframe, was Carlie.

"Good heavens."

Carlie did not reply, not in words, but she gave that little smile that I had seen so often on the teenage Carlie, caught in some mischief. *Yes, I know, I shouldn't have. But done is done.* There was no apology in it. There never was.

I realized I was blocking the doorway and the wind was chasing two dead leaves round my ankles, and the furnace had roared to life behind me. "Come in, come in. I'll put the kettle on, and you can tell me all about it."

So. Carlie had met somebody. *Somebody very special.* She never did say much about the affair (my word, not hers) except to murmur something about it being *incandescent*. But when they had discussed a future together, they had agreed there really wasn't one. In the long run, Carlie did not want to stay in Senegal, and Oumar would never leave. And that is all she seemed prepared to say. She flew to Lisbon, then London, then Toronto, then home, a month earlier than planned. They had both decided it was for the best.

I sipped my tea and pondered, while the wind went on skirling and making mad dashes at the window. "And will you stay in touch?"

"No." The voice was brisk. "Better to have a clean break." Carlie gazed past me for a long time without stirring and finally, in a softer voice, she said, "That's the plan, anyway."

The girls wanted details, of course, especially Ginny. How long had she known him? *Five weeks, five days.* Questions were met mostly with silence and an inward, searching look, as if Carlie were asking herself that very question but did not know how to answer. Eve said she needed time to process everything. Leave her alone. And when Ginny asked what he was like, Carlie just said, *He filled the sky.*

Such a brief time to cause such havoc. You were my friend first and it all grew from there—acorn to tree. Remember those tangled-up birch trees we once found? Someone had looped two saplings together into a kind of knot and they had grown into one tree, the bark enclosing the two of them. You wanted to write our initials on them, but I wouldn't let you; said they were someone else's trees and anyway, we didn't need it in writing.

Carlie has always made up her mind about people immediately. Her instincts have been—not infallible, I suppose, but close. And we should have expected something volcanic from Carlie. But what would it do to her? I needed to stay alert for signs of strain and to help where I could. Would my fuzzy brain pick up the signs?

It was a long time before this, my most rambunctious of daughters, began to regain some sort of daily routine. *Carlie, come and eat. Carlie, turn off the TV and go to bed—it's one in the morning.* She had done nothing with her box of papers, hadn't opened a book, hardly left the house. She did not look at anything as if she were really seeing it. She looked blank when I spoke to her. *Sorry. You just say something?* I gathered up laundry off her floor and cleaned up after her in the bathroom and decided I would tolerate this for one month and no longer.

But before the end of that month, Carlie was showing signs of life: cooked her first meal for the two of us—though just shepherd's pie with a few carrots on the side. She went grocery shopping and asked what I needed, put everything away when she came home. Later, she drove Rosie out to Middle Cove for an outing on a Professional Development Day and picked her up from dance class on a Tuesday. Then one day I asked her where she was going, just to be friendly, and Carlie said *Out* with that irritating saucy smile on her face, so like the old Carlie, and I knew she was back.

ᴥ

I was quietly pleased there had been no mini strokes while Carlie needed my attention. Perhaps my circulation was stabilizing. I still panicked at intersections sometimes, disoriented, forgetting where I was going. When I thought of it in time, I chanted *dentist-dentist-dentist* to myself from halfway up the road. One day, I realized I had no idea where I was, so I turned into a parking lot to get my bearings. My mind was blank. I was holding my breath, hands turning sticky on the steering wheel. There I was in a weedy deserted parking lot, surrounded by trees, not a building in sight, and I might as well have been in the middle of an Amazonian rainforest. Then there was the time I was on my way to meet friends at that nice garden place but forgot how to get there—a place I had visited loads of times. I could picture the café itself, the parking lot, the chalkboard menu—but not how to reach it. I drove miles in the wrong direction before it came back to me.

Finally, there came an episode I could not ignore. I was driving home with a load of groceries and turned right off the main road, checking for traffic crossing in front of me from the other direction. There were no cars, but I suddenly noticed a dog on a leash on the opposite sidewalk. Where had that come from? I looked ahead again, and the dog disappeared along with half of the man leading it. I looked back and the dog reappeared and all of the man. The rest of the way home I kept swinging my head side to side to make sure I was not missing anything. There was a foggy greyness in the middle of the view to the left like a fuzzy hole in my vision. It corrected itself by lunchtime.

But...what if it happened when I was changing lanes? Not that I drove on busy roads or highways anymore, or at peak times or out of town, and very little at night, but still. I absolutely did not want to give up my car entirely. I sat at the kitchen table with my coat on and thought about the simplest routes to take to my regular destinations. I could go round in a circle, plan it out so I was always turning right. If there was no choice but to turn left, I could move into the outside lane and stay there, which was something you used to rant about: *In the outside lane, ready to turn left a hundred miles away. In the overtaking lane doing twenty, holding everyone up*. But what else could I do? It was the unpredictable nature of those episodes that was most unnerving. I could not have foreseen that temporary blindness.

I could not, would not, stop doing everything because of fear of what might or might not happen next.

It was the vision loss and the increasing frequency of episodes that finally convinced me that something totally unexpected, possibly dangerous, could happen at any moment. It was time to give the children an Enduring Power of Attorney, and I should do it while Carlie was home. But who would I appoint? Not Carlie, always on the move. Ginny was the eldest and Eve was more…challenged, but I saw more of Eve and would prefer to ask her, although I did not want to hurt any feelings. We all turned to Ginny in an emergency, but Ginny had enough responsibilities without me. And these powers were not meant just for emergencies; they gave permission for someone else to do my banking or arrange for selling the house, when it came to that. Any one of them would be suitable and they would all share any tasks involved, anyway—but I would be more comfortable with Eve.

So, a week later I sat in the lawyer's waiting room with Eve on that famous leather sofa, then met with the lawyer inside, alone. I answered all of Mr. Thingy's questions, trying to sound half sensible. He must have decided I had made up my own mind and still had enough mind to make up, because there was no hesitation in his manner when he witnessed my signature.

Carlie was negotiating something work-related at Memorial University and also sending off brown envelopes to other universities across the country.

"So where have you applied?" said Ginny at Sunday dinner. Anthony and the Wallace women were lingering over the empty plates, son Jeremy out with friends, daughter Emily taking the SUV to go to a basketball game, and Rosie gone to watch a Disney movie in the rec room.

"Different places, but I think I may have a one-year position here at Memorial starting in September, covering a sabbatical. Then I'll have to wait and see. I want to come home."

There was instant jubilation round the table, and into the noise Ginny said, "So you still think of this as home? I mean... you always...you've been away more than—"

"Yes, what's here that isn't anywhere else?" Eve asked. "What's home?"

There was an expectant silence and Carlie answered in an unusually tentative voice.

"Comfort, I suppose. Safety. Solitude, when I want it." Carlie smiled in a distant sort of way. "Hills and trees." The smile broadened for a moment, "Rain, drizzle, and fog." She pushed a few crumbs into a pile by her plate with one finger, and said life here was easy. She said she was burned out even before... her shoulders hunched up and she shook her head slightly. She still loved so many things about Senegal and its people, but she was worn down from years of seeing smart, enthusiastic girls remaining semi-illiterate because of lack of opportunity, of untreated diseases, malnourishment, unnecessary suffering. And there was nothing she could do—nothing substantial, anyway. The social inequalities...Carlie pressed the crumb pile flat with her thumb.

Then there was the slow swallowing up of the country by the desert, the hopelessness under the colourful, positive exterior. "Worst are the young men," she said. "Full of energy, raring to go but with nothing to go toward. No future. So they're leaving. Three brothers joining a group in the night in a little boat heading for the Canary Islands. Maybe. Then on to Europe: France, Italy, Spain. Maybe. Another mother left with no sons."

She still loved Dakar—it was so vibrant, alive—but it was hard being a single woman in such a patriarchal country. Carlie kept on talking in that dreamy way, so unlike her usual self-assured tone, and there was a concentrated silence in the room, a tension. But I did not want to hear any more. I kept thinking of those boys in the boat. There were worse things than losing one's marbles in old age.

"I'm tired," Carlie was saying. "I talk about it and write about it but nothing..." She sat back in her chair and carefully lifted her napkin off her knees and laid it on her plate. "I'm tired of...I'm just tired."

She was looking around the table now. She had lost that ethereal look. No, that was the wrong word; Eve was the ethereal member of the family. Ginny was totally earthbound and Carlie was...home from the sea?

She was looking at us now, one by one. "And as families go, you guys aren't too bad."

Ginny opened her mouth but closed it again, and Carlie grinned at her. It was a smaller grin than usual, but still. "I've seen a lot of families in a lot of places, and I think the Wallace family measures up quite well. Even my bossy older sister." She held up a hand quickly and said, "I'd like to come home again if you'll have me."

Then everyone was laughing and hugging each other, and Rosie wandered in and said why was everybody crying, and Eve pulled her into the hug-circle and said, "Carlie's not going back to Africa, sweetheart. Carlie's coming home for good."

CHAPTER NINE

2003

LIZ

CARLIE MOVED INTO AN APARTMENT ON 9/11, A THURSDAY. It was two years since the twin towers fell, but the amount of rerun news made it feel as if it was all happening again. And although I enjoyed having peace restored in my house, I did miss Carlie: her unexpectedness, knowing there was someone in the next room to talk to, or that she would be home later. The emptiness echoed back at me.

I liked to chat with the person at the checkout in the supermarket, but it was a snippy young woman that day, a real surlyboots. I made some comment about the bananas but just got a *Hmph* in return. "Would you mind standing the milk upright, please? Now and then, one springs a leak." I smiled, trying to look conspiratorial, but the girl sighed loudly, making a performance of lifting the carton out and standing it up in the bag, her mouth all pinched up.

"Air Miles?" Snarl. I had to dig around for the card and the girl sighed again. You would think I was keeping a line waiting but there was only one person behind me, and he was engrossed in the headlines on the magazine stand: a woman with a spectacular bosom and the title: *Who's the New Man?* Then a royal head and shoulders: *Queen Getting Divorced.*

I paid with two twenties and held my hand out for the change, but the girl kept her hand close to the cash register, so I had to lean over to reach, and she dropped the coins into my hand without really looking so half of them missed and I had to scrabble for them. What if I'd had a back problem? Painful.

I told myself this girl might have a terrible home life. What did I know? But still, there was no need to spread the sourness around.

So I left the checkout without the usual smile but as I reached the door an enthusiastic voice called out, "Liz!"

The owner of the voice looked slightly familiar, but then everyone looked slightly familiar. Carlie said there were only four types of Newfoundland faces and I could believe it. Probably everyone I knew had one of those faces. Someone from Rosie's school? That nice lady from the library?

"I haven't seen you in a dog's age, Liz. How're you doing?"

"Good. Good…yourself?"

"Can't complain. Just back from St. Pete's. Bit of Florida sunshine perks you up."

That voice…this person was connected to the hospital in some way. Yes. She was the lady from the cancer clinic, always reading lurid-looking Harlequin romances while she waited with her husband. Said those stories kept her going. *Little bit of loving does you good when you're feeling down.* Her brother used to sit with her sometimes.

"Saw your brother a while ago," I said, triumphant. "He was looking well."

"I don't have a brother."

"Oh."

"You're mixing me up with So-and-So. Everybody does it." It was an ex-co-worker's wife, and it all came back to me later—her whole life story. We had a little chuckle together, there at the supermarket door, and a joke about senior moments. It did not always end so comfortably. I was having trouble picking faces out of a crowd. Only last week at a fundraiser, I was looking for friends I knew would be out there, when a woman I absolutely should have known came out of the crowd and accused me of avoiding her. *Stared right at me. So rude.* Then she turned her back and walked away.

Despite my careful list, I had forgotten the beans. I had the chili all ready to take to Eve's except for one can of black beans and one of red kidney beans. Eve said she had some. Come on over.

At home, I had my electric can opener, but Eve was into minimizing electrical gadgets in her kitchen. It was not a gadget to me—it was a necessity. Eve had one of those manual affairs where you had to wind a big wing nut thing on the side, which hurt my thumb. This worked the cutting edges, which were anything but cutting edge, and which invariably fell off halfway round the rim of the can, like an old car that loses control on the steep curve in a demolition derby—flies up over the embankment and disappears. And then I would need a Band-Aid and end up scrabbling around on the floor to pick up the damned opener.

So I was feeling grumpy before I even started looking for the opener. There was one big drawer for cooking utensils in Eve's kitchen, the kind of utensils you don't put in the everyday cutlery drawer or with the sharp things. This drawer held wooden spoons and orange measuring spoons and a slotted spoon and oven gloves with singe marks and an ice cream scoop and two ladles of different sizes and spatulas (which sounded so spitty and unhygienic): plastic ones, rubber ones, and a stainless steel one for the barbecue, and a set of chopsticks in a box (from Carlie of course), and a bottle brush and a brush for scrubbing vegetables and a pastry brush, and a knife sharpener with a red handle, which fell off if you looked at it the wrong way, and a cheese grater Ginny had bought at Ikea in Montréal and which fit on top of a red container that caught the cheese shreds, and a meat thermometer and a hard-boiled egg slicer and a whisk and a potato masher and a flat red rubber circle with Parkinson Society Canada written on it for giving a better grip when unscrewing tops off pickle jars, and three beer bottle openers and two wine bottle openers, different styles, one with a cork still in it, and a nut cracker. But No Can Opener. I looked at every item in that drawer and shuffled them around so I didn't miss anything and there was No Can Opener.

"Eve. Where. Do you keep. Your can opener?"

Eve came in from the dining area, reached round and picked it out of the drawer I was staring into. It was a large specimen with pea green handles—can't-miss-it handles, lying in the middle of the drawer I had been rummaging through.

"Oh," I said. "Thought it had red handles."

CHAPTER TEN

2004

ROSIE

ROSIE STOOD AT THE DESK IN HER ROOM AND SPUN THE globe so hard it jiggled on the stand and she had to catch it before it toppled. She put one finger on St. John's at the far eastern edge of Canada, traced a straight line across half the world to the Middle East, and jabbed a vague thumb at the Persian Gulf, where her father was. Qatar. One day she would go to Qatar and find him.

How do you imagine a person you don't remember? You need something to hang your thoughts on: a face, a voice, mannerisms. Hugs. Rosie's father had left when she was a baby and she had no memory of him at all. Her father the blank. Her mother wouldn't talk about him and whenever Rosie asked the rest of the family, they were vague—medium height, brown hair, brown eyes, and *don't keep asking your mother because it upsets her.* There were no pictures of him anywhere. At least Nana had a picture of George to talk to. Maybe Rosie should say Grandad or Grandpa or Pops to be more respectful, but she had heard him called George all her life, so that was how she thought of him. You could talk to absent people if you knew what they looked like, who they were. You couldn't talk to a blank.

On top of all that, Rosie took after her mom so even a mirror gave no clues. At every introduction it was *My, you look just like Eve,* and Rosie had to drag up another here-we-go-again smile. People said Rosie walked like her Aunt Ginny, with those quick light steps, and her sneeze was a conversation-stopper like Aunt Carlie's—not just one explosion, but three in a row. But the rest of her was all Mom. Rosie's only oddity was being left-handed, and that did not belong to anybody at all.

It was 2004, just after her tenth birthday in grade four, and Rosie had to do a project on a country. *Any country except Canada*. Or they could pick one off the list: England, Ireland, France, the United States.... They were all familiar places and Rosie considered doing France because Mom had talked about it so often and had show-and-tell things from when she'd lived there. But loads of kids were doing France. So she chose Qatar.

Mrs. Rossiter said no Google and no Wikipedia please. She wanted them to look things up in books or in journals and magazines like *National Geographic*, to check in the school library—or any library—and to talk to anybody they knew who might have visited that country. Real Research. They spent time in class going over how to ask people questions, do a Real Interview.

Asking Mom about Qatar was a no-no. When Rosie tried Nana, she looked vague, then worried, then said, "I don't think..." but she never said what it was she didn't think. Then there was Aunt Carlie. She might even have been there. The phone at her apartment went to voicemail a few times before she finally answered.

"Aunty Carlie, have you been to Qatar?"

"Why do you ask?"

"I'm doing a project for school."

"Oh. Well...yes, I have. I was just passing through, but I had a quick look around Doha."

"Did you see...anybody you knew?"

"No. I did not see Michel. Nor did I speak to him or contact him in any way. So let's not get into that, okay?"

"Okay. But can I interview you about Qatar?"

There were muffled noises, like a hand over the phone, Aunty Carlie's voice and a man's deep voice and Aunty giggling.

"When's the deadline?"

"Erm...."

"When does the project have to be in?"

Two weeks on Monday. Her aunt had a visitor staying for a few days so they settled on the following Wednesday for the interview and Rosie would stay for supper.

Rosie spent hours on that project. Years later, whenever the word *project* arose, she would think of that one. Aunty Carlie said it was not the end result that mattered so much as the "process." And in the end, there was just a sheet of bristol board with a map showing where Qatar was in the Persian Gulf and pictures of the national flag and the desert and some camels, and three paragraphs about Doha being the capital and the king being an emir with a long name, Sheikh something or other, and a bit about oil.

Aunty Carlie said you had to love the process. *And let's drop this aunty business. Just call me Carlie.* She had books that would help but they were all in boxes and would stay in boxes until Carlie had a permanent home. So she took Rosie to the reference library at the Arts and Culture Centre and showed her how to do a search, how to think what to ask for and who to ask and where. They pored over political maps and physical ones and historical maps and antique maps and Aunty Carlie (Carlie) said she would take Rosie over some other time to the government department that had charts and surveys, to show her topographical maps. *Start with the big picture and work in.*

They went to the library at Memorial University. The library was named after Queen Elizabeth II, and Rosie remembered something on television about Buckingham Palace, seeing a long, long corridor, miles to the far end. In the library the aisles between the stacks looked just as long, only some of them were really narrow, and there were cross-corridors, which made her think of horror movies with a psychotic stalker in the next aisle over (like in the movie she saw at Eryn's that Mom didn't know about). Maybe you would come face to face with the stalker at the end, but Aunty Carlie said you would just wallop him with a book. No worries. She said keep your mind on the books. The aisles were only places where there weren't any.

Carlie made you see the magic. Breathe in that inky, thumbprint smell, Rosie. Notice the scrape of a book being pulled out, see the blur of dingy colours as you walk along, how it changes to a glow when you focus on a single binding—sunset when the light's almost gone, wet spruce, a storm at sea. Feel the paper sucking the juice out of your fingers, these books that have been absorbing the flavour of readers over so many years. Imagine faraway libraries where old men with grooved faces and bushy beards pored over scrolls amongst astrolabes and microscopes.

This was the magic Rosie wanted to remember. This was what she wanted to be when she grew up—a professor like Carlie and her grandfather, George. Her aunt was teaching at Memorial now and writing books about her research, not living out of a backpack. She was tired of backpacks. Rosie did not want to work in a hospital like her mom, worrying about other people worrying, or like Aunt Ginny, sticking needles in people and dishing out pills.

Aunty Carlie took Rosie to a coffee shop afterwards, said that was the proper way to finish a session at the library. Rosie would have preferred McDonalds, but she just said she didn't drink much coffee. So Carlie bought her a latte, which she said was coffee that hadn't hit puberty yet, and if she didn't know what puberty was, go ask her mom. Rosie snickered into her latte. She and Eryn knew all about puberty.

CHAPTER ELEVEN

2005

LIZ

LATE IN THE FALL OF 2005, WHEN CARLIE STARTED LOOKING seriously for a house, I persuaded her to move back home to save on rent. Whether it was Carlie being extra-picky or just a poor time for the housing market I was not sure, but nine months later she was still looking, and the family teasing had become quite inventive.

"This house has some long gestation period."

"Maybe it'll be a duplex."

"Must have a big hedge round it like Sleeping Beauty."

"Welcome to the Hedge of the World."

This particular warm Sunday at the end of June, Carlie had taken over my kitchen for a late lunch and cooked one of her delicious African dishes: grilled chicken marinated in a thick onion and lemon sauce. Everyone was present except for Ginny's children. I had been relegated to table setting. Carlie sat at the head of the table and after the coffee had been handed round, she said, in her CEO voice, "You must be wondering why I've called this meeting." We all perked up from our post-prandial stupor, and Ginny paused in her plate-piling. "I've put in an offer on a house."

There was a chorus of *Oh!* and *Wonderful!* Then the all-important, *Where?*

"Mulberry Street."

One of those awkward silences fell—heavily. A silence that said it all. I pictured row housing right on the street with no front garden, no driveway. I would never find a parking space on a street like that, and if I did, my parallel parking was so bad by then I would not have wanted to risk trying. So, no dropping in. More loss of spontaneity. I would have to rely on one of the others to taxi me over every time.

Anthony's foot tapping had started up again at a slower pace and everyone was carefully not looking at anybody else. Ginny's hands stayed motionless on the plate pile. "But why?" she said, looking upset, offended almost. "Why down there?"

"I want to be in the middle of things. Downtown. Don't want to be out in the burbs. I hate gardening. I don't have children. I'm not looking for a house with a yard and a picket fence near a good school, like you guys. I want to feel part of a neighbourhood and I know people around there. And I only have one paycheque to work with."

There followed a discussion about the benefits of a small house a little farther uptown, nearer the university, or a condo, and yes, Carlie had looked at condos and maybe in twenty years, but they had such an elderly feel to them, and most were tucked away in places she didn't want to be. Anthony commented on the need to have the roof checked and the electrical and plumbing, those structural things, and yes, that was being done. Then back to the pros and cons of condominium living, with Ginny's determined itemizing of people they knew living happily in condos all over creation—*Look at Sherry in Toronto and Jane in Ottawa*—and Carlie's rebuttal about value for money and the hidden cost of condo fees—not so very hidden and rising rapidly.

"I did view one expensive condo out of curiosity," Carlie said. "The view across the harbour was to die for. Everything was to die for. But… So, I went looking for that view in my price range."

Ginny pushed her chair back from the table and tossed her napkin down on top of a messy plate and spoke in that growly voice which Jeremy used when he announced his team had *lost in overtime,* saying, "She bought it for the view."

Then the gloves came off: the forty-five-degree gradient, lethal in icy weather, old-therefore-risky, no insulation, rats, complaints about snow clearing downtown all the time...those bikes roaring around in the middle of the night...fire trap.... Eve frowned at Ginny, shaking her head slightly, and said Carlie would love being down with the arts crowd in the heart of town, and of course row housing could be...cozy...with those shared walls, and some of those old houses had lovely high ceilings with plaster mouldings and beautiful hardwood floors. But Ginny was not ready to take a hint, saying she supposed Carlie could always install sprinklers. And wear earplugs.

Rosie disappeared at some point to channel-flick in the rec room. I vaguely remembered a thank-you-and-excuse-me and hoped I had acknowledged them suitably. I wanted to change the channel in the dining room, too, so I suggested leaving the dishes and going to sit in comfy chairs. My living room furniture was arranged round the room in an irregular oval, a tentative request for democracy. I was glad we were not at Ginny's house, with two long couches facing each other across a big coffee table like opposing armies. When the children were little, those sofas even wore different coloured throws like military uniforms.

The conversation went on for ages, first in the living room, then round the dishwasher, then the whole family drifted off home. Carlie went out with them to say goodbye and I watched from the window. They stood on the sidewalk in a group, still arguing, still looking unconvinced, Ginny waving emphatic arms while Anthony stared at his shoes. Eve put an arm round Ginny's shoulders...what was that about?

Carlie walked back into the house with that swagger that said they were almost getting to her but she would fight them to the death. She disappeared into her room without a word. I turned away from the window, wondering what I had missed down there, wondering about my knees and those tall thin houses with all those tall thin stairs.

CARLIE

Carlie had not expected Ginny to be so perturbed about her house offer. It was not just the usual differences in tastes and opinions, or Ginny's perpetual need to argue over every freaking thing. It was something deeper. They were all standing together on the sidewalk because Eve's car was up the street and Ginny's SUV was two houses down.

"Sorry, Carlie. Didn't mean to shoot you down in flames," Ginny said. It was a bit late for that, but Carlie didn't comment. "It's just that...I was remembering Sophie—you know, from high school—the trouble she had when she rented down there." Sophie would be shovelling out her car before the neighbours were out of bed. Then the folks next door would toss the snow off their frontage right into her empty space while she was gone, so when she came home from work she had to shovel again. And she had rats because all the lofts were joined together, so if one house had rats, they all had rats.

Carlie shook her head. "Well this place has a great attic, completely sealed off from the neighbours, and you can get mean neighbours anywhere—luck of the draw."

"Yes. You're quite right." Ginny sounded abashed. "But then...well, then there's Mom." She had her hands tucked into her armpits, all huddled down as if it were twenty below instead of a beautiful almost-summer afternoon.

So. That was the problem. Ginny always left the real issue until last—Carlie should have remembered. Liz was going to need something soon and Ginny...Ginny didn't think she could handle looking after another elderly person. Ginny was shrinking down even further now, and Eve put an arm round her. "...and Mom could never manage in a house like that."

Carlie froze to the sidewalk. The words seemed to sink to the ground and spread out and the chill creep up Carlie's legs. "So, the spinster daughter should do her thing and take in the aging parent?" Her voice cracked. "So, I should be moving into an old lady condo to prepare?" She brought her voice down, aware of the ugly screech, and hissed, "Well, fuck that!" She turned and stormed back into the house and fumbled opening the door because her hands were shaking. Godgodgodgod....

Carlie stood in her room staring out the window, barely conscious of the SUV pulling away from the curb. Was she making a mistake, buying a house at all? It was a huge change of lifestyle and it still felt like a public admission of a need for permanence, security, stability—things she had scorned all her life. She had a tenure-track position at the university now, one book published and well reviewed, another due out in the fall, first author in various respected journals.... She had thought she was ready to take on this new risk—the risk of tying herself down.

She wandered into her father's office and leaned her two hands on the desk, looking at the place his face would be if he were sitting there. *You understand, George, don't you? I don't just want somewhere to lay my head; I want my own Place—with a heart and an atmosphere. And this is it.* Her father would tell her to stick to her guns. He would advise her not to make a decision until all the data was in but, *once you have all the facts, make up your mind and stick to it.* Carlie stood awhile, remembering him, remembering how they had felt the same way about so many things. Then she heard Liz prowling around and whisked herself back into her own room before she was cornered.

But it was not just Place; it was People too. Eve might still need help while Rosie floundered through puberty, and yes, Liz would need some sort of assisted living down the road and Carlie had every intention of doing her share when the time came. But goddammit, Ginny! Was Carlie making a mistake in committing herself to staying here, in risking her sanity amidst the wrangling and rumbling of family?

Ginny had gone berserk, been totally unreasonable. This needed sorting out. Today. Carlie was not going to be up all night in a stew of anger and upset. She called Eve, who rambled on about Ginny's in-laws and what the frig did they have to do with anything? Eve said they should meet—

"Tonight," Carlie shouted into the phone. "Set it up for tonight." God, she shouldn't be shouting at Eve. She softened her voice. "Sorry. Tonight would be good. Would you arrange it with Ginny, please? I'll lose it if I phone her now. And not here with Mom listening. Besides, I want to be able to walk out if I feel like it."

And Eve giggled. Giggled! Said something about wearing Kevlar.

⁂

The three of them met at eight in a pub near the university, Eve first as usual and Ginny arriving last in her usual flurry but before Carlie had had time to pour herself into the booth. They waffled for a second before the hug, leaving more space than usual, torsos held back stiffly—more a quick jostle of hands on upper arms—and the process of bouncing along the bench and squirming out of jackets all seemed extra noticeable. Then silence. Carlie was willing to negotiate a settlement, but she was damned if she was going to speak first.

"Sorry about the short fuse," Ginny offered. "I'm just at my wits' end with Anthony's family."

"Why? What's going on?" Sounded like malarkey to Carlie. Ginny had been checking on the in-laws forever, so nothing new there.

It turned out that what had begun as an occasional check on Anthony's parents at the family's request had turned into a long, drawn-out daily routine to help both of them prepare for bed, see to their medications, clean up, check on the fridge… "And it's all the way across town so it's at least a couple of hours every night." Carlie remembered a stormy night last winter when Ginny's car slid off the road into a snowdrift on the way back from the Nolans' house, and Anthony and his brother had to drive out in Neil's truck in a blizzard to tow her out. Well, her own family always turned to Ginny in an emergency, so Carlie supposed it made sense that the Nolan family did the same, and Ginny could never say no.

The server was reaching in with the menus and Ginny surprised Carlie by ordering a G&T instead of her usual Something Light, saying she needed fortifying. She described life with Mrs. Nolan: the nitpicking, the constant complaining—and the more she deteriorated the more she complained. The server came with the drinks and deposited them with more haste than grace and Eve passed them around, touching Ginny on the shoulder to draw her attention. Ginny was slumped back against the wooden partition with her eyes closed and her face looked grey, although that could have been the flickering from the television behind the bar. The Leafs were playing some team in white and there was an altercation on the ice between three players. Carlie was a Canadiens fan herself, ever since living in Montréal, so she wasn't too interested. A different server arrived with the nachos.

Help had not been forthcoming when Ginny warned the Nolan family of their mother's increasing dependency. Anthony's brother Neil did what he could, but he worked out on one of the oil rigs and was only in town for two weeks at a time. Anthony's sister, Midge, dropped in with a cooked meal now and then and checked on the fridge, but the rest did nothing. The rest just expected Ginny to look after everything—she was the nurse, after all.

"Like George used to say," Carlie commented, "*Why keep a dog and bark yourself?*"

When Anthony suggested an assessment to place their mother in a senior's home with help from home care in the meantime, the family erupted. Horror at *dumping poor Mother in a home* but multiple reasons why they were unable to do more to help, infighting over what should happen next, and aspersions cast in Ginny's direction. Apparently, Mrs. Nolan had been spreading her complaints by phone to the siblings; everything from Ginny being bossy to putting things in all the wrong places to stealing the teaspoons. But the underlying concern amongst all of them was cost. Who was going to pay for all this? And who was being a dutiful son/daughter and who was trying to wheedle their way into a bigger share in The Will when their parents passed away? (Anthony said there would be nothing much to share anyway.) It was all growing nastier by the day.

Carlie was horrified. "My god, Ginny, you would never put up with that bullshit from us." And Eve was quietly agreeing.

No. Ginny had stopped going since she heard about the teaspoons. Trouble was, Mr. Nolan was a sweetheart and would whisper to Ginny as she was leaving, *You won't give up on us, will you?* And here she was, doing just that.

The commiseration and shock and concern went on for some time, then Carlie said, "Ginny, you have all my sympathy. You've been having a terrible time and I'm sorry I didn't ask more about this earlier." Not that she could have done anything but at least she would have been another sympathetic ear. "I'm sorry for not taking any notice."

She totally understood Ginny not wanting to take on more eldercare responsibilities, but surely there were other ways to look after Liz when the time came—all those things they had discussed over the months, like Carlie coordinating the home care (which she knew from a friend could be a logistical nightmare) and sharing the cost, and maybe taking turns to sleep at Liz's house when necessary (and Carlie would do more than the others because of circumstances), and cooking meals.... Surely there were ways without her, Carlie, having to buy a freaking geriatric condo.

"Right now, I'm buying a house to suit my own needs, not my mother's."

Also, she was offended, hurt, that Ginny would think Carlie would behave like the Nolans.

Then Ginny was waving her hands about, protesting of course she never thought that...never crossed her mind. It was just that maybe Carlie didn't understand what was involved....

"Well, maybe I don't, but there are big differences between Liz and the Nolans, starting with the fact that there is just one of her." And Liz was not like Mrs. Nolan. Not in the least. Good god no, although Eve murmured, "The Mom we know *now* is not."

However. The temperature was cooling, and the hackles and prickles were less hackled and prickly. The nachos had disappeared without Carlie being aware of eating them, leaving a bigger scatter of pepper-olive-chili scraps lying around than usual, which she began picking at in an absent-minded way, and which changed the direction of her muttering to how nothing would be left uneaten in developing countries.

The screen above the bar showed the scoreboard. Game over. The Leafs lost.

❧

There were follow-up phone calls and emails, both Carlie's sisters at their mildest and most accommodating, while Carlie tried to regain the excitement, the euphoria, of buying her very first house. So it wasn't until a few weeks later that Eve mentioned Rosie had also been upset by the squabble over Carlie's new house. Rosie had asked why Nana didn't just come and live with them? Nana could move into Rosie's room on the ground floor and take over that bathroom too, and Rosie could move upstairs.

Sweet child. The lovely girl. And no, Rosie did not understand all the implications—well, none of them did really. Eve had explained about dementia, warned Rosie about the realities. "She asked me about the difference between Alzheimer's and transient ischemic attacks, and I explained as much as I know myself."

Rosie was a little familiar with Alzheimer's, as a friend's grandmother, so afflicted, had stuck fifty of his hockey cards on the wall with Krazy Glue. She understood enough, for now, with no weakening of her resolve. She kept saying, *Poor, poor Nana*, and that it must be like having leprosy—*watching bits of yourself drop off*. Said she would rather have cancer.

"And what about you?" Carlie asked Eve. "Wouldn't that be too hard on you?" But Eve said no, she thought she could manage with home care and two sisters to share the load and to step in if things became overwhelming.

Carlie wondered if she would have volunteered in that way had circumstances been reversed? Hard to know. But there was room for a little guilt.

CHAPTER TWELVE

2006

LIZ

SOMETHING WAS GOING ON. CARLIE WAS ON HER PHONE TOO much. She was not one for phones normally—preferred face to face (or in-your-face, depending on your point of view). She only used the phone to arrange meetings. It was not about the house, as far as I could tell, which was all finalized and the moving date set for—I couldn't remember. Sometimes she sounded angry: *taken all the pleasure out of it.* Sometimes she was more indignant than angry: *shouldn't have to put up with… how dare they….* Then one day I heard the words *poor Ginny.* Carlie must be talking to Eve about Ginny. She had never mentioned anything to me, and I had asked her more than once. Just sighed and said *It's complicated.* That's what people said when they didn't want to explain, when they were hiding something. But I wanted to know. Ginny was my daughter. When I tried to say that to Carlie, she just said Ginny had been having trouble with her in-laws. It would all blow over.

Then yesterday, or maybe it was longer ago than that…it was the day I had my hair cut. Anyway, I was walking past Carlie's room and heard her being angry again. The door was shut but I stopped and listened. Yes, I know. I shouldn't have. *They should stick that awful woman*—mutters and profanities here—*home.* No. That wasn't it. They should *stick her IN a Home.* Ginny's in-laws. Mrs. Nolan. Perhaps that explained Ginny's in-law difficulties. The "awful woman" comment certainly fitted. I had only talked to Mrs. Nolan at weddings and funerals but that was enough. Always criticizing. She was very trying in the run-up to Ginny's own wedding.

But why were they excluding me from this conversation? They must think it would upset me. Why? Were they planning on sticking me in a Home too? No. They wouldn't do that. They couldn't do that, anyway. I was independent and in charge of my own life and would continue to be so until…wait a minute…the Power of Attorney. Does that allow them to move me into a Home against my will? No, of course not. What was I thinking—none of my girls would dream of such a thing. But then why would they not talk about all this in front of me? *Don't leave anybody out.* That was a house rule, all through their growing up. *So why…?*

I was laid up with one of those everlasting summer colds when the family went to view Carlie's house. Their reports were more positive than I expected.

"Bigger rooms than you'd think," Ginny said, "And you can close them off to conserve heat."

Eve said the downstairs bathroom was newly renovated and very elegant.

"And modern vinyl windows everywhere with fantastic views from upstairs." Ginny was overdoing the positives a bit, maybe to make up for the stuff about rats the last time. Anthony assured me he saw no signs of rodents, even little ones, and that the attic was completely divided off from the neighbours' as per current building regulations. In fact it was quite civilized, as attics went, with a new roof and up-to-date insulation.

Ginny was still not back to her normal self. She had been looking harassed for weeks but was still not forthcoming when I probed. All she would say, all any of them would say, was *something to do with the in-laws.* I was getting really tired of that. The girls didn't tell me things like they used to. Did they think I was not capable of rational thought these days? Of rational listening? Little curls of fear stirred in my stomach sometimes. I did not care too much that acquaintances were less inclusive lately but please, please don't let my own family stop consulting or discussing or just plain gossiping with me. That was the power that ran my engine.

Carlie had been in her new house for a week before I saw it for myself, and of course the furnishings were, well…functional. Like the set of ugly chrome and plastic table and chairs in the dining room, which she'd bought on Kijiji—whatever that was. My mother's embroidered tablecloth from the back of my linen closet could improve the table but there was nothing to be done about those chairs. She had brought her creamy sectional sofa from the apartment, which looked good in its new setting, but which I found uncomfortable because it was designed for sprawling not sitting. The only quality furnishings were in her bedroom, which was a truly magnificent room. Yes, I could understand Carlie wanting the house for that room. I wanted a little house out near Topsail once, because of the glorious horse chestnut tree in the garden, but of course it was more practical to live in town. I watched for the *Sold* sign on the house and the first thing the new owners did was chop down that tree.

I donated the desk and chair from your study, George. I knew you would approve. The movers had awful trouble getting the desk out. Remember all our renovations back in the eighties? They made for tighter angles, apparently, so moving that desk was a monumental challenge. The men sweated gallons and drank gallons of Pepsi to make up for it, and I learned some new swear words.

I told Carlie to take the books she wanted from your shelves, too, and we packed up the rest *to go*—Carlie said she would deal with all that. The only thing gone from your office until then was the globe on its stand, which I had given to Rosie back in grade three or thereabouts. I hardly looked into that room after you left. It said *George should be here* louder than anywhere. This unpacking and repacking almost felt like a final goodbye, like spreading your ashes. Yes, I know, you were not cremated. You're still there in the cemetery, where I can come visit you. They kept telling me cremation saved space, but if there's one thing this island has in abundance, it's space—a hundred thousand square kilometres of it. You said that often enough. But this still felt like spreading your ashes.

In addition to parking problems at Carlie's new house—and it turned out there was a perfect little parking area next to an office building at the top of the street—what worried me most was the slipperiness of the main stairs. They were made of beautiful wood with probably ten layers of that Varathane varnish so you could see your reflection, but Carlie was going to kill herself one day, running down those slippery steps in her woolly socks and falling. Nobody there to help. Days lying all bent out of shape before anyone found her. Carlie just ignored me when I brought this up. Everyone ignored me all the time.

Weeks later, on a chill February day, Carlie had a compression bandage on her ankle. It was something she could not disguise or she certainly would have done. She said she twisted it slipping on black ice, but I knew she did it on those stairs. Carlie had on that bland face she used to hide what she was thinking, but I knew. The very absence of expression was an admission of guilt. Later we were all over for Saturday lunch and there was an attractive, very new strip of carpet up the middle of the stairs, echoing the colours in the stained-glass window on the landing. Victorian. No, Edwardian. I could do the bland face too.

"Nice carpet," I said.

Whatever triggered the flare-up between Carlie and Ginny over the house seemed to have sorted itself out. I didn't inquire any more. I remember trying to separate the two of them when they were arguing growing up. There was one particular fight over... goodness knows what...they were always squabbling over something. Eve had been a baby, so it must have been around kindergarten or grade one for the other two. People said I should leave them alone; they were learning to be assertive, learning to differentiate between assertiveness and aggression, and now was the time to sort it out, when they were children. It was harder if they didn't understand the difference until their twenties when people were less tolerant. So I should let the squabble run its course, unless somebody was about to lose a limb. I have often wondered if that was why Eve avoided arguments—just kept to the sidelines instead, and learned by taking it all in.

The girls did learn the difference between assertiveness and aggression though, all three of them, so something worked. We didn't make too bad a job of their upbringing, did we? How would Rosie learn with no siblings to observe or practice on? Even cousins were thin on the ground, spread across the country or the wrong age. I grew up with a ton of cousins, all living close by. We grew up in each others' kitchens.

I worried sometimes about how Rosie would cope when she learned about her parentage. She would need all the self-confidence she could muster to know she was still her own self, still Rosie. She was heading into puberty already and it would soon be time to tell her. They would survive it I supposed, she and Eve. I hoped. But I also hoped I would still have enough faculties left to help, so it had better happen sooner rather than later. Hugs and reassurance might be all that I could offer but I've had lots of practice with those.

I was just home from morning coffee with two ladies I had not seen for ages. It was a pleasant change being in a coffee shop instead of somebody's living room. There were people to watch and action outside the window: traffic and a line at a bus stop and a girl marching along in purple tights, all by herself but talking (wearing those big headphones) and gesticulating. There were conversations to overhear too. Not that I eavesdropped deliberately, but when someone says *don't let him get away with it,* it does make you wonder.

The three of us discussed the problems of babysitting while we played with our muffins, (too dry, not enough berries) and sipped the excellent coffee. (Should jot down what I ordered, for next time.) One friend had been taking care of two grandchildren since babyhood while the parents worked. I could imagine how exhausting that would be. They still came to her after school, so she was always tied down in the afternoons. Hence the morning coffee. I admired her fortitude. She seemed to think that was what being a grandmother had to be. *What can you do?* Well, you could say no, now and again. That's what you could do.

The other friend said she brought up her own crowd without outside help from anybody and no way was she doing it a second time. She helped in emergencies of course, if the sitter was sick or someone needed ferrying to an appointment. *And we want to travel while we still can. Can't count on there being a "next year" at our age.*

I was relaxing in my recliner afterwards with soothing guitar music playing—that Spanish piece you loved, George, that you hear on movies sometimes, with the hero riding off into the sunset. *Aranjuez*. I sat wondering about the role of a grandparent. It was not the same as being a parent. Some children were brought up entirely by a grandparent out of necessity but then that person was really a substitute parent. Even when Eve was out of commission and I was standing in, it was only temporary, a kind of holding pattern. I deferred any decisions that might arise for Eve to make when she was available, even when I knew I would disagree with her decision. I had heard of families where the patriarch (or matriarch) tried to force the following generations into their vision of the future. It never worked. Some of my favourite murder mysteries had that as a plot.

But we did not listen to our grandparents enough, or to our parents. We missed opportunities. How many times, since my own parents died, have I wanted to know what happened to them through the Second World War or my grandparents in the First World War. My grandfather was in the navy. My mother taught in a little outport, where the children walked long distances sometimes, in all weathers, and each brought a log to put in the stove in the one-room school. So many fascinating things that I had no interest in until it was too late.

Grandparents had more time to remind everyone of their roots, too, their relationships and togetherness. Why else did my generation sit around at family gatherings talking about who was related to whom and in what degree, or who went to school with this one, or married that one (or should not have done). It was like those *griots* Carlie talked about in Senegal—and like the one on that old TV series, *Roots,* where the griot recited every tribe member's name right back to the name of the main character. This family reminiscing might be uncomfortable for Rosie when she finds out about her father—not that anyone else would know. At least Michel would not be around, nor his family, to underline her lack of Simard features. There were lots of safe Wallace faces here, and all those blond blue-eyed Robinsons on my side. No question that Rosie was one of us.

CHAPTER THIRTEEN

2006

CARLIE

CARLIE KNEW THE HOUSE WAS MEANT FOR HER FROM THE moment she saw it. She took a day off work to move in and enjoyed every minute: the good, the bad, and the farcical. This last was when a tightly packed plastic bag fell off a pile and rolled down the stairs, out the door, and into the street. The back wheel of a passing car ran over it so the bag burst, dumping lacy underwear in the middle of the road. A black pickup going the other way paused as Carlie gathered her belongings, then disappeared round the corner trailing laughter.

For weeks after she moved in, Carlie walked up and down, looking out each window, basking in the knowledge of it being her Very Own House. It was close to the top of the hill overlooking the harbour and the Southside Hills beyond. She had had a wall knocked down between two rooms, so now her bedroom stretched almost across the whole harbour side of the top floor. Below was a steep slope of roofs cobbled together like beach rocks, with chimneys poking up in places, some with smoke streaming, others with starlings popping in and out.

The first time Carlie noticed the little flashes in a window two streets over was after she had been in the house long enough to stop tallying days. She realized it was not actually the first time she had seen the flashes, just the first time it made her think about binoculars and peeping Toms. The roofs were too crowded to show much pavement, but you could see top floors in the spaces where streets would be, and some showed windows. Most were small and frosted, like bathroom windows. A larger one had a sheet or something draped across, pinned up permanently in a function-only way. Then there was the window with the twinkles. Carlie dug out her own binoculars, unused since Senegal, and a few nights later she confirmed that some invisible person was aiming just-visible binoculars at her bedroom.

No way was Carlie putting up drapes. She had bought the house for that panorama, and she wanted to feel part of it. She spent hours up here at the window writing and now she sat at her father's lovely old desk, where he had done his thinking and studying. The family's past had soaked into that desk and the cityscape outside held the bigger history. She had an old sepia photograph of St. John's Harbour full of sailing ships on her back wall, next to a black-and-white of the Portuguese White Fleet from the 1950s and a couple more showing battle ships from two world wars. There was a smaller coloured picture of the *Matthew* she had taken herself in 1997. She had explored the replica of the original *Matthew* when it was berthed down there in the harbour, astounded at the size of it—so tiny to brave the vast North Atlantic. Of course the original had braved far more dangers, five hundred years before, bringing John Cabot from Bristol to North America in 1497. They may have made landfall at Bonavista, farther up the coast. Here, in this room above St. John's Harbour, time and place met, and Carlie felt centred.

Her first choice for privacy had been one-way glass, but apparently anything that would effectively stop the peeper from seeing in when the light was on would look varying degrees of milky the rest of the time. She researched blinds (horizontal, vertical, solid, wooden, faux-wooden, woven-wooden, woven-bamboo, pleated, roller, solar, aluminum, vinyl, Venetian…) but she had fought too many contrary classroom blinds over the years to seriously consider them.

Finally, Carlie stood in her closet, staring at the top shelf, then lifted a package from the back and laid it on her bed. She unfolded the gleaming blue fabric from its layers of tissue paper, spreading it out. She had bought it her first year in Senegal, intending to turn it into a robe for herself. It had been woven and dyed locally then beaten with heavy wooden clubs to give it the desired shine. Bazin. She had seen the place where they did the beating, and the noise was worse than a dozen jackhammers. You could feel it up through your feet a mile away. The fabric was every tint and shade of blue, from an almost-white hot summer sky to the blue-black depths of ocean, plain in the centre and patterned down the sides. Carlie left it spread out all day, returning to study it, deciding.

She had it made up in a single panel, with a light-proof lining to protect it from fading. It hung in stiff folds, covering that segment of window. It could be steered round the corner onto the adjoining wall during the day. She could not have hung such a reminder when first she left Senegal, but now she told herself she could focus on its beauty rather than on her loss. The very blueness of the fabric caught her eye when she came into the room. It stood out, glorious and brash and alien. Oumar had not been in her life when she bought it, but it was him. The rest of the room, the rest of the house, was so very northern—those subtle green-gray, blue-grey, gold tones leaking into each other with the occasional splash of red. This fabric had a voice of its own.

For a moment she saw an image which had haunted her for years, of flat saffron-coloured scrub stretching to the horizon, with one poor scraggy tree on what had once been endless grasslands—the only tree in sight with any greenery left—and five camels standing around it, eating every last leaf. She shook off the vision and focused on the here and now: greenery everywhere, water, and steep slopes. Home.

Carlie still wondered about the scumbag who had caused all this trouble, so she strolled over to that street, to the house with the window, picking it out easily by the height and roof shape and red trim. She noted the address: 31 Carbury. There was a *For Sale* sign two houses down.

"Another house for sale," she mentioned to Mrs. Murphy from next door during one of their doorstep exchanges. "Carbury Street. Number 27, or maybe 29…or 31. Know who lives there?"

Mrs. Murphy knew the history of every inhabitant back generations to two decimal points and recited all kinds of fascinating details about the people at all three addresses. "Man called Frank Hughes is in number 31," she said. "Lives alone. Divorced. Works for Hydro. Son lives with the mother but stays with the father on weekends. Hangs around here a bit. Teenager."

Carlie was tempted to put a copy of the sewing invoice in the Carbury Street mailbox, in an envelope addressed to The Person with the Binoculars, but she did nothing. She did not tell the family in case it triggered evil memories for Eve. It was Africa she thought of whenever she moved the bazin panel, not binoculars, and no more twinkles caught her eye, so eventually she forgot all about them.

Until Rosie was in grade eleven.

CHAPTER FOURTEEN

2007

ROSIE

FOR ROSIE'S THIRTEENTH BIRTHDAY, MOM GAVE HER A DOG. She said now Rosie was responsible enough to look after a pet and think about a dog's needs and not just her own. Rosie had been asking for a puppy (pestering, Mom called it) since she was old enough to tell a dog from a horse.

So they went to the rescue place to choose one.

"Just don't fall for a huge dog that will fill up the kitchen and knock Nana off her feet," her mom said. "And remember, little puppies with big paws will probably turn into big dogs."

"Okay, Mom. I'll check their feet."

They were parked outside the building now and Rosie could hear barking.

"Or a guard dog."

"What's wrong with a guard dog?"

"Some breeds can be aggressive. Police dog types are trained to attack. We don't want it taking a bite out of the mailman."

"But puppies won't be trained yet, will they? Are guard dogs aggressive when they're little?"

Mom went all quiet and Rosie wondered why for a second, but by then she had reached the door, so she just turned and beamed at her mother and walked in.

Rosie had pictured a dozen or so dogs behind a chain-link barricade all on their hind legs straining to reach her, and she would see a cuddly little fluffy one she would fall in love with, and it would lick her lovingly and snuggle up in her arms.

But when she walked into the reception area there was not an animal in sight. It looked like any old waiting room except smaller and a bit scruffy and there were photographs of dogs and cats all over the walls instead of a bunch of teeth or a person peeled down to the bones. A chalkboard had the names of animals adopted this week in slanty handwriting like Eryn's and two printed black-and-white signs said *Thirteen Pets Placed in Care* and *Thirty-One Pets Adopted in 2006.* That looked hopeful, but what was the difference between being in Care and being Adopted? Care was temporary, the receptionist said. Adoption was permanent.

Rosie did not see a single cat while she was there. They were probably behind those closed doors behind the reception desk. Anyway, Rosie was not interested in cats. The woman said no, they couldn't see into the room where all the dogs were, it would make the animals too excited, but they could see the outside pens if they wanted to go out back behind the building. But it was cold out there and the two rows of kennels were empty—little igloo shapes the colour of gingerbread, ten of them, each in its own wire-mesh run.

A girl came, said she was Amy, and led them down the hall to a small room like the secretary's office at school, with four chairs round the walls.

"There are hardly any animal smells, Amy," Mom said. "Everything's lovely and clean."

The girl beamed and gave a little pep talk on the importance of hygiene with so many animals. "And we're at full capacity right now with ten dogs." Six of those were big breeds so she would only show the four small ones, one at a time.

"We can come back every week, Rosie," Mom said when Amy had gone. "You don't have to take one today."

Hah! As if Rosie was going to wait one minute longer.

And the first dog was a pretty little ball of white fluff just as she had pictured. But it stood with its back to the door and barked at them, a shrill yip that went on and on. Rosie crouched down in front of it and put her hand out and the yipping only sped up.

"Will we see the next one?" Mom asked, and Rosie sighed and said *yes* and sat down again with her dreams in little yappy pieces.

The next dog was a purebred Scottish terrier and when Rosie approached with her hand out, Amy tightened the leash a little and said, "Not too close," and the dog backed off, growling. "We think this dog may have had a rough start in life. He's beginning to calm down and be less snappy, but you would need to be patient at first."

He was a maybe. He needed a good home. But could they see the other two first?

The third dog looked from Rosie to Eve as he walked in and sat down in the middle of the floor facing them, all calm and cool, wrapping his tail round his toes and settling in to wait. He was a brown suitcase of a dog: part terrier, a bit of this, a bit of that. Waiting.

"Look, Mom! It's Paddington. He looks just like Paddington Bear." Rosie went down on her knees and hugged him and he smiled at her, tongue lolling, tail thumping.

Later, Rosie remembered him as standing next to a suitcase, although she knew that was ridiculous. Maybe it was his stillness. Expectant. He was the right colour brown for a bear, with a rough-haired terrier coat and a squashed face and small neat ears that stood up straight, turning towards sounds, collecting signals. He looked Left Behind. He looked left on a station platform when everyone else has gone back to Africa or Peru or wherever. He looked patient and alert but not worried. *It is what it is. I have a past. I've brought it with me in my suitcase, but you can't see in.*

That first day home, Paddington anchored his feet close to the front door, nostrils wide, mouth closed tight, ears twitching, and Rosie's mom said to leave him until he was ready. He stayed there for ages. He had seemed so confident when Rosie first saw him, so comfortable in his skin, but who knew what he had endured before this. They both spoke to him softly each time they passed the porch—*you're part of the family now, Paddington; you're a Wallace now*—and after a while he began to investigate, touring the house in instalments, and by evening he was curled up on the living room floor next to his brand new sleep cushion with his nose close to Rosie's feet.

He had trouble going up the stairs with those short little legs, and even more coming down. His first time up, he left his back feet in a safe place and stretched his body round the bend in the stairs for a look, before risking the second half-flight. For the longest time he dithered on the top step before coming down, peering over the edge, and pacing across and back. The way he floundered and flapped in the snow in the backyard was the reason for his nickname, Paddles. Most of the snow had blown off the left-hand side of the yard so he used that side as his bathroom and did so forever more, and Rosie said he must be left-handed like her.

Eryn came over to meet him on Saturday and they took him into the den while Mom was cooking something that smelled fantastic, something with gravy and onions. Eryn wanted to try the dog in a hat to see if he looked more like Paddington and that set them off on a dressing-up binge, using everything they could find that was small enough: gloves on his feet and a scarf round his neck and Rosie's hat with ear flaps that Carlie had brought back from Peru—a chullo.

"And Paddington Bear came from Peru, didn't he?"

"How do you like your uniform, Paddles?"

"You look cute, Paddles."

They tied on the hat and had to wrap the ties round his neck to keep it there and giggled as the dog pushed his head along the floor, trying to get it off. It was over his eyes and his tail was tight between his legs and he shook his head hard, which only made things worse.

Then the door opened. "Get that off him. Immediately." Eryn and Rosie looked up, surprised at the anger in Mom's voice, and she roared, "Now!" Well, it was not a roar exactly, her mom never shouted, but the sort of tone where you jumped to it and didn't ask questions. The dog started to whimper, frantically rubbing first one side of his head along the carpet then the other, then he peed on the floor.

"You're upsetting him, Mom."

"Not another word, Rose. Just. Get. It. Off."

Rosie tried, but the knots had pulled tight and the dog was trying to pull away.

"I'll hold him, Eryn. You try unpicking the knots. You've got fingernails."

"The wool's stretched. I can't see…it's all hairy."

Mom disappeared and a drawer rattled and she came back with the kitchen scissors.

"Hold his head." She cut through the ties and unwound the hat and threw it on the floor then untied the scarf. The gloves had fallen off ages ago. That was Rosie's favourite hat. Mom picked up the dog and carried him away, talking to him in a soothing voice and shutting the door behind her. Eryn and Rosie sat on the floor looking at each other.

"Wow, I've never seen your mom get mad before. She's kind of scary."

"I was going to ask if you could stay for lunch."

"Guess that's out." This was going to be such a special time, taking Paddles for a walk with Eryn and eating whatever Mom was cooking that smelled so good…. Why did Mom have to spoil it? She could have just helped them get the hat off. Rosie picked it up and one string was just a couple of inches long now. Useless. The other still had the knot attached. Might as well cut that off too, have a matching set.

They watched television for a while, flicking channels, but couldn't settle on anything. Eryn had lost her bounce and after a while she phoned and asked her mom to come pick her up. Mrs. Brown came on her way back from the supermarket and Eryn gave Rosie a hug as she left and said, "Call you."

"Rose, come into the kitchen please." Paddles had been taking a drink from his bowl with his back to the door, but he turned round to face Rosie. Was he keeping an eye on her? Was he scared? Scared of her, Rosie?

"That was plain schoolyard bullying."

"We were only playing."

"*You* might have been playing. Paddles wasn't. And he didn't have any choice. You forced all those clothes on him, two on one, and you must have seen he didn't like it." Paddles waddled out of the room and turned left towards the back door.

"I didn't know he'd get upset."

The lecture went on and on: how the dog couldn't see round that hat and probably couldn't hear, and it was pulled tight round his neck and how frightened he must have been. Her mom didn't sound angry anymore, just firm. Calm, like always.

"Never force something on another person—or on any living creature—especially if they are weaker than you. They have no redress, no comeback. A bad-tempered dog would have bitten you. Paddles is a gentle dog and he didn't known what to do."

Rosie could feel tears building at the back of her nose. "Sorry, Mom."

"That's okay sweetheart. It was thoughtlessness, not cruelty. You'll know not to do it again." Mom put an arm round her and Rosie didn't trust her voice, so she didn't say anything and made herself all stiff so she didn't blubber and anyway, she wasn't sure she wanted a hug from her mother right now. "At least." Mom didn't sound as certain suddenly. She stepped back and looked into Rosie's face. "At least I hope you will."

What did that mean? Did her mother think Rosie would go around bullying people? Did she really think…? And Mom looked like she was thinking exactly that.

Rosie wrenched herself away from her and snapped, "I wouldn't...I'm not."

Her mother turned away and drifted away to the stairs like she always did, and words stuck in Rosie's throat, but she stomped over to the bottom step and yelled up, "Why do you always—you never..."

Her mother paused for a moment then went on, pulling herself up by the handrail like she was an old lady, and Rosie was sobbing and trying to get the words out. ...*always think the worst. I'm not...ruined my whole day...everything.*

Her mother had stopped climbing but didn't look around, wouldn't even bother to look at her, and Rosie screamed, "You can take the stupid dog back. I don't want him."

She rushed into the porch and hauled on her boots and jacket, could not see a hat and just pulled up her hood and fled out of the door and started to run, almost falling on black ice, and then slowing to a fast walk, placing each foot flat so she wouldn't skid. No gloves in her pocket so she buried her hands deep and curled them into fists.

She didn't notice where she was walking and next thing she was outside school, which looked all locked up and deserted on a Saturday. The air temperature was only a bit below freezing but the wind chill was something fierce. Carlie was out of town and Aunty Ginny's house was too far to walk to and Rosie was too embarrassed to go to one of her friends. She wriggled her toes and kept on going but after another ten minutes the cold drove her home.

Rosie expected her mother to be shut away in her room but this time she was standing in the porch, had the door open before Rosie reached it, and before the door was fully closed she was saying, "I'm sorry, sweetheart. That was awful. I know you wouldn't hurt anyone deliberately, person or animal. I'm so sorry."

Rosie didn't look at her straight away, tried to pull off her boots with hands that were too cold to grip, and her mom said, "Forgive me. Please." And when Rosie stood up, Mom put her arms round her and said sorry again and how cold she must be and there was hot chocolate almost ready in the kitchen, and Rosie could feel herself starting to thaw from the inside out, and by the time her hands had warmed up she was almost ready for a proper hug with nothing held back.

CHAPTER FIFTEEN

2008

LIZ

CARLIE WAS PRESENTING A PAPER IN BRUSSELS AT A FIVE-day international conference on social anthropology, and her friend Juan would also be attending. Carlie had been getting itchy lately, so a trip would do her good.

The day before she was due home, she emailed her sisters to say she was taking some banked holiday time for a four-day side trip to Paris and please could someone water her plants. Ginny had questions. Of course she had questions. Carlie would do the round trip by train and still fly home from Brussels. She would be staying at a hotel in the centre of Paris. Ginny checked it out online and found it was a much fancier hotel than her usual Holiday Inn level and would probably cost an arm and a leg. Then she discovered there was to be a trade delegation from Senegal staying there at the same time.

Was Carlie meeting that Senegalese man—Oumar—the one she was never going to see again? I was in an uproar. Carlie came home in March 2003, Ginny said. Yes, I remembered then, because it was around the same time as the start of that dreadful war in Iraq. Now it was almost March 2008, so five years later. How could she afford it when she had just taken on all the expenses of a new house? What was she thinking?

How did Carlie know about the trade mission, and had she been in touch with that Oumar person, and what was going on? *Oh, Carlie, you've got through the hardest part, why are you stirring things up again?* You're fifty-three years old. (Maybe that's why.) But that was far too late to be chasing some man halfway across the world. Better not say that. Carlie never *chased.* She *arranged to meet.* And who knew what age was too late? But still. She met Juan sometimes, or that other man with a Russian-sounding name. I liked Juan, that time he came to visit—very dashing, but kind too. It was usually around Eastertime when they met, in New York or Amsterdam—halfway to wherever they were. Maybe this was the same sort of thing, but she had been friends with those other two for decades. This felt infinitely more dangerous.

My insides were in knots the whole four days. Don't you give me another of those stroke-things, Caroline Wallace, with all these shenanigans. I thought maybe I did have one, the day before Carlie was due home; I woke up feeling dreadful and stayed in bed until noon, dozing and half waking and dozing again. No rule to say those things had to stick to office hours.

Carlie sailed home without a feather out of her, arriving on that dreadful three-in-the-morning flight from Toronto. I phoned her at breakfast. "How was it?"

"Wonderful," she said (in such a matter-of-fact voice). She was not pleased at the family inquisition, as she called it. All that prying.

Carlie was never the confiding kind. It was not that she was secretive, exactly, more that she did not need affirmation or suggestions (certainly not suggestions), or a shoulder to cry on, although she had come close to that five years ago.

"Did you see Oumar?"

"Briefly."

"Will you be seeing him again?"

"Probably not."

And really, that was all she ever did say. She did not seem distraught or delirious with joy or disappointed or emotional in any way. As Ginny commented, it was just another day at the office.

CHAPTER SIXTEEN

2008

ROSIE

IT WAS HALFWAY THROUGH GRADE EIGHT WHEN ROSIE finally saw what Michel looked like, and she was sorry afterwards because of the trouble it caused.

"You've been in my writing desk."

For two thumps of her heart Rosie thought of denying it, but it was a waste of time. Her mom knew. She looked taller than usual, standing in the doorway, stiff armed, stiff faced. "How *dare* you."

Eryn had giggled about how her brother had broken into the liquor cupboard. *Got a skinny-looking nail from the shed and jiggled it in the lock. Easy-peasy.* More a joke than a crime. Then they all sat around drinking a bottle of wine from the back of the cupboard one Saturday. *Doesn't like this kind—someone brought it last Christmas. She'll never notice.* And so far, Eryn's mom hadn't. And the wine was gross.

Rosie wasn't even sure why she had done it, but last week Eryn had said how she couldn't believe Rosie didn't know what her father looked like and did he even exist? And then there were these nails at the back of the kitchen drawer…

"Just having a look," said Rosie to her mother. She tried to sound casual, "Didn't hurt anything."

"You have hurt something." Mom's words were coming out in spits. "Now I can't trust you. You looked in my private things when you knew—you *knew*—I wouldn't let you in there." On and on about *can't believe it* and *how could you* and then *violated.*

Opening the drawer had been easy enough but she had not realized you couldn't lock it again with the nail. Not even Eryn could carry this off—not that drawer. That was Mom's private place. Rosie had not known what she would find when she opened it,. just hoped there would be something of her father's. It might have been all bank stuff and legal things and, yes, there were some official-looking envelopes in there, but she didn't bother with those. Her eyes went straight to the baggie full of photographs, all of her father. There he was at his graduation, and him and Mom on Signal Hill in front of those signposts pointing to *London 3733 kilometres*, *Montréal 1619*, above the entrance to the Narrows. There was another picture in a restaurant and of a group hiking—it looked like the Spout Trail near that rusty old lighthouse.

There was one of those fat wedding albums too, a silver bride with a two-inch waist embossed on a padded white cover. Rosie pored over that album taking in every detail of her father: the thick dark wedge of eyebrows, so French looking, the cleft in his chin, the thin nose—an aristocratic nose. But overall it was a nice face, a friendly face—friendlier than his rose greeting card suggested all those years ago. She had tried to imagine Michel when she was growing up, but he'd been nothing but a blur, really. A blur with brown hair.

Rosie wanted to take a picture to show Eryn, just one. Her mom would notice if something was gone from the album, or if the graduation picture was missing from its cardboard frame, but maybe Rosie could take one of the snapshots. She spread them out, picking out the best ones. Did she like him most when he was serious or laughing, full face or a quarter turned? Would she risk taking more than one? Finally, she took the one of him standing by himself on a hiking trail, silhouetted against cliffs and ocean, handsome and laughing in a carefree, outdoors way. It didn't show his features as clearly as some, but it showed the person he was.

The album had the best close-ups. There were pictures of Old Montréal and a gorgeous photo of her parents coming out of the church, which looked so old and elegant, another looking out of the window of the limo, one cutting the cake, all with her father looking at Mom as if she were a chocolate éclair and he was starving. He looked so in love. Mom looked happy, laughing and smiling, but he looked beyond happy. He shone. How could he possible leave?

"I only looked at the photographs." Rosie tried to sound casual. It wasn't fair. It was so not fair. Her voice wobbled a bit and came out higher than usual. "You never tell me anything about my father. Ever. Now at least I know what he looks like."

But her mom had frozen solid, did not seem to be hearing her anymore. Her arms had come up in front, squeezed together, hands clenched by her chin. Her face had gone paler and paler until it looked sheet white, and she swayed a bit, moved so she could lean on the doorframe. Then she was walking away without a word. You could hear her shoulder rubbing slowly along the wall and the stairs creaking then her room door closing. Then everything went silent.

Rosie was left quivering, everything quivering. She huddled under her duvet and curled up in a ball, shivering, tears welling up and sliding everywhere. The dog peered round the door, a nose, an eye, an ear. Rosie put her hand down, whispered *Paddles*, and he climbed up. She edged back on the bed so he could nudge his way in and settle in his usual place, the tip of his nose under her chin, licking it now and then, and she cried into the top of his head. She had taken that one photograph, hidden it in last year's diary, but then she was so upset she didn't look at it for weeks. And she never did show Eryn.

Mom did not come out of her room for three days after the desk event. She may have gone to the bathroom when Rosie wasn't around, may have filled up her water bottle, but nothing was moved in the kitchen: not the coffee or the bread or an apple from the bowl. The cereal was undisturbed—Rosie folded the inside waxed paper in a certain way. Rosie fed Paddles and let him out, took him for a walk each evening. She made her own lunch, ate sandwiches for supper, took ten dollars from the emergency money in the kitchen drawer and bought milk and bread on the way home from school.

She knocked on her mother's door but there was never an answer so she didn't go in, although she hovered there, debating. She did not make her mother a sandwich. Let her make her own sandwich. She heard movement in there sometimes, so she was not too worried at first. But when Friday came, she phoned Aunt Ginny, and her aunt came round immediately. *What happened? Tell me exactly.*

Aunt Ginny got Mom ready to go to that twenty-four-hour place, the Upton Clinic. She ran a bath for her, made her sit at the kitchen table and eat an egg sandwich, talked all the time in that down-to-earth way. *Better pack layers. You know how that old building feels so stuffy but there's always a cold draft round your ankles.* Mom seemed half asleep, staring at things as if she didn't know what she was looking at. She did not look at Rosie at all.

"Mom...?"

Her mother still did not look up and Aunt Ginny put an arm round Rosie's shoulders saying, "She's in a muddle right now. She'll be alright, just give her time."

Rosie packed an overnight bag, and Carlie took her back to her house for the weekend.

"Can I bring Paddles, Carlie? There'll be nobody here to let him out and things."

"What do you mean by *and things*?"

Well, they would have to feed him and everything, but Rosie would bring some food and his dishes and see to taking him out. She would do everything.

"Can't we just drop by morning and evening and let him out? Leave him food and water?"

But he would need letting out more than that and he might be frightened and when he was frightened, he peed on the floor.

So Rosie gathered his things with Carlie muttering all the while about all that ridiculous paraphernalia: three bowls for water and hard food and soft food and that sleeping cushion and his own personal towel with his name on it—*that was a Christmas present*—and little green booties for god's sake—*that's only in the middle of winter*. More possessions than half the population of Senegal. Out of all proportion…

"So, can we take him?"

"I suppose."

The ground floor at Carlie's house just had the hallway, then a big dining room and a kitchen with one of those cute little hatches for passing dishes from one to the other, and a bathroom and some kind of storage room at the back. The living room was on the next floor. Paddles looked up from the hallway at those mountainous stairs and his tail sank between his legs. Rosie loved those stairs because they were elegant, gracious, and the stained-glass window turned the polished wood to orange-gold, warm and glowing, with splashes of red and purple when the sun shone right on the glass. But she had to admit they were not dog friendly.

Paddles struggled up the first few steps and Carlie said, "Here, give me that bag and you carry the damn dog."

"He's not a damn dog. And he can't help having short legs."

Carlie snorted. "Those aren't legs. They're disadvantages. One on each corner. God, Rosie, you didn't pick that animal for its looks."

"He's a *dog* not an animal!" Rosie could feel tears building. This was too much, on top of everything else.

"Well, we won't get into classification—"

"And he's a *him* not an *it*!" Rosie was shouting now. "And Mom was pleased I picked a dog with disadvantages and not a trophy dog." Mom didn't voice an opinion too often, but the whole world knew what Carlie thought as soon as she thought it.

Paddles had started quivering in Rosie's arms, so she kissed his head furiously and said, "Don't take any notice of Aunt Caroline, she's just being mean." Then she realized the dog was squirming because she was squeezing so hard so she relaxed her grip and whispered, "Sorry, Paddles. I'm sorry."

When they reached the living room Carlie said, "Okay, Paddington, make yourself at home. Just...try not to smell like a dog. And you can tell Rosie there's a lemon meringue pie in the fridge and she can cut two big pieces for us and bring them upstairs. The tray's in the pantry, left-hand side."

The snack was eaten in silence. No way was Rosie having a conversation with her nasty mean aunt. Carlie kept looking at her over her fork with no expression on her face and after the snack she set Rosie to organizing books.

"I suppose you know your alphabet."

That made Rosie giggle and she gave up on the cold shoulder. The books were still in dozens of cardboard boxes, even though Carlie had moved here back when Rosie was in grade seven. "Just line them up on these shelves, heaviest on the bottom, by subject where possible, until you run out of space." The shelves were planks of wood with bricks at each end to hold up the plank above. "Just for now, until I get around to doing something permanent."

Mom said Carlie took a geological view of *now,* meaning sometime this century.

Carlie ordered pizza with all those delicious extras on it that they never had at home because Mom said they were all fat and bad for you, and she opened a bottle of apple cider. Carlie taught Rosie to play Scrabble and they played for hours, all weekend, sprawled across from each other on those two squashy love seats with the box of tiles on the table between. They took turns getting up to refill the chip bowl, and Paddles stretched out on the floor near the bowl with one eye on the chips. Rosie started winning a game now and then, and her aunt said she showed *promise*, which was a word Carlie had all the letters for but couldn't fit in.

When Rosie went home her mom was better—quiet and slow moving, but better. She was only gone two days this time.

The first time had been the longest and Rosie had stayed at Nana's, but that was one Easter, back when she was in nursery school, after some burglars kicked in the back door.

"I'm sorry, Mom. Sorry I made you sick." Rosie started to give her a hug then wasn't sure if Mom wanted one, but Nana always said don't be scared of wasting a hug. *Plenty more where that came from.*

"Don't be sorry, sweetheart." And Mom wrapped her arms round Rosie and said how much she loved her, and she was sorry too for giving Rosie a fright. "Not your fault. None of this was your fault. Just some little thing sets me off sometimes. A thought—nothing you said." And Rosie wanted to know what the little thing was this time but was afraid to ask.

CHAPTER SEVENTEEN

2008

LIZ

EVE HAD A MAJOR EPISODE, JUST WHEN I THOUGHT SHE WAS stabilizing nicely. It was severe enough for Ginny to take her into the Whatsit Centre...that psychiatric place. Surely that was only needed if Eve was suicidal. Oh, my god! Was she? Ginny said no. Eve would never consider anything like that while she had Rosie to look after. No. Of course she wouldn't. Well, not if she was thinking straight, she wouldn't, but that was the whole point. Then I came down to earth again and realized I had gone through this whole thought process a million times and had come to the same conclusion each time. Eve had dropped down into depression again, almost catatonic, and she just needed supervision for a spell, observation, adjustments to her medications maybe—that sort of thing.

I myself was not consulted. I only found out because I went over to Eve's house and it was deserted—not even the dog there—and blinds closed in the middle of the day. The girls said they planned to tell me but hadn't got around to it...rushing about too much. Anyway, Rosie called Ginny, not me. Well, of course she did. Everyone called Ginny. Although in the old days, I would have been the first choice.... *Stop that, Liz Wallace. Things are evolving and Ginny is better able to handle emergencies now.* And to be honest, I would not have wanted to handle it.

This all reminded me of how I felt when I first allowed you to file my tax returns. Not that I missed doing the damn things, but I had always done my own, and my own banking and the paying of household bills. I was my own woman. But you wanted to see if we could claim more tax rebates as a married couple and you could do this better if you did both our returns at the same time, which made sense. Then suddenly it made more sense for you to go to the bank for both of us as it was on your daily route, and I was weighed down with babies. Taking toddlers into a bank was a nightmare back in those days: all those shiny metal bollards to control customer traffic, with enticing loops of yellow nylon rope between them for swinging on and jiggling, so the bollards would fall with the least touch and make hollow, echoing clangs, and every face would look disapproving as if nobody in there had ever seen a child before. I was happy enough to give up the bank trips. And next thing you were doing it all and I was left feeling like one of those old-fashioned wives who wouldn't know if a tax return was fit to eat.

What had I been thinking about?

Eve.

Well, she was back home and recovering, which was all that mattered. The girls said the episode was triggered by Rosie breaking into Eve's locked drawer. The word *violated* was mentioned. Yes, that would do it. *Breaking in* would do it too. They were mostly worried about Rosie seeing photographs of Michel. That must have been what she was looking for. Eve thought there might be one or two small photos missing. We had always been so careful not to put a face on Rosie's non-father, not to give him a physical presence. This was troubling.

I wanted to help, so I made a lasagna and took it over to Eve's house. It was not up to my usual standard, and I was not sure why, which was disappointing. Rosie was in the kitchen and brought me a cup of tea and said not to worry, my lasagna was always delicious.

That dog was eating its supper, its name tag jingling against the bowl. I couldn't recall his name, but it was a He. I remembered back when our girls wanted a dog—Ginny mostly. She liked looking after things. Carlie just thought it might be a great excuse to take it for a long walk when she wanted to be out *on the go*, but she was not keen on the *looking after* part. Eve would have liked one but thought a dog would be too lonely when everyone was gone all day. You were not keen, although you would have agreed if we had insisted. It was me who said no.

Animals were work. I was on speaking terms with the cat next door, although I did not like it doing its business in my flowerbed, but I was not a dog enthusiast. Dogs demanded attention. Some barked too much and the big ones ate enormous amounts of food, official and unofficial; a friend's golden was known to swipe her morning toast right off her plate, not to mention nudging the lid off the garbage can, looking for leftovers. Newfoundland dogs drooled and left long ropes of saliva festooned over everything; when you walked across Maudie's rec room you ended up with slimy knees. Most dogs left hair all over too—fluffy hair, which floated into the farthest corners and showed up as dust bunnies at embarrassing moments, or long wiry hairs that wound themselves round the houseplants and half strangled them to death. Hair had been problem enough with three daughters. But still. A small, non-yappy short-haired dog like this one was probably a good idea for an only child.

After the dog had finished its dinner, it—no...*he*—came over to investigate me, starting at my feet. I hoped all that sniffing indicated novelty, not the degree of smelliness, and I kept discreetly pulling my feet away, but his nose kept indiscreetly following. It was mildly embarrassing but less so than those two English setters next door when I was sixteen or so: straight for the crotch, the pair of them—one to the back and one to the front.

I would not mention this to Rosie. I would not mention Eve's mental health either, except for the usual *How's your mom?* So we talked about...*Paddles, Nana.* Yes. We talked about Paddles.

Rosie loved lasagna. She loved all pasta and made her own favourite pasta sauce a week or so after my lasagna offering and invited me for supper. I had promised to bring French bread to go with it but I forgot, which was a shame. I would have loved a good baguette. I hadn't made a baguette for a hundred years, not since we came back from your sabbatical in Paris, but the memory was carved into my brain because of Madame…what was her name? Veronique. You must remember her—lived next door and worked as a pastry chef. I told her my mother had taught me how to make bread, which was a mistake. She said I could not leave France until I could make a baguette.

You do not knead baguette dough, you leave it to ferment. It's wet and sticky and I kept wanting to add more flour. *Pas plus, pas plus*. She said it was a test or something in baking school—couldn't move to the next level until you had made a perfect baguette. I thought she might confiscate my passport. I lost count of the failures. Not that she said anything other than *bon, bon*; it was the eyebrows. They tilted at different angles for different levels of *Non, alors!* When I finally got it right, I thought they might fly off the top of her head.

Do not punch down.

Do not deflate the air bubbles.

Leave the poolish (starter mixture) covered, to let the bubbles rise—five hours *comme ça*, eight hours make more bubbles, *come ça*—and on and on. It should end up with a crispy crust and big holes in the chewy centre. I always thought it was bad baking when I saw holes in a loaf—thought the baker had not punched it down enough. And he hadn't, but it was deliberate. Those holes were bubbles. Trapped air. You worked very hard for those bubbles.

Anyway, we were eating Rosie's pasta concoction and I was enjoying it, in spite of the lack of French bread, and I was about to tell Rosie how tasty it was when out of the blue she said, "A girl was attacked last night." She said it to her mom round a forkful of spaghetti. "In the laneway between the school and that supermarket."

My hand jerked and a pile of noodles whiplashed through the meat sauce, spraying it down the front of my sweater. Rosie had a hand over her mouth as if she expected a reprimand for talking with her mouth full, but Eve just swivelled a fast ninety degrees to stare at Rosie and said, in a compressed voice, "Is she alright?"

"Don't know. She's in Mr. McAllister's class. Don't know her very well. Off school today, though."

"You don't go down that alleyway, do you?"

"No, but it's not bad in daylight. Loads of people use it."

And that should have been the end of it, but Eve went on, saying, *Don't Use It Any Time*, as if each word weighed a ton. Did it happen after dark? It had been after orchestra practice, so it must have been getting dark, and they had taken her violin out of its case and smashed it. A couple coming out of the supermarket heard the racket and looked down the lane and the guys took off.

"Guys. How many guys?"

I held my breath and avoided looking directly at Eve. Rosie did not know how many, and Eve asked if they got there in time—the people from the store.

"What d'you mean?"

Silence.

"Oh. Rape. I don't know, Mom. That's what everyone's asking. People are saying she was stupid to go down that ally at dusk by herself."

"Blame the victim. Of course."

Rosie turned defensive then and said her mother had just told her not to do that—go down that lane any time. But the bus stopped outside the supermarket and it only came every thirty minutes after four o'clock and it was a long way round the other way.

I realized I was still holding my breath and let it out in a whoosh, then dabbed at the sauce stains with a serviette to hide my agitation. Futile exercise. This sweater would need washing now—handwashing, dammit.

Eve was still speaking in that catastrophic voice. "Rosie, you're at an age now where you have to be careful."

Rosie was staring back, starting to look worried. "I know, Mom."

"No. You don't know. If you knew, you'd be terrified."

Oh, Eve, keep it casual. My heart was pounding and I could feel my body heating up and that loud thumping in my ears. Rosie had stopped eating altogether and sat looking frozen, eyes wide, mouth half open, and Eve went on in that urgent voice about how they come at you when you least expect it, and you're helpless. Helpless. If you try to punch them, someone grabs your arm. If you kick, they grab your leg. If you scream, they stuff something in your mouth. You can't—

"Eve..." I began, although I had no idea what to say to stop the avalanche.

"Mom!" Rosie said, looking more and more horrified. "How do you—?"

"It's happened to some of my clients."

Eve slowed down a little then but went on saying how important it was that Rosie avoid risky places: public bathrooms, parking lots, shady areas. Well, she didn't drive yet but...shortcuts. Better to go the long way around than risk a deserted shortcut. Stick with crowds. Wait in the entrance of the mall, not outside in the dark....

"Eve..." She didn't hear me—no glancing my way or changing her voice.

"Don't stand next to one of these big vans that hide things. Watch out for boys, men, one man, sitting in a parked car, especially if they've been there for a while. They might just be waiting for someone, but they might be lurking. Be careful where you arrange to meet friends. Be sure to pick a place with people around."

Finally, a pause, then an extra command—to ensure there would be people around whenever and wherever she was going. Some places looked entirely different after work hours.

"When you're learning to drive, they say *assume every other driver on the road is an idiot*. Well, for your own safety, assume everyone out there is—"

"A rapist?"

The silence was painful.

Nobody finished their food, and I escaped home as soon as I had finished helping clean up. I could think of nothing at all to say. I just hoped Rosie would accept this as a psychology thing—Eve's professional experience talking—not a personal thing.

Perhaps we should have given the girls warnings like this, growing up, but it didn't cross my mind. Well, we both warned them against getting into cars with strangers, going into creepy places alone (but what would Rosie consider creepy?) and we insisted on checking their loot bags at Halloween. It would not have made any difference in Eve's case, anyway. Who would think of saying *Don't lie too close to the dunes.*

I did not sleep well that night and felt dreadful the next morning. Was it just lack of sleep or one of those Things again? I stayed in bed until lunchtime anyway. Who would care? Only then did it occur to me that maybe Eve could have used the opportunity to tell Rosie about her real father. That would make her careful about shortcuts and dark places. But no, it was too soon. She was not through puberty yet, and anyway springing it on her like that on a weekday without planning what to say… and Eve would not want to tell her with me hanging around. But still. Rosie needed to know soon.

CHAPTER EIGHTEEN

2008

ROSIE

GRADE EIGHT WAS ALMOST OVER BEFORE ROSIE LOOKED AT Michel's photograph again. There he was in front of her, a real, solid, honest-to-god person. Her father. She began studying the picture regularly before she went to sleep, so often that she had to take it into Staples for a protective plastic coating. She still couldn't talk to him, though. Maybe she should have picked a close-up. Here, he was still too far away.

Rosie piled the pillows up against the headboard and lay back in her favourite reading position and studied Michel's photograph again. He was handsome, her father. She could be proud of that. She kept her knees bent up so Mom would not see the photo in her hands if she opened the door. Not that her mom would ever barge in without knocking, but in case Mom came over for a good night kiss, Rosie left *To Kill a Mockingbird* lying on her stomach ready to slip the photo inside. That was one of her favourite re-reads that Mom would never question—a book about an exemplary father.

Eryn would be off to North Carolina in July to stay with her dad's family. She had written him at Easter to ask if he had bought her ticket yet. As Nana would say, Eryn was never backward in coming forward. So why didn't Rosie write to her own father? Why hadn't she? The more she thought about it the better the idea seemed, but she could not tell her mother.

She started searching for him again on Facebook. It should be easier to find somebody this time, but she had not realized just how many people there were in the world called Michel

Simard and a million more just plain M. Simard. And maybe he used a pseudonym online. Mom did. She tried including his company name plus Qatar, and then Montréal—nothing narrowed it down much.

Finally, Rosie decided this would need a hard-copy letter, and to reach the correct person it would have to be sent through the lawyer. She would have to warn the lawyer not to tell her mother. No, she couldn't be as sneaky as that, and maybe he would tell Mom anyway. Rosie thought about it and thought about it, but why shouldn't she write to her very own father?

Another problem she ruminated about was what to write. She kept starting a letter in her head:

Please come...

I am writing to invite you...

If you can't come, perhaps a letter...?

Why have you never come...?

When are you coming...?

The deciding moment came a week before the end of school.

Rosie fumbled her hand down on top of the alarm clock to turn it off and then just lay there with her hand still on the clock, eyes closed, curled up in her cozy duvet-hole. She managed to mumble *I'm up* when Mom knocked on the door and instantly fell asleep again, and Mom did not realize until Rosie had not appeared for breakfast. Her mother banged on the door a second time.

"It's almost eight, Rose, and this is the day I have to be in early for a meeting."

Right. Mom had a million meetings a week. Rosie was halfway through the bathroom routine before her eyes were fully open. She walked into the kitchen, trying to push her arm down into her sleeve, all turned inside out and bunched up, and instead of helping, Mom said, "If you would pick your clothes off the floor and straighten them out before you went to bed that wouldn't happen."

Rosie rammed her fist into the sleeve so hard that she bumped the milk jug on the table and the jug almost tipped over. She caught it with the other hand, but not before some milk sprayed out onto the toast, and of course Mom heard her say *shit* under her breath and glowered at her. Ears like a frigging bat.

"From now on, on school nights you can leave your phone here on the table when you go to bed and not spend half the night texting Eryn."

Rosie decided right then to send the letter to Michel, and from that moment it was a matter of Content, Style, and Presentation, through rewrite after rewrite. In the end the letter was so brief it looked lost on the page, even with her address at the top, and Rosie wrote it out three times before it was centred to her satisfaction.

Dear Father,

I am writing this to ask you to please come home, even if it is only for a short visit.

If you do not want to see Mom, I could meet you somewhere else.

Kind regards,
Rosie

She agonized over how to finish off the letter. She so wanted to put *Love Rosie*, but how could she? There was nothing to love. When she checked online, the business endings were too businesslike and none of the informal ones said what she really wanted to say: *I would love you if you'd let me.*

Rosie went down personally to the lawyer's office on Duckworth Street and had to entrust it to his secretary. She told herself not to expect anything from Michel for at least a month, although she started counting down after only ten days.

There was a call from the lawyer's office after forty days, which felt almost biblical. There was a letter for Rose Wallace. Would Ms. Wallace like him to mail it to her or would she pick it up at his office? Rosie almost ran down to Duckworth Street. She was faster than usual climbing back up the hill too, but only went as far as Carlie's house to avoid waiting any longer. Her aunt was out of town. She sat on the first chair she came to in the dining room and tore open the envelope with shaking hands.

Hello Rosie,
I spend my time in the Middle East these days or in France. I rarely come back to Canada and never to Newfoundland, so a visit is out of the question.
I wish you well in your endeavours and in all the years ahead of you, but I cannot be part of your life.
Sincerely,
Michel

Rosie sat staring at the letter for eons, feeling empty. Feeling the way she did when she fell and hit her head on the ice that time and for a moment had not known who, where, what she was. *I cannot be part of your life.* What did that mean? *Cannot be part of*...yes he could! He just had to send a letter now and then, even a picture of a frigging camel. *Cannot.* What he really meant was he didn't want to. Her own father. What had she done to deserve...? Nothing. He knew nothing about her. His own daughter. He wasn't interested. Indifferent. She tried to remember what it was her social studies teacher had said about that—they had been discussing homelessness. Yes, and he should be half of Rosie's home. Her teacher had said something about hate not being the opposite of love; indifference was. How could she fight that?

CHAPTER NINETEEN

2008

LIZ

WHEN I LOOKED UP AND DOWN THE STREET ALL I COULD see were yellow lawns. June was dandelion month. There was one pure green lawn. Mr. Whatsit up the street swore he didn't use chemicals but his was the only green lawn. I would just have to wait for—Whatshisname?—to come and mow mine. Did I phone him? Must check when I went in—if I remembered to make a note of it. If I remembered when I went in…

My whole garden was a mess with all those groundcover plants growing into each other, periwinkles amongst the pink things, and pink things in the periwinkles. When I bent down to pull up a dandelion, my head swam, so I had to grab a branch and hold onto it until the buzzing stopped. I creaked down to the basement and rummaged around for the kneeler. Really, George, it's time you cleared this up.

Oh.

No.

I stood still and felt the weight of *Musts* and *Shoulds* pressing down on me.

Maybe just weed this little corner. It caught my eye every time I stood at the kitchen sink. A few prods with the trowel and my thumb hurt and that knee, and those roots must go down to Australia and my hip twinged and I was breathing heavily, and the buzzing was back. Dammit, I had only been there two minutes. I tried again but the buzz grew to hornet proportions and I had spots before my eyes, and I did not want to collapse in the garden for the neighbours to see. Mrs. Are up the street would get all superior and tell me how much better *she* managed when her Herbert died—or was it Hubert? Or Howard? Maybe I should stop calling her Mrs. Are before I made a Big Mistake. But her real name conjured up that classic Trojan beauty—what was it…? Helen—and a beauty she definitely was not. Her surname was…it was a mouthful that sounded like a firm on Wall Street. Yes. Arbuthnott. Not too many of those around here. *You one of the Carbonear Arbuthnotts?* Smirk.

I walked into the house and looked at the kitchen floor and was afraid I would stick to it if I tried to cross. How long before somebody found me? The cleaning lady was not due until next week. I pulled out the floor-wiper thing with the long handle and the squirt bottle on the end, and made one pass across the floor. Maybe I should do stripes like you do on lawns, or just two lanes with stop signs.

Did I just hear myself?

Was I talking out loud?

Holy moly, Mrs. Are would have a field day.

Later, as I reviewed my lack of accomplishments, I finally saw what everyone kept telling me. This house was too much, and I should move. But where? People said condo but they were unaware of the dementia. How long before I needed looking after? I could put my name down for that Home we both liked. It took a year or two for a vacancy to come up in the nice ones. As long as I had my own room and a window with trees outside, I could handle it. I was not sharing a room. I would sit right down on the floor in the corridor and scream if they tried to make me share a room. A sit-in, like you see on the news. But I suppose they'd just tranquilize me and…

A wave of fear swallowed me, and I could hardly breathe—the loss of control. No matter how we had planned for old age, the two of us, no matter how long-sighted and frugal we had been, I was going to become one of the dispossessed. Oh, George. I need you, George. I know the girls will be loving daughters and look after me, but my life will be at the mercy of others and mercy is one of those qualities on a scale; the girls will be at the compassionate end, but it is still someone else's version of compassion—*not that damn broccoli, I want the cream bun.* And there was another end to that scale which you saw in Homes run by overworked staff with troubles of their own—cold charity, measured and labelled. Or being talked down to like a toddler, in a well-meaning way. And if anyone stuck a stuffed toy on my bed, I would kick it into next week.

I closed my eyes and sagged back in my chair. Just thinking about it was exhausting. I could not…I would not put this off any longer. This weekend. I would have the girls over for coffee on Saturday to discuss it, go to that nice bakery in the morning.

ஃ

I had been to the bakery and was driving west on Empire Avenue, turning left onto the Crosstown Arterial. It was lunch-time, which I usually avoided, but everything that morning had taken twenty minutes longer than I'd expected, maybe because it was Friday, and every light across town was red. So there I was, first in line, waiting to turn left at noon in all that hectic traffic, with a lofty SUV on either side and one of those bossy big trucks grinding its teeth right behind.

The arrow turned green and my two lanes roared off like the Indy 500, but as I curved left I saw the red lights swinging in the wind above me. They were pointing to the stopped, waiting traffic way over on my right but for a moment I panicked—*My god, I'm going through a red light*—and I stood on the brakes and there was a thump and then the horns started.

I gripped the steering wheel to keep it steady and glided round the rest of the curve, aimed the car into the side of the road out of the way. The truck man came charging up to my window: *What the fuck are you doing? Moving your vehicle. My new truck… See your licence… wouldn't drive a nail.* Another man appeared then, the one who had bumped into the back of Mr. Truculent. He was saying *calm down* in a civilized way, so then the two of them went at it for a minute, and I had time to open the glove thingy with dithery hands to find my…those papers in that blue folder. By then a police car had stopped on the outside of us, back a little, with its lights flashing, and everything became orderly. All I could think of afterwards was that I would never drive again.

Can't phone Eve. Have to protect Eve.

Was Caroline home or in Africa?

Anyway, Ginny was the one in emergencies. I tried to phone Ginny but my fingers wouldn't work and old Truculent was back to raging at me through the window, making my brain rattle. *Sir, you're addling me.* The police officer started up the phone for me and asked who I wanted to contact, and next thing there was Ginny's voice saying it was lucky I had caught her; she was on her way to a meeting. I said *Oh, Ginny* and tried to explain, and the words were there in my head but they wouldn't come out, and I tried again but my tongue just would not work. I handed the phone back to the police officer, shaking my head, with Ginny's voice saying, *Mom, Mom, where are you, Mom...?* and the officer's voice droned, faded, droned into the phone like radio interference, and I had to lean back and close my eyes.

Ginny came and took charge, and I found myself in Emergency, but really there was nothing wrong that a cup of tea couldn't put right. They told me later that I kept saying I was going home, arguing about taking a taxi, but all I remembered was a confusion of voices and people, then being helped into a strange bed.

I lie still, wondering about the orange sneakers on the floor by the closet. Ugly sneakers. Not my floor. I know the voice outside the door but can't place it...Caroline's? And that laugh. Someone I know laughs like that. I roll over in my cocoon of bedclothes, and a pain stabs through the back of my head so I roll back onto my side. After a minute the pain fades, and I push myself up so I'm sitting. The room swings sideways, swoops, then steadies, and I feel a bit squeamish so I sit very still.

Feet appear in front of me. "How are you feeling, Mom?"

I squint up at the face but I'm not sure… "Eve?"

"You're looking pale. Do you want to stay here, and I'll bring you a cup of tea?"

"Rather sit at a table."

"We're all in the kitchen if you're up for it. Can you walk?"

"'Course I can walk," but the floor is misbehaving and that knee gives way and I have to let Eve pull me up and hold on. Eve wraps a housecoat round me. "Nice," I say, examining the sleeve. "That new?"

I shuffle a foot into an unfamiliar slipper, then the other one, and we set off across the floor—acres of floor, two doorways, more floor, and I'm almost collapsing by the time we reach a chair in the kitchen.

What a racket.

I can't untangle the voices and everyone is staring at me: Eve and…yes, Caroline…and Ginny. And Eve again. No. I look away, look down at my hands. I should know that young one but I don't. It's happening. Right now. I'm turning senile right now.

Then there are arms round me and someone is wiping my eyes, my face, and they are patting my shoulder, holding my hands. *You need a rest. You only feel like that because of the accident. You'll feel better in the morning*—the only comments I can pick out of the tangle. I lean my head against someone's stomach where they stand next to me and I close my eyes. I want to ask what they mean about an accident, but I'm just too tired.

⁂

They're right. It's all for the best. It makes perfect sense. The girls are packing up my things to move me into Eve's house, sorting them into three piles: take, give away, throw.

"You're not giving that away, Ginny. I might need that."

"Eve has a fancy big food processor, Mom. When's the last time you used this old blender?"

"I use it all the time. Every time I make soup."

"No," Eve goes past with a box of glasses in her arms. "You use that little hand one. We'll take that. It's a great little mixer." She puts the box out by the porch and comes back and crouches down by my chair and says she is weeding things out of her cupboards too, to make room for my things. We have to squeeze two houses into one now. Why don't I stretch out in the living room with my book, so all this sorting doesn't upset me? Yes. I pat Eve on the knee and struggle up out of the chair. It's all for the best. But still…

Don't make such a fuss about possessions, Liz Wallace. Think about all those refugees having to run for it without taking even the…what do you call important things? Essentials. Probably didn't even have the essentials in the first place. I always wonder about people's photographs when their houses are threatened by something awful. Ours are stashed all over the place—any spare corner of a cupboard, in albums, bags, and envelopes. Of course, nowadays they put them all on these computerstick things. Ours would be logs not sticks, whole trees, even. And refugees won't have those memory whatsits. Have to carry memories in their heads. Yes, but my head is not holding much these days. I need reminders. What happens to old lady refugees with those mini stroke things? Stress, the need to keep up, no meds…they'd be dead in no time. Nature's way. So stop your fussing over…what was I fussing over?

I picture a man pushing an old lady in a wheelchair across a ploughed field. I see it over and over. On the news maybe? Why that, when I can't remember things I want to remember? Terrified children. Big hungry eyes. Hard to push that chair over ruts…the old lady being jostled and rattled. Does she know what's going on? Careful ruts ruined…crop ruined. Where's the poor farmer? Where are the people who should be eating that crop? Poor wheelchair. How long before a wheel falls off or the camshaft breaks? And fancy me remembering camshafts. I can see you fuming about that, years ago—one wheel down in a pothole.

Little bits of past still roll about, beads fallen off the thread. I have to live in the present now, in the moment. But the present leans on the past and my past is missing. Threadbare. No future. Just a present full of holes.

PART TWO

CHAPTER TWENTY

2008

ROSIE

HER GRANDMOTHER'S MOVING IN WAS THE MAIN EVENT that summer of 2008.

On a sunny Saturday in June, the family swung into action to empty Nana's house with coordinated efficiency. Rosie was impressed. Nana spent the day with her friend Maudie. Rosie helped mom and the aunts with sorting and bagging and the wrapping of breakables, and helped her uncle load *the good stuff* into the SUV for delivery to family and friends and Goodwill. Commercial companies would come the following week to empty, clean, and paint, and Nana's Mr. Whatsit would mow the lawn. Mom and the aunts were sad over the loss of their childhood home, but there was so much laughing and teasing, and *remember this* and *remember when.* They said it felt just like a wake. What Rosie remembered most was the togetherness she felt when everyone was sitting in Nana's half-empty living room finishing off a box of donuts at the end of that exhausting day—feeling so happy that she rushed around to give each of them a hug, saying, "I love, love, love my family."

But Nana's permanent presence in their house was more of a disruption than Rosie had expected—not the change of rooms, which was organized quite quickly, but the fact that Nana was always there, needing attention; standing in the middle of the kitchen at breakfast so they had to dodge round her, making Mom late; getting confused with the channels on the TV again and again, and needing help so she could watch Usain Bolt in the Olympics all that August.

There was suddenly an extra layer of confusion in all their normal routines. Even Paddles looked put out with all the stair climbing to and from Rosie's new room. Rosie had not anticipated it quite like this. Somehow, she had thought of Helping Nana being like an extra bit of homework, added onto the normal routines in an organised chunk—and she was delighted to help. Nana was special and she deserved all the help they could give. But this was someone else's needs intruding into every task and thought and action, so Rosie could not finish things the usual way, could not plan and schedule and know that this is how it would be. The interruptions were random, interfering with Rosie's own chores and causing her to lose focus and make mistakes. Rosie wondered if this was how life would be with siblings, all wanting the bathroom at the same time or blasting their music when she needed quiet—maybe being an only child was not all bad.

It was the kettle that brought home care into the picture. Nana would forget to press the button to start it for her tea then complain that it was broken. Once, she filled a saucepan instead then wandered off, and the pan boiled dry and set off the fire alarm. At bad times she was no longer safe on her own. Mrs. Murphy began coming over at eight on workdays. She was a comforting pillow of a lady with pink cheeks and a cheery voice. Unflappable. Nana accepted her from the start as if they were old friends, though just occasionally she would stare at her and say, *Who are you?* But over the summer, life at Rosie's settled gradually into its new shape.

Nana had always been so wise and now she was all bewildered. It brought a lump to Rosie's throat, the unfairness of it all. When Rosie was growing up, Nana was the person who listened the most. She didn't keep making suggestions like Aunt Ginny, or drift off looking sad like Mom, and back when Rosie was little, Carlie had always seemed a bit fierce. Nana had been perfect.

Of course, the other big event that summer was the letter to Michel. It loomed: the thinking about it, the sending of it, the waiting for an answer. His reply put a big cloud over the start of grade nine. Eryn was so full of her trip south she didn't notice, but Mom looked concerned and kept asking if there was anything wrong. Like Rosie could tell her mom! And in the days after the reply arrived, Rosie went from black depression to a roaring red fury. *Didn't care. Couldn't be bothered. How dare he?*

Mom had taken Nana for an appointment, so Rosie pulled her father's letter out from its hiding place between her box spring and mattress. Not that she needed to hide things from her mom, but Eryn would quite openly poke around in Rosie's stuff and laugh because she never found anything juicy.

Rosie had also kept that one card with the embossed rose from grade three along with the photo from grade eight, all in a blue folder. The folder had held fancy writing paper once, back when people still wrote personalized thank you letters. Carlie said each Christmas, Nana used to make the girls sit down together before they went back to school and write careful thank you notes to absolutely everyone who had given them so much as a candy cane. The folder had caught Rosie's attention at Nana's house because of the colour—the purple-blue of those harebells which grew in wind-blasted crevices in cliffs: so fragile-looking but so tough.

She re-read the wording in Michel's grade three card. How stiff and dry it was, generic and empty. How could she not have noticed before? Well, maybe she had, but had chosen not to see—all those perfectly positioned, perfectly round lowercase letters that now she wanted to stick a pin in, to scratch right out of existence.

Michel was such a cold fish. (Yuck. Fish.) He had left Mom to struggle on her own and never bothered to check on Rosie growing up, on how either of them was managing. If only Rosie could have met him, just once. All her dreams of meeting him had gone up in smoke now. Toast. She was going to rip up that letter and the photo too. Well maybe not the photo, not yet anyway, but that card was going down the toilet. No, in the shredder—no, she wanted the satisfaction of tearing it limb from limb herself, into microscopic bits. No. Better still—

Rosie grabbed the card and rushed out to the kitchen and pushed it down in the nearest toaster slot. It was about the same width as a slice of bread and went in easily, but it stuck up above the top, so she pulled it out and ripped it in half and pushed the two halves down again, one in each slot. She went back for the letter and put that in too. Then she turned the dial up on high and waited, smiling, jiggling up and down on her toes. She'd show him. She watched and watched but nothing happened. The metal coils were red, and heat was coming out of the top, but the paper refused to burn. Then there was a dirty sort of smell not a bit like toast, more like a bonfire, and something chemical that made her eyes sting. She held her breath, turned away to inhale.

The card was blackening and buckling now so it pressed onto the coils at the sides, sticking to them, and there was a stink of metal or maybe paint from the frying gold rose and whiskers of smoke started to rise. The alarm screamed, and out of the corner of her eye Rosie saw Paddles scrabble to his feet and take off. She tried to pop up the toaster but it was stuck in the down position, so she turned the dial to low although there was a real blaze rising from it now. The power. Turn off the power. And maybe she was making a draft because the flames kept bending towards the plug in the wall.

OhgodOhgod.

Oven mitts. Rosie yanked open the drawer and grabbed the ones that came up to her elbow, but they were tangled up at the back and it took precious seconds to unravel them. Finally, she managed to pull out the plug. The metal coils darkened. The paper went on burning.

That frigging alarm. Rosie hauled over a chair and stood on it to reach and had to take out the battery before it would stop. The silence was heaven. Thin smoke was rising to the ceiling now and slowly rolling over and drifting to the window, so Rosie rushed across and opened it. She wanted to take the paper out of the toaster, but it was falling apart, and wisps and sparks were floating over towards the window and Rosie was afraid they might set something else alight, so she swept all the papers and envelopes spread over the counter down onto the floor. The flapping made the smoke bend, and something hot landed on her nose. She jerked backwards and swiped at it with her sleeve.

But overall things were calming down, enough so that she could hear Paddles whining at the back door, and when she went through, he was skittering about, nudging the door crack with his nose. Rosie said *okay, okay, Paddles*, and he squeezed out as soon as the door started to open, which was the fastest he had ever moved. She was picking up the papers when the hammering and ringing at the front door started, and Rosie knew who that would be.

"Oh, Mrs. Noseworthy—"

"My goodness. Are you alright? I've phoned the Fire Department. What on earth happened?"

Gaaaaah! Well, there was this bit of paper...No, no damage. Yes, she'd be more careful next time. Yes, they had a fire extinguisher, right here in the kitchen...forgot about it in the heat of the moment. No pun intended. No, it wasn't a laughing matter...*Shit. Shit. Shit.*

CHAPTER TWENTY-ONE

2008

LIZ

ANOTHER DOCTOR'S APPOINTMENT. AND WHICH ONE IS THE doctor? I've seen three people already, or was it two? Anyway, I'm tired of trudging down hospital corridors and sitting on hard chairs in waiting rooms. They don't fit a small person like me. If I sit back so my spine is comfortable, my legs stick out straight and my knees hurt, but if I sit on the edge so my legs reach the floor, I have to sit up tall, with nothing against my back, which is tiring. I've been preaching *Stand Tall* for years, but there is a limit to how long you can keep that up at my age. How long are they going to leave me sitting here for heaven's sake?

The questions they ask are confusing and some are just plain stupid. I'm not in kindergarten. It's insulting. And I've never remembered the day of the week, haven't since I retired, so it's no good asking me. And I know that yellow stick thing is for drawing and writing—I just can't think of the name. It will come to me...only she won't wait, keeps rushing me. Irritating. I just get into the flow and she says *that's fine*, and I have to move onto the next item. I like to finish things. I'm deadly slow, counting in steps these days. Sevens. I know my times tables backwards and forwards. So does all my generation. I cannot understand why it is not taught these days—so useful when you're working out figures in your head. Although...in the old days, I could change ounces to grams in my head, and now I go straight to those whatsit tables in my cookbook instead. But at least I can work it out if I have to. Well, I could before. Anyway, it's shocking how children today can't do anything without their machines.

⁂

I'm home again—no, not home. We're pulling into Eve's drive. Oh, dear. How I would love to go back to my own house and curl up in my recliner with a cup of tea. I sink back into the seat and sigh. At least I can have the cup of tea. But a lady bursts out of a house two doors down and comes rushing up to Eve, all out of breath, grabbing her arm and saying something about the Fire Department and Rosie and damage. The kitchen is freezing when we walk in, and the window is wide open.

Rosie has burnt something in the toaster and nearly taken the house down with it? Surely not. Mrs. Thingy must have it all wrong. Although there is a smell of smoke. And Rosie has actually demolished a card Michel sent her in grade three. Why ever would she do that? A vague thought floats just out of reach: something about little Rosie waiting and waiting for the mail...crying. I look over at the garbage, wondering why Rosie hasn't...but we did want to turn Rosie against...didn't we? I can't remember why for the moment, but maybe this is worth a bit of smoke. Anyway, it can't mean anything bad because Eve is standing in the middle of the kitchen, laughing. She should laugh more often—such a beautiful sound, like bells pealing, chime after chime round the kitchen. Eve says it's about time they bought a new toaster—one that would maybe brown both sides at once. I head for the living room. It's too cold to sit in the kitchen.

"Can I have a cup of tea?"

⁂

They need an electrician to see about the plug in the kitchen and he says the wire has burned out, so they need new wiring. He is in my way all day when I try to boil the kettle, and that kettle is no good either, but the man says his job doesn't include kettles.

Right after that—wait, no, Eve says the electrician was a week ago. At any rate, now there are two plumbers in my bathroom all day because the toilet keeps overflowing. They ask me if I've knocked something else into the toilet, say they've been here before. Well, I know I do silly things these days, but I would have noticed something like that.

Terry is the young one doing all the work with that metal snake. He's wearing the biggest pair of workboots I've ever seen, as big as those old cabin trunks in my basement. If you fell in, you could hurt yourself. Terry has to coil himself down to fit into the room. I wonder how tall he is. Almost up to the ceiling. Calvin, the older man, does all the observing and supervising. He fills up the room sideways. I used to think this bathroom was quite spacious.

Eve—no, Rosie—is passing just as Calvin says, "It was while I was working in Saudi Arabia," and Rosie stops and asks if he ever worked in Qatar and starts telling him about her father. Calvin says no, not Qatar, but Saudi is close. I'm in my bedroom next door, but Calvin has one of those voices you can hear all over the house. He should have been a politician. He tells Rosie about being a welder over there and living in a compound, which was fantastic, he said, with everything you could possibly want. He was given a top-of-the-line face mask for work because he was Canadian. Filipinos were only given a little piece of plastic to hold in front of their face with one hand while they welded with the other one. Dangerous. Heavens, yes—all those sparks. And something about Filipinos working on little platforms hundreds of feet up in the air with no safety net, no harness, hopping about over eight-lane highways. I miss the next part because I'm visualizing someone falling off and I am trying not to—appalling. Didn't anybody care? Well, Calvin did. He was invited for tea with one of the Filipinos, but it almost made him sick: shack made from bits of cardboard and tin...open sewage down the middle of the street...drinking water out of a bucket...the Filipinos were not allowed in the compound.

After the plumbers are gone, I say Qatar doesn't sound very nice.

"That was Saudi Arabia, Nana, not Qatar," says Eve. But still…she has tears in her eyes and says she hopes Calvin's friend is alright. Calvin bought him a good mask and gave him his own safety gear when he left. The man sent all his money back to his family in the Philippines…a pittance compared to the Canadians, who earned good money. Calvin meant to stay long enough to earn a down payment on a house, but he left as soon as his contract ran out. Couldn't face staying longer. Says he gets goose bumps whenever he hears what's going on over there. Rosie mutters something about her father, too, wondering if he's made friends with any Filipinos or if he is indifferent. Said that word twice. *Indifferent.*

CHAPTER TWENTY-TWO

2010

ROSIE

"WHICH PART OF MONTRÉAL DO MY GRANDPARENTS LIVE in?"

Rosie started with Carlie because the family always said she spoke first and thought second. Not this time. She was peering at books on those elegant new floor-to-ceiling shelves at the back of her living room, nose to the bindings, tilting her head different ways to read titles. She said she was looking for something about Russia under the tsars, muttering about it having a gold cover, but she turned and looked Rosie straight in the eye. "Why do you want to know?"

"Just wondered." Rosie made her voice casual and shrugged all the way down to her fingertips as if it really didn't matter one way or the other. "Just talking about Montréal in class yesterday."

"I don't know." There was a period at the end of that. Carlie's voice went downhill and braked, and the engine turned off. Frig. Then Rosie had to ask Aunt Ginny and Uncle Anthony, one at a time of course, and that was harder, and they also frowned at her and asked why and said they didn't know.

So, in desperation, she asked Nana.

"Don't know, but it was very grand," Nana said. "I remember counting the windows across the front of the house and wondering about the number of bedrooms."

"How many were there?" Shouldn't have interrupted. Should not. Nana looked flustered and said *erm* a few times and dried up. *Was it near downtown? Was it near the airport? Was it by the river, a lake, a church?* Nana couldn't remember.

"There were beautiful roses in the garden. I remember that. Talked to their gardener. Standards all neatly…those pole things…staked, yes, and ramblers climbing everywhere over walls and…those wooden things…trellises. And there were a lot of high walls. They were Keep Out kind of people." She pursed her lips for a second. "The gardener said pink ones were the hardiest, yellow ones were the weakest. Well, I knew that. Could never keep that pretty yellow one through a winter here." She smiled out at the garden, eyes dreamy. "China roses and whattayoucallems—hybrid teas, cabbage roses, flori—something—" There was a long silence.

"What about the family, Nana?"

"The parents were very formal. I preferred talking to the gardener."

⁂

"I have a letter for you, Mom. From Miss Robinson. It's about an exchange with some French grade ten students from Chicoutimi." Rosie held out the letter. Mom just looked at it, took her time getting hold of it. "Can we have a French girl staying with us here for four nights? Please?"

"Don't see why not."

So far so good. Rosie took a big breath and dived into the rest, about her class going to Québec in June, staying with families, plane to Montréal, bus to Chicoutimi, one night in Montréal on the way back, Musée des beaux-arts, bake sales and stuff to raise funds. The prices and everything were in the letter. Rosie put on a hopeful, you-can't-say-no expression and waited.

"Is this why you were asking where Michel's parents live?"

Frig. The Wallace grapevine. "Well, I just wondered, while I'm up there…"

Mom was opening the envelope by sliding her finger in, not bothering with the letter opener, and it tore messily across the back. She read it through and said it sounded like a good opportunity. Too good to miss. "You'll like Chicoutimi." Relief flooded through Rosie and she couldn't help smiling—beaming, even.

"But." Mom looked at her like she had bad news, told Rosie to sit down for a minute, said this was a big But. "There must be no attempt to communicate in any way with the Simard family." She was staring at Rosie as if she was counting the pores in her skin. "I mean it, Rosie. If I thought you would try to phone or write or go to their house, even just to look, I would not let you go on this trip."

Rosie didn't understand. Why couldn't she contact them? It would just be hello and goodbye—she wouldn't pester them or anything. They were her grandparents. Eryn saw her grandma all the time and Justin Halfyard saw his at Christmas and they talked on the phone, and their parents were divorced too.

"I can't tell you, Rosie. I'm sorry. It all happened before you were born, and I try not to think about it because it makes me very sad." Mom's face was getting that frozen look she got when one of her bad times was on the way. God, she couldn't get sick now. Please. She had to sign the paper for Miss Robinson by the end of the week.

"But can I go to Chicoutimi if I promise, absolutely promise, not to contact them in any way?"

Mom came and sat next to Rosie on the sofa and put an arm round her and said yes, of course she could go, and Mom would give her a cheque and go to the parent information meeting next Monday. Rosie started jiggling up and down saying, *thank you, thank you* and about how they were planning a car wash next Saturday, but her mother sat staring into space. "They wouldn't be nice to you, you see. If you contacted them. And I don't want you to get in the middle."

Nana had wandered in halfway through the conversation and was looking from Mom to Rosie and back again. "Michel was much nicer than his parents, you know," Nana said. "He…" She was staring at Rosie now, really staring. Nana looked as if she had something important to say but maybe she couldn't get her thoughts in order, because all she said in the end was, "We can all be much nicer than our parents if we work at it."

Mom stood up and put her arm round Nana, turning her away, saying that nobody could be nicer than Liz Wallace and why didn't they go and start dinner. What was all that about? Her Simard grandparents must be really mean.

There was no time to do anything about them anyway, even if Rosie had been tempted. Every minute of that trip had something in it, something new and different, something to store up and talk about when she came home. She began picking up differences between accents: the kids' in Chicoutimi and her French teacher's and her mom's. When Rosie phoned home, Mom said it was because of her year in France; she never did pick up the Québécois accent, although she was in Montréal a lot longer. Yes, and Michel must have sounded Québécois, so Rosie asked about that and if they had spoken French at home. Her mother said yes to both questions, and had it stopped raining yet?

Rosie did think of her grandparents on the last night of the trip. She was amazed at the size and number of volumes that made up the Montréal telephone directory compared to the one for little old St. John's and before she had made a conscious decision she was rifling through pages, looking—not to phone, she told herself, just to see. And there were dozens, columns on columns, of Simards. Well, it was a pure laine name after all. She still had no contact details—Robert Simard was one name she looked for, but there were a ton of just R. Simards too and Robert could be a middle name for all Rosie knew. There was a W. R. L. Simard, which sounded impressive. Eryn looked over her shoulder at that moment and asked if she was going to phone her grandparents, and when Rosie mumbled something about them being estranged and that they wouldn't like it, Eryn said, "Why wouldn't they?" And Rosie didn't know how to answer, didn't know herself. But she tried to sound casual, saying they were not very nice. Anything to put Eryn off.

But Eryn brought it up again as they were getting ready for bed and started parading around in her underwear inventing wilder and wilder stories about Rosie's paternal grandparents: how they were afraid Rosie would turn up and claim a fortune that was rightfully hers; how her father had gone insane, and they had locked him up in the attic with Grace Poole; how they were not really her grandparents because her mom had run off with the mailman, or that caretaker guy at school whose eyes pointed in different directions, or a pirate. Yes, a pirate. And Eryn mimed climbing a ladder with a knife between her teeth making *arrrr* noises. He'd look just like Johnny Depp. One of the parent-chaperones walked in just then and said *quiet down, girls*, and she hung around until they were all tucked in with the lights off, and by the time she left, Eryn was whispering about Raoul Papineau instead—one of the cute guys in Chicoutimi.

Back at home, the mystery around her grandparents was something Rosie wondered about now and then, late at night or curled up on the sofa with Paddles on her feet. She did not put it into words in her head, the way she would normally lay out facts and possibilities. This wondering was like something Gothic drifting around in a long white nightgown, always floating away or across a distant doorway, so you never saw a face.

In between all the drooling over Raoul in Chicoutimi, (with lots of throaty r-rolling), Eryn teased Rosie about Sean, another classmate on the trip. "He couldn't take his eyes off you, girl. Fell over that chair 'cause he wasn't looking where he was going. Went red as fire."

Eryn laughed about that. Eryn had never blushed in her life. Rosie had—not very often, but when she did you couldn't miss it. It was the fair skin. She was not concerned about Sean, but Rosie did not want Eryn finding out that she liked Joel. Absolutely not.

Sean was chatty and friendly and talked to everyone. Girls liked him, but more in a one-of-the-girls way than a crush-on-you way. He was a friend who happened to be a guy and Rosie approved of that. He'd invited her to the Junior High Grad weeks before the event, and Rosie had laughed and said ask me again in a month, and he did. So then of course she had to say yes and spent the evening of the grad trying not to notice that girl Brittany from the other class dancing with Joel.

Maybe her mom was right about being careful with teasing. Rosie had dismissed it as one of Mom's psychologist quirks, but what Eryn was doing lately did seem like a power thing. She was doing it more often and to more people, and somehow it felt nastier. It used to be funny. *Your dad hang you on a hook at night, Pete? You've grown a foot since last week.* And it was okay for a guy to be tallest in class, so Pete didn't mind, just grinned and went on. And Amy didn't mind being called *Paint by Numbers* when she started with the streaks in green and orange and purple. But Pat did not like being called *Pudding* when she put on weight, and told Eryn so, but Eryn kept saying it. Nobody liked having the parts of themselves they were embarrassed about pointed out or mimicked, like that boy in Mr. Murphy's class with the flat feet that turned out at ten and two. Eryn would get behind him and walk like Charlie Chaplin and giggle and make a fuss so the boy would be sure to know what she was doing. Shy kids in school avoided Eryn. And Rosie did not, not, *not* want to be teased about Joel.

There was a time Rosie shared everything with Eryn. It was the trip to Chicoutimi when that started to change. Eryn told the rest of the kids about Rosie's mom and grandparents being *estranged* and made up all those wild stories about Rosie's father. They were funny, in a way, and nobody took them seriously, but…Eryn should have known that Rosie would be hurt. Then again, Eryn didn't keep anything secret about her own father, told everybody everything, so maybe she really didn't understand. So once they were back home Rosie had tried to explain. Eryn just laughed. *Oh, poor little Rosie misses her daddy.* Rosie was too shocked to say anything at the time.

She should have said it was mean.

Something.

Too late now.

CHAPTER TWENTY-THREE

2010

CARLIE

FOR A LONG TIME CARLIE SAW ROSIE AS A CONSEQUENCE, AND, after Michel left, as a cause, but never as a little person. Maybe she'd been thinking like an anthropologist rather than an aunt. Her deep attachment to Rosie-the-girl took Carlie by surprise.

Ginny's children developed in leaps and bounds because Carlie would be in The Gambia for two leaps and Senegal for three bounds, and on each trip home she was astounded all over again at how the children had aged while she wasn't looking. And it was just like Ginny to be statistically correct and have One Boy who looked like Anthony and One Girl, the image of Ginny, two years later. Ginny was so freaking traditional. Carlie brought the children gifts from her travels and went to their concerts and sports events when pressed. They were nice kids, but they did not need her and never made her feel the least bit maternal.

Rosie was different; maybe because of having one parent and no siblings, with Carlie always on alert to step into the parental shoes in a crisis; maybe because Carlie was afraid of what Rosie might learn one day and wanted her to have the best growing-up experience possible before it happened. Through the early years Carlie was merely an extra babysitter who was away a lot. It was only at age ten, after Rosie sought help with a school project, that she and Carlie developed a real rapport. Then gradually Rosie became one of Carlie's special people, and Carlie became one of Rosie's confidantes and also, according to Eve, the ultimate in glamour.

Some traits in Rosie reminded Carlie of herself, like her fondness for puzzles. Whenever Carlie and Rosie were together Rosie would demand they play more Scrabble, until their murderous games became a family fixture. They would find a quiet spot away from the kitchen and, when called to dinner, drive the family nuts by insisting on finishing their game. Later, they began a long-term relationship with cryptic crosswords. Nowadays Carlie would buy a paperback volume of puzzles for the two of them, but George had introduced Carlie to cryptic crosswords back when he still bought British newspapers in their flimsy airmail form: *The Daily Telegraph*, *The Guardian*, *The Times*. Those newspaper puzzles put vocabulary in a competitive light and required a passing knowledge of Roman numerals, literary quotations, Greek mythology, cricket, gastronomy, and the difference between *adagio* and *lento* on a musical score. In later days, the puzzles also triggered rambling conversations between herself and Rosie, and Google searches into obscure topics, and planted seeds of inquiry in Rosie's hungry brain.

And around all those positive feelings Carlie had for Rosie there was a nebulous wish to atone for what Eve had suffered in Mexico. Survivor guilt. Eve had been thoughtful and mature as a girl, never going to extremes, never in trouble—a goody two-shoes to balance Caroline's brattiness. Eve was always agreeable, and yes, Carlie admitted to being born contrary. It had passed into family law that, as a toddler, whenever someone said what a pretty little girl Caroline was, she would look grumpy and say, *I'm a boy*. Some would laugh then and say she was a cute little boy, and she would scowl even more and reply, *I'm a girl*. There was no pleasing Carlie.

During Carlie's adolescence, the fire department had been called a time or two. Once, she was chasing a squirrel and was going to jump after it into the next tree but wimped out (to her lasting shame), then could not back up because her shorts caught on something spiky. So, Carlie sat and yelled for Ginny. The second time was not an emergency because she had been quite safe, rescuing a kitten, but some interfering do-gooders on the ground had called the fire department because the branch she was on was bending down and creaking a bit.

During her teenage years, each new emotion had carried her off on a tidal wave of destruction, so it was pure luck she made it through to her twenties without ruining her life…or somebody else's. Now, she recognized her good fortune, because for all her recklessness and her venturing quite deliberately into the kind of places lone women did not go, nobody had ever harmed Carlie.

It had been unseasonably hot all week, with daytime temperatures in the mid-twenties, the highest across Canada. The seasons in Newfoundland always lagged a couple of weeks behind the rest of the country, which was depressing in spring but highly satisfying in October. It was a frisky blue-and-white day, with trees at their absolute best—still half green, a perfect backdrop for the other half, running the gamut of gold, orange, and scarlet. This Saturday morning Carlie was not setting foot in the car. She would walk up to Eve's and help out, then walk the Rennie's River trail.

Her phone pinged with a text from Rosie. Could Rosie come over for the books Carlie had promised? She was downtown with friends. Carlie replied, *Leaving soon for your place* and was surprised by the response, *Wait. Go with you*. Teenage Rosie would not normally be seen in public with an aunt on a Saturday. Rosie had "discovered" science fiction recently and had been surprised that Carlie read such books too, let alone owned a few. Of course Carlie gave her the lecture on stereotyping. Afterwards Rosie said, "So sci-fi is like anthropology—walking a mile in someone else's shoes?" Well, the good ones were.

Today's conversation began with an innocuous question about anthropology as they walked up Mulberry Street. Why had Carlie chosen it as a career?

"It was for that exact reason—to walk a mile in someone else's world: to find out why people do what they do, think how they think, and what contributes to people's differences. And similarities." It was also about the travel, but not as a tourist. Carlie had not wanted to flutter from place to place as a temporary visitor, always with a mental return ticket ready, just staying until the novelty wore off. She wanted to really Be in the place where she was living, to understand, to belong. She had not realized how difficult that last one would be.

Anthropology had moved on (somewhat) from the days of rich colonialists taking a paternalistic look at the "savages" in foreign lands. These days, real scholars tried not to judge people through European or American eyes. They tried to view a person's world through that person's own eyes, in a non-judgmental way, which required total immersion—learning the language(s) and living as the local people lived—and *close observation*. That was what Carlie had tried to do.

"But why Senegal?" Rosie wanted to know. "It's not a place you hear much about."

Carlie had hung around with Senegalese students living in her building when she was doing her undergrad at McGill. She was still in touch with two of them, twenty-five years later. She did a minor in French—the official language in Senegal. Her friends taught her a few bits of Wolof too, although she never risked using it in front of strangers because of the smirks and sniggers from those same untrustworthy friends. "I just thought Senegal sounded a fun place to go and I'd have some connections."

In Montréal, Carlie had not realized those students were all from powerful, elite families. So few Senegalese teens had the opportunity even to graduate from high school, especially girls, and there had been only one university in the whole of Senegal at the time, the Université Cheikh Anta Diop in Dakar. (There were maybe six now.) And that one had been extremely overcrowded. So the rich often sent their children out of the country.

It was hard to talk while climbing a hill after a beery Friday night at The Ship. Carlie had chosen a longer, more oblique route up to Eve's house rather than the direct, vertical one, but it was still steep. And somehow, as they slowly mounted the broad shallow steps on Garrison Hill (three paces per step), the questions veered around to why Carlie had left Senegal and had she ever had a Grand Passion?

Aha. Rosie must have heard something about Oumar and was wanting to know more. Carlie looked sideways at her niece. "Are you planning a grand passion, Rosie?"

"You don't plan something like that. It just happens."

"So, has it happened?"

"No! I just wondered...How you—how—You know..."

"No, I don't know." (One, two, three paces. One, two three...)

Rosie tried a different tack. "Don't they have polygamy in Senegal?" The rumble of traffic grew louder as they reached Military Road and a siren started up in the distance. "I mean, it's common in a lot of countries around there, isn't it?" A hairy little dog with its head out through the half-open window of a passing car aimed a volley of yaps at a German shepherd on the sidewalk. The car stopped for a pedestrian, and the little hairy head retreated so fast it bounced off the glass.

"Okay. Let's sit over here and talk." Carlie led the way across Military Road to an old bench. "So," she said. "Polygamy." Islam allowed men to have up to four wives. Back when Carlie was still working in Senegal and was aware of such statistics, the UN estimated 47 percent of Senegalese marriages were polygamous. Most monogamous marriages were in the cities. Plenty of men still approved of polygamy. Well, of course they did—it was all in their favour; in most instances a wife's rights were totally at the mercy of her husband. He might allow a great deal of freedom, or none at all, and then there was the balance of power between wives one through four to consider... "And an unmarried woman is generally held in contempt, so choices are limited."

Carlie had masses of facts and figures that Rosie could read—academic papers, reports—if she was interested. But it might be more fun to read a couple of novels, also sitting on Carlie's shelves, both written decades ago but still relevant. One was *God's Bits of Wood* by Ousmane Sembène. Polygamy was just there as a fact of life, woven through the background of his novel, the main story being the fight against French colonialism and racism, and a strike by Black railway workers after the Second World War. Carlie sighed, remembering Thiès, the Railway City. She had lived there for a while.

Traffic hiccupped and stuttered to the west, where the crossroads met at awkward angles. Drivers were being remarkably patient. Carlie smiled to herself. Maybe their good behaviour was due to there being so many churches nearby: the Roman Catholic Basilica behind them, the Kirk, the United Church, and the Anglican Cathedral just over the brow of the hill. They would not go much for polygamy. Rosie was probably only asking about it as a means to find out about Carlie's love life, but then she surprised Carlie by saying yes, she would like to read that book and what was the other one?

"*So Long a Letter* is a novel by a Senegalese woman," Carlie said. "Mariama Bâ wrote a letter-cum-diary to her lifelong friend all about polygamy, from a female perspective, obviously." The friends had both been happily married for years (they thought) until each hubby sneakily took a second wife. The friends were both educated, teachers with more opportunities than most women, so one of them applied for a divorce and moved to the US. The other, the writer, followed the traditional passive acceptance of the situation and wrote about her life as a dutiful first wife. *Yesterday you were divorced. Today I was widowed.* Polygamy was the main issue here but behind it were questions about the writer's place in the extended family and in the world, and of the growth of modern Senegal and, most of all, the growth of the author's own self in spite of all the difficulties. It was a good book for Rosie to think about.

Traffic had cleared for the moment, and it was peaceful, sitting there, with a breeze lifting their hair and two blue jays flashing from tree to tree across the road. Finally, Rosie said, "But you came home." It was a statement with a question in it.

"Indeed," Carlie said, pulling a what-can-I-tell-you face. "I left in the end, like a lot of Toubabs."

"Why?" Rosie said, still digging. "I thought you'd stay forever."

The truth was, Carlie had run away. But she was not about to tell Rosie that. "After my studies were finished, I worked in the so-called civil society, which was trying to do what the government should have been doing but wasn't: look after the people." Carlie explained about the NGOs, national and international, and the smaller local associations, and that there were well over two hundred such groups based in Dakar—still considered the capital of French West Africa. Her favourite local group, where she volunteered, had raised money by running an internet café and having the Senegalese version of bake sales and craft sales, and by giving French and English classes, but they still needed outside financial help for bigger projects.

This particular time her group was starting an ambitious educational project, and two teenage sisters she knew quite well were ecstatic about beginning business-training the following week. Then the outside funding was pulled at the last minute, and Carlie had to tell them it was all cancelled—had to watch the hope drain out of their faces. Such failures happened regularly, but this time Carlie's own heart sank and sank and did not come up again. She was done. Part of her job was to inspire hope, hope for something better. She just couldn't do it anymore. Alternate funding was found months later, and the program went ahead eventually, with the two sisters, but by then the reasons to leave had far outweighed the reasons to stay, and Carlie fled. Home.

"Why did I leave?" she said out loud. "Because I guess, in the end, I was just another homesick Newfoundlander."

A bus puffed out fumes as it roared past their bench. Carlie could only see two passengers in that whole hardworking vehicle. If this were Dakar, it would be packed. She summoned her breeziest voice. "Why all these questions?"

Rosie slouched down and didn't answer.

"There's something going on. What's wrong?"

After a minute Rosie straightened a little, saying, "Oh, nothing new, I suppose." She made to stand up, so they set off up the slow rise of Bonaventure Avenue, and after a long pause, the dam opened. Rosie had lost her cool with Eryn and had yelled at her in front of people—something Rosie always hated, and here she was, doing it to her best friend. Well, she used to be her best friend. Should have waited and said it in private, only she never saw her in private anymore. Didn't think she wanted to, either.

This was routine teenage behaviour, but Carlie wondered about the reason for all the acrimony and whether Rosie would tell her later. She tried to console Rosie, saying her friend needed standing up to from time to time, and Eryn was very public in her own behaviour, so not to worry about the audience.

"But I was awful," Rosie said. "Screeching and cursing like...words I don't ever say, don't even *think*. Awful." She was hunched down again, looking miserable.

"Well, next time you can work on having a more normal voice and no curse words."

There was an almost inaudible mumble, then—"Too late."

Maybe some nice young man had heard her tantrum—this Joel that Rosie was so very offhand and casual about. If he was a nice young man? He was the one Carlie had noticed in the movie lineup that time, behind Rosie's crowd, had noticed him particularly because his smile was just like Michel's. Rosie had turned and looked at him. It was only for a moment, but her face said it all: shy, noticing, please-notice-me-too. So, Carlie had taken a second look at this boy, whose smile had dropped off so very quickly when Rosie turned away. Then there was no resemblance to Michel at all, in fact his face looked…furtive. All Carlie's instincts said Do Not Trust. Ginny would call that rash judgement, but Carlie lived by her instincts. Mom had noticed too. Carlie had taken her out for some window-shopping and a stroll in the mall that evening; she did that sometimes on Fridays.

"That boy," Mom had said, then stopped. "The one our girl was looking at." Stopped again.

"What are you thinking?"

"Not nice."

"No. Smile's like Michel's though."

Her mother was still shaking her head. "Not nice."

Liz could still recognize a threat, pick up on bad vibes. Was there a primitive warning reflex tucked away in some ancient part of the brain, which zinged or lit up in response to subtle signs? *Beware!* Or did one have to learn it as a skill? Whatever it was, Liz's was still in working order.

They were at Eve's door now, so Carlie said, "Well, Rosie, it's sometimes a good idea to let someone know they can't walk all over you." Rosie gave a minimal nod and went straight to her room, saying thanks for the books.

She would probably go on brooding over that young man. Girls her age all wanted a Romeo. It was worrying when the first candidate for the part was an unsavoury character, but that was how you learned the difference. There had been plenty of creeps in Carlie's life and she had never come to any harm—and, inborn or learned, she could detect the warning signs from outer space. Carlie was glad this part of growing-up was behind her.

CHAPTER TWENTY-FOUR

2010

ROSIE

"CAN I COME OVER, ROSIE? MOM'S IN A MOOD." IT WAS THE first text from Eryn in ages. They had hardly talked since their fight, which Joel had overheard, and Rosie still felt badly about that. So she was glad of the chance to get together. Eryn's mother was often in difficult moods, but Eryn said this one was worse than usual. The regular ones involved a lot of stomping around the house and banging things, but this time Eryn's mother had gone all quiet and was going through bills and receipts and bank stuff. All she would say was, *Your father's really done it this time.*

"And he's always *your father*, never *my ex* or *Jim*." Eryn and Rosie were sitting on Rosie's bed with Paddles lying between them. "Well, she calls him *her ex* to other people but never to Allan and me. Like it's our fault." Eryn stopped talking, stopped petting Paddles, and folded her arms, then pulled up her knees and wrapped her arms round her knees instead.

"So what's he done?"

"Something to do with support payments. Don't think he's been paying them." Eyrn sighed. "Heard Mom telling her friend Jodi she was going to have to do extra overtime."

Rosie did not think Michel had ever done anything like that—although would Rosie even know? Mom never freaked out over unexpected expenses like plumbers and electricians, but nor did she go on expensive trips overseas (unfortunately) and she never went to the more exclusive restaurants that some girls at school talked about. Mom's one extravagance was expensive clothing (although usually from the sale rack). She stressed *quality* to Rosie whenever they went shopping together, which usually meant more moolah, but she insisted the good stuff lasted longer so it was more economical in the long run. Mom was careful but had never been in a panic over money.

Rosie was not sure about dollar amounts, but she thought a mortgage was the same as rent only more so…a big chunk to pay out every month. And Michel had made life a lot easier for them by paying into it all these years. So he couldn't be all bad—although he was probably rolling in money, and it's not like he had another family to buy things for, like Eryn's father had.

"Mom asked me if I would cook supper on Tuesdays," Eryn was saying. "She showed me her book of recipes, so she really means it."

"I can come over and help if you want."

Eryn pounced on that idea. Rosie knew so much more about cooking than she did. Like, how did you sauté, and what was the difference between a simmer and a rolling boil?

They talked about cooking and meals they might try. Nana had given Rosie all kinds of tips and old-fashioned rules you didn't see in cookbooks, like putting a mint leaf in with boiling potatoes to make the starch easier to digest. She made little sermons out of everything too, only you didn't mind because it was Nana, and it didn't feel like a sermon. *Light on the salt, Rosie. You can always add more but you can't take it out again. You can never take back what you've said, so watch that tongue of yours.* Eryn said her mother said something like that too.

But it wasn't only Nana and her Life Lessons; Rosie was used to helping in the kitchen because her mom didn't want her growing up not knowing how to boil water, like some of her roommates in Montréal.

"Your mom had roommates?" Eryn said she couldn't picture that.

"As a student. In the ghetto. Before Michel."

Rosie found it strange too, as if the stories were about a different person. Mom had gone away to McGill on her own and taken trips all over Canada and the US; Greyhound buses and hostels and crashing on people's floors. Excitement. Risk. And before that, just after grade twelve, she had backpacked around Europe with two girlfriends for a month. But after Rosie was born, Eve had become a real dead-end, stay-at-home mom. Rosie grouched about that every year when her friends went south, one after the other, during the endless Newfoundland winter. *Everyone but me has been to Florida, Mom. Why do we never go farther than Terra Nova National Park?*

Carlie had spent years going to all kinds of interesting places, and Rosie loved to hear about them. Some of the posters on Rosie's walls were from Carlie's travels: an ornate temple in a jungle, a fantastic waterfall, a sphinx. Eryn had given Rosie one of the Whitewater Center in Charlotte, North Carolina, and Aunt Ginny had given her an Olympic poster showing a gymnast on the parallel bars. Nana gave her a 2010 dog calendar, which Rosie felt slightly guilty about displaying…all those perfect purebreds when poor Paddington was so obviously not.

Back during her Chicoutimi trip, Rosie had taken money out of her precious Qatar Savings Account to buy a little Picasso print at the Musée des beaux-arts. Mom had found a frame for it in the basement. Rosie worried about dipping into her savings because Christmas and birthday money was not building up fast enough to cover plane fares for her Qatar trip (whenever that might be). She'd have to get a summer job because the family might not want to lend her anything for a visit to Michel. The thought that her father also might not want her to visit fluttered past, but she ignored that. The only way to overcome Michel's indifference was to get right in his face and show him what a great person she was. End of subject.

Mom was ironing in the kitchen when Eryn left, so Rosie wandered in and told her about Eryn's mother's troubles. Mom just said *Oh, dear* but made no other comment. As usual. The iron had more to say than her mother, hissing and gurgling and puffing out steam so the whole kitchen felt tropical. But Rosie persisted: "Mom, why do you always say *Michel* and not *Your Father*?"

Her mom didn't look up, just turned her blue flowery shirt over and started on the other sleeve. She loved ironing—liked calming things, smoothing things out. Rosie would rather forget the iron and wear wrinkles. Finally her mother did look up and said, "Because you're all Wallace. And not just in obvious things like features and colouring, but in little mannerisms. You tilt your head when you're thinking, like Ginny, and when you raise your eyebrows you have three lines across your forehead in the exact same place as Mom and me."

"But I must have Michel's genes too. Do you see anything of him in me?"

Mom arranged the shirt on a hanger then hung it on a door handle. "No. I don't. You must have paternal genes, of course, but they don't show. I always think of you as ninety per cent Wallace and ten per cent Other."

As the day wore on, Rosie thought more and more about that casual *Other*. All her life she had been described as a Wallace—her mother and aunts too—although their colouring, hair, and eyes were all from Nana's side. But collectively they were all Wallace now. Rosie had to admit there was nothing of Simard in her face when she compared herself with Michel's photograph. But to claim her whole being for the Wallace / Robinson clan and dismiss half her genes as Other was insulting. It was not like her mother at all.

It was just after Eryn's visit that Mom had a call from the lawyer, so of course support payments jumped into Rosie's mind. Lawyerly calls always involved Michel. Rosie answered the phone and the guy reeled off his name and spelling, Wojcik, in a mechanical way that suggested he did it every time. It was just six letters but those consonants would be high-scoring letters in Scrabble if you were allowed to use proper nouns: twenty points, not including the vowels.

Mom took the call in her room with the door shut but later she came to Rosie's room and said the lawyer had news about Michel that she thought Rosie should know. "Michel is getting married again. To a French lady. And they're moving to Paris. He—"

First, Rosie stopped breathing, just stared at her mother and stopped breathing. Then her heart dropped. She felt it physically drop, as if her whole framework had given way and her heart had fallen down through the scaffolding.

Now she'd never have the chance to show him what a great daughter she was.

Rosie lay in bed feeling all purpose had been taken out of her life. What could she do? The new wife would not want to know anything about Rosie, nor want Michel to have anything to do with her. She would stomp over everything from Michel's previous life, boycott the least little connection. Rosie hated the new wife already.

Rosie wanted to stay in bed, pull the covers up over her head, and ignore everything, only it was the absolute last day to hand in that English paper which had taken so much work. She dragged herself out, grabbed the nearest clean underwear, and slapped on the same clothes she had worn the day before. Mom kept giving her little sideways looks all through breakfast, finally leaning over and laying her hand on Rosie's cheek, and later gave her an extra big hug as she was leaving for work. As if that would help. Then her mom said in a matter-of-fact voice that she was surprised it hadn't happened sooner. *He left fifteen years ago, after all.* Like it didn't matter now. Mothers just did not understand.

When Rosie got to school, Eryn said she had a face like Monday morning instead of the start of the weekend, but Rosie was not in the mood for prying. After school, the girls were all going up to the Square to hang out. Rosie said she was going down to Carlie's, but she had something else to do first. She started rooting around in her locker, hoping they would just leave, because what she really wanted to do was go home and snuggle under the blanket in the rec room and be a blob in front of the TV. She made a show of folding her old green fleece, zipping it, resting it on her knee as she stood on one leg and folding it Martha Stewart–style. She did the same with her hoodie, laying it precisely on top of the fleece in that fanatical way the guy in her math class lined up pens in order of size and colour.

The girls were still standing around outside when Rosie came out so she had to turn down the hill after all and head towards Carlie's, but her aunt would certainly not be there on a Friday. Rosie was trudging, she knew, and looking at the sidewalk. Carlie would tell her to pick up her feet and look the world in the eye. Nana would say, *You might be feeling down and out, but there's no need to announce it.*

Then a voice came out of nowhere: "Don't see you down this way too often."

Joel. Joel!

"Going to my aunt's. How about you?" Rosie wasn't looking at the sidewalk anymore.

"Going to my dad's," Joel said and fell into step beside her.

"Your parents separated?"

"Never together, really. I mean…single parents and all that. You?"

"Oh, they were married but my father walked out when I was a baby. I've never even met him."

There was a gap in the traffic, so they jaywalked across the road before they reached the crossing, and Rosie said her father was getting married again soon. She tried to keep her voice casual but there was a little hitch in it after the word *married* and she hoped he wouldn't notice, but he was looking at her as if he had.

"Want a hot chocolate or something? A Tim Hortons just opened on the corner by the traffic lights."

Rosie tried not to beam and took a mental inventory of the money in her backpack. *Enough*, she thought, so she said ,"Sure," and he smiled that gorgeous, long, sexy curve of a smile.

She had just enough for a double double, and Joel bought the same and they carried their coffees to a table in the window. Not that there was much of a view—just a row of cars, parallel parked, and traffic—but Rosie didn't care about the view. She noticed a strong smell of pot from Joel's clothes, now that they were indoors. She wondered if any teachers had commented on that in school or if he had only been smoking since the last bell—it was the weekend after all. Where had he appeared from just now?

"You play hooky this afternoon?" she said.

He didn't answer and his face was blank, so Rosie said, "Don't worry, I won't report you to the hooky police or anything." He was looking at her a bit narrow-eyed with his mouth tight shut, so she changed direction, saying, "Where does your dad live?"

His face tightened up even more, so that was a mistake too. Crap! No more questions.

"Carbury Street," he said after a minute. "I'm living with my father now. That's why I changed schools. Used to live in Mount Pearl with my mother." He said it all in a closing-the-door kind of voice, and Rosie felt her face turning pink, so she rushed into saying how hot the coffee was.

He sat a bit sideways to the table so he could stretch out his legs—he had very long legs—and he rested one elbow on the table and toyed with his cup. He never did look at her straight on and it made her want to say something brilliant so he would turn toward her completely. He had dark, opaque eyes, with low-slung eyelids. Come-to-bed eyes, Eryn would call them. Rosie could only see one at a time anyway and she chuckled to herself, thinking maybe that was a good thing. There was something about him; something that made her heart beat faster.

He seemed more…worldly than the other boys, more exciting. Although maybe that was just because he was a bit older and he'd come from a different school, so she didn't know him as well. But it was the smile that did it most of all.

Afterwards, Rosie could not remember the details of their conversation, only that he asked a lot of questions and she didn't want to ask too many back. But when they parted there was a warm feeling of being understood—someone from a broken home commiserating with someone else from a broken home.

He had drifted off in the opposite direction after they came out of Tim's with a half-smile, half pointed look, half wave. She, Rosie, was going to change the half part. He was going to give her his full attention. If Joel ever asked her out, she would wear her favourite blue top. *Your eyeballs are going to fall out, Joel Walsh—both of them.* But he and Rosie had to be together in the same place for anything interesting to happen, and he didn't go to the parties Rosie's friends attended, and there was no way Rosie was going to invite him to something first. She fell asleep that night, plotting.

CHAPTER TWENTY-FIVE

2010

LIZ

EVE...*NO, I'M ROSIE, NANA*...HAS HER ARMS IN THE DISHPAN up to the elbows in bubbles. She says the dishwasher is broken, which explains the long face. I loved mine too. Who was it that said she'd rather do without her indoor toilet? It was Ginny. It was something I would have said if I'd thought of it first.

I pick up a plate to dry it, but it slips out of my fingers and falls on its lip on the floor. I stand, watching it doing one of those ice-skating things where a girl in a frothy skirt spins on the spot and reaches her arms up in the air, going faster and faster. I could never understand the physics behind that. The plate is so pretty, flashing blue then white then blue again, going round-roun-roou-rooouu-rrrrrr... Then Eve—no, Rosie—is picking it up and telling me to go and sit down, the dishes can air dry. No need for her to be so snippy. The plate didn't break. I go to the kitchen table and sit down. I'm always doing as I'm told these days.

It's Rosie doing the dishes...the snippy one. Anyway, Rosie is ploughing through those bubbles, making them mound up above the dishpan.

"You put too much of that green liquid in," I say.

Silence.

"Happened to me once," I say, remembering the bubbles piled high in the sink. "Tried to swill them away but they wouldn't melt. Just floated round in a circle. Carlie says they go round the other way in Africa."

Rosie goes on clattering dishes. She's going to crack something. I open my mouth to tell her, but close it again. Rosie is not rinsing them enough, and the bubbles are spreading everywhere. "My bubbles were from the washing machine though. Baby soap. Sweaters. The whole thing stopped in the middle of the spin cycle. Jammed up with bubbles. Had to scoop them out with a bowl, over and over." I can see the inside of the washing machine now, the mass of bubbles set solid with bowl-shaped scoops out of it, like ice cream. Looked like that stuff they put Chinese takeout into as well...poly-something, only more delicate. Like wedding veils, maybe.

"What happened to the sweaters, Nana?" Rosie has turned towards me, looking interested. I think back but all I can remember are the bubbles.

CHAPTER TWENTY-SIX

2011

CARLIE

ROSIE'S DRIVING LESSONS HAD BECOME A STAPLE IN Carlie's week, while Eve stayed home with Liz. Mostly they were short trips around town for Traffic Practice. You could probably cope with any city in North America if you could drive (and park) around downtown St. John's, with its tangle of one-way streets and awkward intersections, steep hills and blind corners. The founders had never heard of the grid system. Huge piles of snow often exacerbated the narrowness and poor visibility, and then there was the ice. It was not that the city was bitterly cold—in fact, it was milder than most Canadian cities, being farther south and on the ocean—but for months, the temperature would hover around zero degrees centigrade: first the ice, then the thaw or rain—just enough to wash the municipal salt away—and then the flash freeze again. Over and over. Sooner or later, everyone got stuck on one of the hills, wheels spinning with that ugly rubbery whine. Everyone had a horror story of losing control: of sliding down a hill through a stop sign and coming to a stop halfway up the old museum steps, or seeing a whole line of cars parked at an angle on Cathedral Street sliding sideways into each other.

When Rosie suggested driving up Signal Hill to look at an iceberg at the end of one lesson, Carlie suspected there was a question looming. Well, it was as good a place as any for signals to be received. Marconi's first transatlantic radio signal had been transmitted to this very spot on the twelfth hour of the twelfth day of the twelfth month in 1901. Maybe it had left a vibe.

It was the first clear day in a week: clear road surfaces, clear skies, and someone had told Rosie there was an iceberg out there. It seemed a bit early for icebergs to Carlie, but then again, the *Titanic* had had its iceberg problem around the same time in April, a century or so ago. Today, the ocean was just a sullen stretch of winter grey, heaving and grumbling out to a grey horizon. There were a few bergy-bits out there but nothing substantial. Maybe Rosie's Someone needed better glasses. They sat there in the car, silent for a few minutes, before Rosie asked her question.

"Carlie, why does Mom have PTSD when you don't?"

Ah. Carlie had anticipated a question like this at some point and had considered some answers, but it was still tricky in the moment. "I'm harder-hearted."

Rosie huffed and said, "But think of all the awful things you've seen with your own eyes and have seen for years...way worse than anything Mom might have heard second-hand as a therapist."

"Don't underestimate the dreadful things Eve has had to deal with through clients. Body and mind. Every bit as traumatizing—"

"But still...yours was personal. I would expect *you* to be the one...."

This would be the time to tell Rosie the truth. Carlie so wanted to tell her the truth, but of course it was not her place, not her choice, and this was peak homework time building up to exams so perhaps it would not be a good moment anyway.

"Is it something to do with her and Michel's trip to Mexico?"

Carlie pulled out a sponge from the pocket on the door and wiped the condensation off the inside of the windshield, passed it to Rosie to do her side. The sponge was too dry to absorb anything properly and just smeared the fog into two misty arcs, with droplets forming here and there.

"Your mom has been absorbing other people's pain for decades, Rosie, but things did seem to come to a head around that time, so Mexico is a reminder, for sure. Lots of things are reminders and we don't know the half of them so they're hard to avoid."

Rosie was all hunched down now, looking sideways out the window, saying she did more stuff that reminded her mom than anybody else.

"Eve doesn't care about that. She loves you more than anybody else in the world and that's what matters." There was more talk about signs and symptoms, but no more awkward questions—for now.

Carlie tackled Eve with this the next time she arrived for Liz duty at Eve's house, when Rosie was gone somewhere and before Eve disappeared for choir practice. *Rosie's questions are getting more specific. She's zeroing in on Mexico. Asking why I don't have PTSD like you.* Eve said *yes*, she had been considering telling Rosie everything straight after her exams, only now Rosie wanted to attend a gymnastics camp in Gros Morne soon after school finished, so Eve would have to save it until after the camp because Rosie would need recovery time. Eve thought the two of them could go on a little trip, to Toronto or maybe New York—do some shopping and see a show. Whatever Rosie would like. No, she had not made any reservations yet. No, she had not mentioned the trip to Rosie....

Then after the gymnastics event, Rosie was invited to the summer cottage of one of the girls at the camp, and after that the girl came to stay with Rosie while her parents were away, and next thing it was past the middle of August, and Eve said there was not enough recovery time before school started. And Carlie had a sinking feeling about all this but there was nothing she could do.

Carlie was sitting at her desk one evening in July, gazing out at a ripening sunset, when Eve phoned to ask a favour. "There's a big psych conference in Boston on PTSD in September, and I would like to go because—"

"—and will I stay at your place while you're gone. Of course I will. No need to give me a ton of reasons. I'd do it if you were going mud wrestling." Thank heavens. First time out of the country since Mexico. First time out of the province.

Eve was gone for four nights the week after Labour Day and arrived home just after supper. There was no stress in her face—only the usual fatigue and glad-to-be-home look of anyone just in after two planes and Customs and a lot of waiting around in airports.

When everyone was settled away, the two sisters sat back with a glass of red and Carlie said, "So. Learn anything useful at the conference?"

"Yes, actually. I did. There's much more information out there now about sexual assault trauma, rather than just combat trauma." Then she changed the subject to her shopping spree—she loved shopping in "away" places for clothes that were a bit different, and taxes were so much less in the States that she could be extravagant without feeling guilty.

They were alone in the living room now, Eve curled up at the end of the loveseat and Carlie sprawled on the couch. Liz was in bed. Rosie had done the runway thing, modelling all the clothes Eve had brought back for her from Boston, before she'd gone off to a movie with Eryn. She was wearing three of the tops all at once, hanging down one below the other: grey, blue stripes, then solid blue. Liz would hate it. It was lucky that Rosie and Eve were identical in size and shape. Only their carriage showed differences: Rosie's bouncy athleticism versus Eve's grace.

"So, did you buy anything for yourself?"

"A gorgeous outfit in *nude*..." Eve wiggled her eyebrows. It had aqua embroidery and a matching aqua shirt—the right kind of aqua that didn't drain the colour out of one's face.

"Oooh, let's see it." But it was all bundled up ready for the dry cleaner the next day. First time on and Eve had spilled red wine down the front.

"That's not like you."

Eve shrugged but turned away, and there was something about the way she turned...something furtive. She spiralled up off the sofa, still turned away, and left the room, and Carlie's antennae stood on end. Eve came back with a scarf in her hand. "For you," she said, holding it out. Carlie tried to catch her eye, but Eve was not looking, just started waving that scarf in her face, saying how well it would go with her green outfit. Evasive. Very evasive.

Carlie ignored the scarf. "You met someone."

Eve was sitting now, and she dropped the scarf on her knees and sat very still for a moment then said, in a neutral voice, "Well, that was a non sequitur. What makes you think that?"

"You're embarrassed. This is plain old embarrassment."

"Don't be silly."

"I'll tell Ginny…"

Eve sat forwards, straight-backed on the edge of her seat, and said, "Don't you tell a soul, Caroline Wallace, not a soul." She looked almost threatening.

Carlie could feel her eyebrows stretched right up on top of her head. "Well! That hit a nerve."

Eve's eyes were hard and sharp, and she said if Carlie couldn't keep quiet about this, Eve would never speak to her again. And yes, she had met someone. He was staying in the same hotel for some engineering conference, but she did not want to share this with anybody because it was so new, so fragile. She felt superstitious about it. She growled about Carlie's sixth sense and how difficult it was to keep secrets around her and reiterated the need for Carlie to keep it to herself. "I'll let you know if and when I'm ready to go public."

"Well at least you've met this guy face to face, haven't been taken in by some online dating affair."

"Give me some credit."

Carlie swallowed the lecture on being cautious because what Eve really needed was to cut the caution, undo some of the knots, and loosen up. But she could not prevent a little wave of fear that, for Eve, loosening up with the wrong person could be a disaster. *Caroline Wallace, stop being such a nervous Nellie.*

Eve said, "You think I'm being naïve."

"Just thinking it over." Carlie got to her feet and sat down by Eve on the loveseat, and gave her a bear hug. "I'm glad you've met somebody. Really, I am. As long as he's a nice guy."

Eve was smiling. "He is."

CHAPTER TWENTY-SEVEN

2011

ROSIE

THEY CAME OUT OF THE HOCKEY ARENA PUMPED UP AND bouncing, chanting *Go Crazies* because their school team had just made it to the finals. They huddled, then spread widthways onto the street, re-formed, and wandered down the icy sidewalk in twos and threes. Rosie was arm-in-arm with Eryn, and Joel was somewhere on her left, just behind. Joel! The sky was an endless indigo-black with tiny pot lights, and the wind had given up and gone home so it was hats-off singing. Even Rosie, with the voice of a crow, was singing. They marched and danced and fooled about, all the while heading for the nearest nachos.

At the restaurant, they pushed tables together and sat in a messy big square of winter jackets and noise. Waiters tried to make sense of shouted orders and corrections and additions, and to pin down the winner of the olives/no olives argument. Gradually the steam level rose, and jackets came off. The soft drinks arrived. The decibel level dropped marginally from Ultra High to a Medium High hubbub. Rosie was on the edge of her seat because there, across the table, sat Joel, smiling at her. He'd leaned over her shoulder from the row behind, halfway through the game, and said *Hi*. And here he was, and here Rosie was, in the new blue sweater she had chosen with him in mind. Life was good. The only improvement would be for him to sit next to her but somehow, when Rosie sat down, there were Eryn and Mark grabbing the next chairs, and Sean and

Craig on her other side, and Melanie's crowd all in a group just beyond, and Joel hanging back and moving around the table, so he ended up opposite. But at least she got the full force of that smile.

Rosie was starving and shovelling nachos into her mouth, leaning forward so she didn't drop salsa down her front. As the pickings thinned, she reached more to the middle of the nearest plate, lifting off her chair a little. Then a race for the last bit of olive broke out between herself and Mark, and they chased it as it flipped off the pile and skidded north, and Rosie was saying, *No fair, you've got longer arms*, just as he grabbed it and turned to grin at her. And at that moment she noticed Joel's phone down low on the table and wondered who he could be texting, right in the thick of things.

"I saw that!" Eryn's voice over the top of everything. "I saw you, Joel Walsh. Taking a picture of Rosie's cleavage." She was out of her chair, squeezing past people to reach him, and some of the guys were looking round, surprised. Others went on eating and talking until maybe the change in the noise level registered, or the tone of it, and they turned to see, too. Rosie was sitting up straight now and her hand came up to the front of her sweater and she looked down to check her neckline. She reached behind to pull it down at the back.

"What are you talking about?" Joel looked half amused, half annoyed. "Just texting a friend."

"Show me," said Eryn, reaching for his phone.

Joel was glancing at his phone and pulling it back, away from Eryn. "None of your freaking business." His thumbs were on the screen, twiddling.

"Better show her your latest picture, b'y. She won't stop bugging you until she's had a look." That was Mark.

Then Eryn had it in her hands, looking. "You've deleted it. I saw you just now, clear as anything."

"I wouldn't do that to Rosie—or anyone," Joel said, his voice indignant. "It's you that has the dirty mind. You should apologize. Apologize and sit down out of it."

He was staring at Eryn by now, but he had flicked a little smile at Rosie when he mentioned her name and she felt a wave of—what? Emotion. Call it emotion. And there was anger at Eryn too for doing her centre-of-attention thing again, for spoiling Rosie's evening.

"Oh, sit down Eryn, you're imagining things." The moment the words left her mouth, Rosie wished she could take them back. Eryn stood motionless for a minute, staring open-mouthed at Rosie. *God, she should not, not, not have said that.*

"Sorry. I'm sorry, Eryn. I didn't mean that." Rosie stood up and tried to squeeze behind Mark's chair towards Eryn, wanting to hug her, make amends, but Eryn said, "Stay right where you are, Rose Wallace. Don't come near me." She tossed a look of disgust at Joel, which made Rosie look at him too. And he was smirking. A little blaze of anger fizzed up inside Rosie, but it was smothered almost immediately by a wave of wanting—wanting a Grand Passion like Carlie. Wanting it now.

So she stopped, undecided, and in that tiny moment Eryn forced her way round the table and yanked her jacket off the back of her chair, rummaging through pockets for money and dropping loonies and toonies in front of Melanie. Then she headed for the door.

Here we go with the drama again. Why couldn't…? Rosie shuffled back to her seat and sank into it, not looking at anyone. How fast everything could fall apart. Gradually, voices started up until there was a comfortable-enough rumble that Rosie could raise her eyes.

And there was Joel's smile, wide and beautiful and just for her.

But Rosie could only manage a small smile back, and at that moment Mark asked her if she wanted the last nacho in a cheerful, let's-get-back-to-normal voice, and by the time she had declined and tried to crack a joke and be normal, Joel was heading for the door too.

Now she'd lost them both.

ꟼ

Rosie slept badly and woke late. What to do about Joel? Nothing. What to do about Eryn? Rosie emailed and texted and phoned, but Eryn wouldn't answer. So, very late on Saturday morning Rosie went to Eryn's house. Her brother answered the door. *Ho! Are you ever in the doghouse. I'll come check on you every five minutes if you like, call the ambulance…*

So Rosie expected a tirade. But instead Eryn was scary calm. "You gotta watch out for him, Rosie. He's bad news."

"What makes you say that?"

"That creepy bastard followed me all the way home."

What? Rosie's heart thumped faster. "Well, that was nice of him, in the circumstances."

"No. It wasn't." Eryn's voice sounded harsh. "I thought he was going to attack me somewhere quiet. I went the long way around to be in places where there were people. Only there were hardly any, and they were all going the other way. And I couldn't avoid that shady part near Chris's house." Eryn was huddled down on the sofa, arms crossed and clutching the opposite shoulders. Like Mom did sometimes. "He scared me, Rosie."

Rosie resisted saying anything caustic about Eryn's imagination and tried Mom's tactic instead. "What was it that made you afraid, exactly?"

Eryn's head shot up and she glared at Rosie. "No need to be sarcastic. You would've been scared too. He kept saying things about being alone, and weird people being around with Swiss army knives and scarves they could pull nice and tight. Big people. And he is big, Rosie—tall anyway. He'd be hard to fight off. He said people could force me down on the ground and…" Eryn swallowed and took a few deep breaths. Said she'd kept telling herself he was just trying to scare the shit out of her, but then she'd looked behind and he had this evil smile, like the bad guys in vampire movies.

"He kept it up all the way home, Rosie, making threats in that creepy voice—kind of soft but clear at the same time." Eryn was visibly shaking now and there were tears in her eyes. Rosie sat next to her, put her arm round her. Her whole body was quivering.

"He started asking what I was going to do on that shady stretch, how I'd better keep checking in case he got too close. And then he sped up. I was too scared to turn around but I could hear him right behind me, and he laughed." Eryn huddled down on the sofa. "I felt like an insect he could step on at any moment but wanted to play with first." And when they'd reached that block with the trees, she picked up her heels and ran. "You should have seen me, Rosie. I could have kept up with you. Never ran so fast in my life." He had run as well, laughing.

And all that night Eryn had kept wondering what would have happened if she'd tripped and fallen. Surprising she hadn't really, with the uneven pavement and the ice and everything. And all because she called him out. "He's evil, Rosie. Keep away from him."

Rosie was trying not to be convinced about the calling-out part, even now. She just did not want to believe Joel had taken a picture. But Eryn was still terrified and she was not easily scared. Over the next hour Eryn kept adding pieces she had forgotten, such as his parting shot when she unlocked the door and her hands were shaking so much she could hardly get the key in. He'd said in that soft voice, *Don't go thinking anyone will believe you if you tell some story about this. I've just been a gentleman and seen you safely home.* "And he laughed again, Rosie. That creepy laugh."

Twice, Eryn clutched Rosie's arm during that hour, looking her in the eye and saying, "You believe me, Rosie, don't you?"

And Rosie did.

A few days later, though, Rosie was wondering if this may have been just heavy-handed humour—bad, but not as malicious as Eryn made out. He'd been laughing the whole time, after all. That meant fun, right? Not evil intentions. Rosie had not seen a sign of Joel since Friday, so the following weekend she decided to talk to Carlie.

"Well, if this is going to be a serious conversation let's go down to the harbour and look at the boats." Carlie could always find an excuse to watch the action down by the water. "And yes, you can drive."

Rosie still had a few months to go before she could take her final driving test and legally she could still only drive with an experienced driver next to her, which was ridiculous. She'd been driving since her sixteenth birthday in January of last year, so almost through two whole winters with all that snow and ice, storm conditions, hydroplaning conditions, fog—everything. She did not consider herself a novice anymore. Carlie picked her up as soon as Mom was back with the groceries, and Rosie drove along the waterfront, past the huge orange offshore supply boats lined up down by the Port Authority—three at that moment, all with predator seabird names such as *Atlantic Shrike* and *Osprey*. One was being off-loaded by little cranes scurrying around behind a muddle of trucks and boxes on the apron.

"I remember ospreys in Senegal," Carlie said. "There were so many gorgeous birds flashing about: beautiful to hear, beautiful to see. Then there were those awful birds of prey, circling, waiting…hawks, eagles, vultures, falcons and, on the ocean, the ospreys. They drop feet-first for the fish, you know. Vicious talons."

Farther west was the towering Coast Guard boat, the *Cowley*, looking military-scary because it was all grey and aggressively shipshape. Farther still was an elegant Portuguese ship painted blue and white, the *Princess Maria* something, followed by a double row of smaller boats all with girls' names. Then came the Maersk container ships down at the dry dock end and more cranes, then stacks and stacks of Oceanex containers.

Rosie drove across the bridge to the south side then back along the far side of the harbour to the Small Boat Basin at Prosser's Rock. There was not a soul in sight, and Carlie said yes, let's park here.

The engine was barely off when Rosie burst out with it: "Carlie, how do you know if you can trust someone?"

"That's a loaded question. Why are you asking?" Carlie did not inquire as to why Rosie hadn't asked her mother, like she usually did. She must have realized it was the kind of question that might upset Mom.

Rosie shrugged. "Nana always said you make up your mind about a person within the first five minutes of meeting them, and that you're always right."

Carlie said she was not sure about that, although she supposed she usually had the basics right. She was looking at Rosie now. "Who are we talking about here?"

Her aunt had a knack of getting straight to the part Rosie didn't want to discuss. She thought of stalling, of inventing someone, but decided that was a waste of time. So she took a breath and said, "Joel."

Carlie nodded, kept on looking at her, and said if Rosie had reached a point of wondering whether she could trust him, then she probably couldn't. Something was trying to warn her. "Trust your instincts."

But the trouble was Rosie *did* trust him, a little, or she wanted to. It was other people who didn't. The question hung in the air until finally Rosie admitted "other people" was Eryn.

"Ah. So, what's poor old Joe done to get Eryn upset?"

Rosie tried to assemble her thoughts and could not, even though she had been thinking about this nonstop, so she muttered that the name was Joel, not Joe.

"Joel. Joe. Not an 'L' of a difference."

Rosie wondered why Carlie was grinning in that inane way. This was serious. Anyway, there was a huge difference. His father called him Joe and he hated it, said it sounded like a plumber—Joel was a great name.

"What's wrong with sounding like a plumber? A good plumber is worth his weight in gold."

A gull wheeled across in front of the car, crying, and landed on the bow of the nearest boat. They always sounded so grouchy, gulls—either screeching at each other or whining and complaining by themselves. "Did you say his father lives somewhere near me?" Carlie said.

Rosie nodded, still watching the gull. "Somewhere. Carbury Street, I think."

Carlie turned abruptly to stare at Rosie, frowning. It made Rosie ask why, but there was no answer, and Carlie turned back to look at the boats. They were lined up the way Rosie pictured horses would stand in their stalls, shifting in their sleep. They were longliners, all rocking unevenly, bumping the wharf now and then, creaking with the bigger waves. She wished she had thought of that when she was writing her paper on "Deserting the Outports." These were the fishing boats they'd talked about in school, waiting for the start of the season: fifty-five- and sixty-five-footers from all round the island, not wintering in their own harbours anymore but berthed here, near the biggest market.

Carlie asked if Rosie knew Joel's father's name. No. So then Carlie really started interrogating and Rosie ended up telling her the whole thing, and she knew from Carlie's face what she was going to say. *Do not trust him. Keep Away.* It was what Rosie had been afraid of, what some wriggling discomfort had been warning her about.

"Analyze," Carlie said. "Keep the facts separate from your crush on Joel and being annoyed with Eryn. Cover up *I Want* and *I Don't Want*. What's left?" Like examining a crime scene: look for details; replay the whole incident over and over. Rosie might have noticed things without registering them at the time: Joel's facial expression or body language, a sound, a movement... her own stray thought or feeling—her subconscious analyzing.

It was hours later, spread out on the couch with Paddles, when Rosie finally acknowledged the satisfied smirk on Joel's face for what it was. It had been nudging at her since the morning and yes, maybe the *I Don't Want* had been keeping it out. But did he look that way because he really had taken a picture and managed to delete it in time, or because Rosie took his side rather than Eryn's? She rather liked that last idea. But something else was nagging her too. What made her suddenly notice the phone down low on the table? She still half-wanted to see Joel again, but her doubts were a lot more solid, and he really had frightened Eryn.

So, when she was at the mall the next Saturday, looking for a birthday gift for Melanie, Rosie almost yelped when Joel appeared in front of her out of nowhere.

"Oh! You surprised me," she said, taking a step backwards.

He smiled that special smile and said if she needed soothing, they could try Second Cup, with a nod in that direction. Loyalty to Eryn, the wish to give Joel another chance, caution, attraction, wanting—they all boiled up together. But the smile won. Rosie sat with him for almost an hour, sipping a sparkling water, there at the edge of the shoppers and browsers. A group from Mr. McAllister's class ambled by, sizing them up and grinning. Joel talked about the school hockey game they had watched and how he had never taken up hockey because the equipment was so expensive, but he used to like soccer and did Rosie play any sports? She told him how she had moved from dancing to gymnastics, but did not mention her mother insisting she learn karate for self-defense. When she went back to her gift hunting, Joel asked for her phone number. Rosie watched him plug the numbers into his phone, and while she was beaming at him, some little voice was saying maybe it was not good to have her number in Joel Walsh's phone.

"You went out with that monster again!" Rosie and Eryn were walking from Eryn's house to Rosie's the next day because it was such a glorious spring day after a string of mauzy ones.

"No. Not *Out*. And it wasn't planned or anything, and I couldn't be in a safer, more public place. And he was nice at Second Cup. Funny. He can tell a good story."

"I bet." Eryn flipped her hair back and raised her chin into fighting position. "So. Are you going out again, if he asks you?"

Rosie sighed. She linked arms with Eryn and said, "I don't think so. And it's not that I don't believe you...but he really is cute."

They had been walking along in a companionable way, but Eryn yanked her arm out, saying, "I think he's a psycho. And not a cute psycho, either."

"Is there such a thing?" Rosie said, to lighten the mood.

"There was one on the radio the other day. Mom was listening to CBC in the car." Rosie smiled—that was not Eryn's favourite radio station. "Some big-name professor dude with a snooty British accent was being interviewed. He'd done this personality study and filled out a questionnaire, along with another million people, and his profile fit the psychopathic personality profile down to the last detail."

Rosie laughed. "Bet he was sorry he'd done that questionnaire."

"Yes. He hadn't believed it at first, but started asking people if he had ever done this or said that, and they all said yes, he had. Even his wife."

"The psychopath has a wife?" Rosie stopped and turned to face Eryn. "Holy moly."

"Anyway, buddy decided if he really was a psychopath, he was going to be a nice one, and before he did even the simplest thing, he would try to think how a nice person would do it and he'd do it that way. Apparently it slowed him way down and was exhausting, because he couldn't just do everything on automatic anymore. He was wiped by the end of the day. It changed his sleep cycle and everything. But it was working."

Rosie wondered if you could keep that up all your life, and Eryn shrugged. "Who knows? At least he's trying, which is more than that Walsh creep can say."

Monday after school, Rosie was still on the porch taking off her heavy jacket when Carlie arrived. It was the changing of the guard. Nana's helper, Mrs. Murphy, was struggling into her boots on her way out. Nana was calling from the living room to *close that outer door, quick*. Mom always said that door was perfectly placed to catch the least breath of the prevailing northwesterly, and it was certainly prevailing today.

Carlie was in a rush. No, she would not stop for a cup of tea thank you, but they could make one for Nana if she wanted? She gave Nana a quick kiss, tucking in the throw around her knees, but nodded at Rosie in a significant way, flicking her eyes towards the kitchen.

"Just a quick visit," she said, once they were out of earshot. "I don't like checking up on people, but I thought this was important."

Rosie tried to take Carlie's coat, but Carlie just shook her head, left it hanging open, and perched on the edge of the table. She said her neighbour knew everyone around, so Carlie had asked if she knew a young guy called Joel. Straight away Mrs. Murphy said, *Frank Hughes's son, Joe. Likes to be called Joel—Frank Hughes that lives on Carbury. Number 31. The son goes by the mother's name.* She had to think for a minute then said his name was Joel Walsh.

"So now we—"

Carlie cut her off. "The thing is, Rosie, I've had…trouble with this young man before." Carlie had forgotten all about it until Rosie mentioned Carbury Street. She would have been in grade seven. "Joel Walsh was a peeping Tom with a pair of binoculars looking into my bedroom window just after I moved in. That's why I have that blue panel hanging in the end section."

Holy shit. Yuck. But…how could Carlie know it was Joel and not his father? She couldn't know that. But it only happened on weekends, Carlie said, which was when Joel stayed with his father. He stayed with his mother the rest of the time.

And the flashes came from the small bedroom facing up the hill; the window on the bigger room was on the harbour side.

Carlie was standing up. She was supposed to be at a meeting. "Rosie, please think it through. And keep away from this Joel. He sounds like a predator in the making." She headed out to the porch, saying, "Call me with any questions. I will be home in an hour or so," and left.

The information sank down, down, down, and even though there was still a little flame of denial that flickered, persistent, reaching for anything the least bit flammable, it was being smothered, inch by inch, by all those deadening facts.

CHAPTER TWENTY-EIGHT

2011

CARLIE

CARLIE DID NOT THINK ROSIE'S HEART WAS TOO INVOLVED, it was more her desire for romance, but it could still cause trouble. Carlie hoped Rosie's common sense would stop her from making a hero out of this questionable young man. (But what did common sense have to do with being in love?) *Patience, my darling. Love will come one day*—although Carlie had had to wait until her forties for the real heartbreaker. No need to mention that. There had been romances along the way, of course, but nothing else had made her feel, when it was finished, that the best of her life was over.

Could five weeks and five days of utter madness be considered a Grand Passion? Surely if she had really loved Oumar as wildly as she thought, she would have stayed, despite everything. But she had been too sensible. God, Carlie had spent her whole youth despising anything sensible, even the word (it was the worst insult in her repertoire to throw at Ginny when they were on the outs). So why, why, *why* had she walked out on the love of her life?

Because she was burned out: from being a single woman in a man's country; from seeing the lives around her become more difficult every day; from comparing life here and life back home more and more often. Living in such a very foreign place was, in a small way, what Eve found so trying about her PTSD—the mental fatigue of constantly applying coping mechanisms. It was risky being spontaneous in Senegal because Carlie's reactions and expectations were often scarily different from those of everyone around her, which led to misunderstandings. Caution had never been her strong suit.

She was tired of endless flat countryside with just a thorn tree and a few huts for relief. She was tired of constant dust from December to March because the Harmattan was full of Saharan sand. Hazy skies. She'd rather have fog any day—it was more soothing on the eyeballs. She was tired of talking in somebody else's language and tired of trying to live as a Senegalese woman lived when she would never think like one.

Oumar was a microcosm of everything Senegalese, the epitome of everything that was best about his country. His country: that was the whole point. They had reached decision time, a place where their differences were pulling them in opposite directions. Carlie had been so sure then. She had known in her gut, heart, soul—wherever it is you keep your innermost self. Instinct told her she could not do it, not over the long term, not forever.

She could never belong in that place, in that life. Better to quit while they were ahead. When she left, she had to cut the knot completely, otherwise she would not be able to withstand the pull to return, the wanting of him. There had to be no tokens from him, no reminders, nothing to pull her back. There were no accidental reminders in Newfoundland, like the smell of spruce, which comes home with you after a day in the woods. There were no Senegal smells or sounds back home. Air, land, water—they were all so specific, so different. She needed have a clean break, not a long, drawn-out demise.

Oumar had tried to give Carlie a djembe drum because she so loved the music, but she had refused it. That sound played straight to her emotions, back to some primitive innocent place before rules, back to a time of instincts and simplicity—if there was ever such a time. Now, she regretted that decision. There was a drum circle in town. She could have learned. She had some reminders of course: carvings, basketwork, a beautiful piece of traditional glass painting (sous verre), photographs—

all the usual things. But they were reminders of Senegal itself. Now, the blue fabric in her window had become a symbol for Oumar.

But over this last year, Carlie had started having doubts and she was not used to doubting herself. She had been engulfed in flames over Oumar. Surely she could have made it work, had she stayed. He was worth it. Should she have made a bigger effort? Did coming home make her a cold and selfish person, as Ginny had so often accused her of being? No. Never cold. Selfish, maybe. Probably.

She had presented a paper at a conference on social anthropology in Brussels, and Juan had emailed to say he was attending too. As always, they shared a room. He told her Oumar was in Paris with a trade delegation. It was 2008, and she had not seen Oumar since 2003. Five years. Was it safe to go and see? She had hovered on the edge of a decision for two days, but it was the sound of djembe drums in the metro station in Brussels that made the decision for her. Five young men at the back of the platform, sitting in a row, slapping their drums: tall, slim, Black, and passionate. Two slaps with fingers open on the rim of the skin drumhead, then two with fingers closed, then a slap with the hand relaxed in the centre... All the different rhythms intermingled. All fluid shoulders and arms, music flowing right through their bodies—one young man with his head thrown back and eyes closed, one pounding his foot with such fervour, lifting his whole foot clear of the ground between thumps. Carlie stood, entranced, letting two trains go by without her before dropping twenty euros in the bowl in front of them and nodding and moving away.

And so, she had bought a train ticket after the conference and gone to the hotel in Paris where he was staying. She chose a corner seat with a view of everything, far from the busy main desk in the huge lobby/ lounge, with its two bars along the sides, partly hidden by decorative screens, ranks of elevators, and elegant groupings of armchairs set amongst the potted plants. And she waited. She saw them eventually, first in their robes, trailing wheeled bags, then again, later, in western suits. She heard snatches of Wolof and French and English and other African languages, voices sliding from one language to the other so easily as they circled and mingled. She saw them move as a group to the dining room and he was there, tall and glorious and unchanged. She heard his voice. And she knew she was foolish to have come.

He never saw her. This was not Oumar, her friend and lover. This was Oumar, part of an all-male delegation, a representative of his country on official business. She could not interfere, cause embarrassment, perhaps weaken his position as a delegate. It had been ridiculous of her to come, menopausal and pitiful. She checked out, paying without protest whatever they demanded for a cancellation *à cette heure tardive, Madame,* and caught an overnight train back to Brussels.

Disaster averted. At least, that was what she told herself.

CHAPTER TWENTY-NINE

2011

ROSIE

RELATIONS WITH ERYN WERE BACK TO NORMAL ON THE SURFACE, but Rosie still felt uncomfortable with her. When they were in a group—in the mall, in a hallway, even in the classroom—sometimes Eryn was so loud it was embarrassing. She had always been boisterous and outspoken, and Rosie had admired her for her aliveness and her self-confidence, and envied her ability to start conversations so easily. She was fun. Now Rosie found it irritating: the way Eryn bent forward so her hair fell in a curtain, then straightened up and whisked it back off her face with both hands. It was too theatrical, and she did it every few minutes. Or she'd pull her hair down over one shoulder and roll it into a big ringlet, leaning into the person next to her as she did it. *Look at me.* Walking in a group, she would link arms with people and tow them along faster, or she would step in front, so they had to stop. It was starting to feel more like a power trip than exuberance.

So Rosie brought it up at home. "D'you think Eryn's changed, Mom?"

Eve frowned into the chocolate chip cookie dough she was mixing. "In what way?"

One day her mother might answer a straight question with a straight answer.

"Her behaviour."

Mom went on beating butter and sugar in that big earthenware bowl, made three full circles with the wooden spoon before she answered. "She's not as relaxed these days. Looks like she's trying too hard." Mom put the spoon down and stood looking at Rosie as if she were measuring her, like she might add her to the bowl, two tablespoons at a time, and whisk her in. "She's trying to be the person she thinks she should be, the person she wants to be. All that bouncy personality was unconscious before. Natural. Now she's working at it, so it's a mite overdone." She started beating again. "She's just finding her feet. Being a teenager."

Then Rosie went along with Eryn's plans to meet up with a group she had been talking about. They met in the park one evening. One of the guys was sitting on a swing, pushing himself idly with one foot, chatting to the girls standing around. A big guy had started whacking a swing seat as high as he could, making the chains screech, and it was crashing down and bouncing wildly. Another boy was cheering him on, but the rest wandered a safe distance away. Eryn rushed into the middle of them, but Rosie hung back, stopping near two guys and a girl talking together.

One of the guys looked over at Rosie and said, "Hey, you run, don't you? I've seen you on the Rennie's River trail."

"You one of that group running the opposite way?"

"Yep. Five of us, three times a week."

Guess that was why they were so fast. Rosie only went now and then, and it was more of a jog than a run. They chit-chatted about the trails around town and their favourite trails up the coast.

The guy with the swing had wrapped it round the overhead bar two or three times by now with a lot of clattering and yelling, and Rosie's group drifted farther away from the noise.

The running guy stuck out his hand and said, "Name's Kit. Born in Saint Kitts, although I only lived there for a month."

"Glad they dropped the saint part. My aunt was born on a snow plough."

"No kidding. She called Snow White?"

Rosie smiled and shook her head. "But her middle name's Erica, after the snow plough driver."

"Must've had the fright of his life."

They had given Eric a nice thank-you gift, and he had given her grandmother a medal of Saint Christopher—the patron saint of travellers—for the baby. Carlie carried it everywhere on her key ring.

When Eryn told Rosie about a plan for a bonfire on the beach that weekend with the same group, Rosie decided to go too.

"Have another little toke," Pete said to Rosie, holding out the end of a soggy joint. "Free up your mind for that masterpiece you're going to write."

"Masterpiece? What're you talking about?"

"Eryn says you're going to be a writer, so..."

Rosie pulled a face. "She's making that up. Just thinking of doing an English degree, is all."

"Writer, English degree...whatever."

They were sitting on the beach at Middle Cove and one of the other guys, Jason, was trying to get the fire going but the wind was gusting in unpredictable spirals, snuffing out the sparks before they could take hold. Three of the guys crouched down next to each other to make a barricade of legs and elbows and jacket wings, and slowly coaxed some life into it. And all the time they were cooking hot dogs and roasting marshmallows, passing joints around, Rosie was realizing this was not her scene. She pretended to take a puff and passed it to the guy on her other side, who was so busy getting friendly with Amanda Somebody that he didn't notice anything Rosie might or might not be doing.

The nice one, Kit, was not here tonight nor were the friends he had been with, which was too bad as they had been the reason she'd come. These were *the others*: the ones Rosie didn't trust. She did not like the c-word coming from one of the guys, the one who had been messing with the swing, or the screechy laugh from the girl he was talking to, and she did not like the way some of them crowded round Alec when he showed them a picture on his phone in that sneaky way, and the smirks and nasty titters. She had made it through an hour or two, but she was not looking forward to whatever came next.

What would Carlie do?

If you're not enjoying yourself, leave.

Rosie's head had started to ache but that was probably the cold wind. She pulled her hat out of her pocket, snuggled into her collar. The temperature had been dropping since suppertime. But maybe her head hurt because Pete kept putting his arm around her waist and yanking her closer, giving her full-body whiplash, which was driving her nuts. She would edge away as soon as he was distracted but then he'd do it again. She was so not enjoying this. They were all pairing off, which she had not anticipated, and she was left with this Pete guy. Eryn had said it was just a big crowd, only one or two couples. She had also said Kit would be there. But if he hung around with this crowd maybe Rosie did not want to further his acquaintance anyway. And this crowd would scoff if she used a word like *acquaintance.* Kit would come back with something funny. Maybe.

"Carlie, can I borrow your car, just this once?" Rosie had said two days ago.

If Carlie had been available to phone for a ride this would not have been necessary, but this night, of all nights, Carlie was going to a play with her friends because the tall one, Mo, was acting in it. Not only that, but they were all going to the cast party backstage afterwards. Carlie would have her phone switched off all night. And Mom could never leave Nana alone in the house these days—she would likely end up on the harbourfront in her slippers. So.

"Do you have your mother's permission?" Carlie had said.

Long pause. "I haven't asked."

There was too much silence on the phone so Rosie listed off reasons: test in less than three months, certain to pass, couldn't just call a cab out at Middle Cove—might be trapped for ages waiting for someone. Not that she expected trouble but… "Like you always say, Carlie, *always have an escape route.*"

"Isn't there somebody going who can give you a ride? Somebody you trust?"

Eryn was going with someone called Dave in his car, so Rosie could maybe hitch a ride, but she had never met him and…well….

"Must you go to this particular party?"

Rosie thought of Kit and of taking her mind off Joel. "Yes."

Her aunt agreed it would be safer for her to have her own vehicle in this instance. Rosie started to say thanks, but Carlie kept going. "But. And I mean But. No alcohol or drugs of any sort. Nothing."

"I don't—"

"And *no* passengers. I trust you but I do *not* trust passengers."

And Rosie promised. She also agreed to all the other stipulations about not parking too near the beach where she could be boxed in, and about reversing into a parking spot, and don't forget to lock up and….

When the time came, Rosie had put soft drinks and the makings for hot dogs in her backpack, and a can of sour cream and onion Pringles to share. Then she had walked down to Carlie's for the car, telling her mom she had her phone and that she would be with Eryn.

⁂

Eryn was sitting across from her now. She was acting weird, falling over onto that Dave guy next to her so he had to push her back up again, laughing and saying, *Up you get, girl.* Then she flopped forward over her knees so that, from where Rosie sat, her hair seemed to float dangerously near the fire. She moaned in a way that was beyond her usual theatrics. It sounded all wrong.

Rosie struggled to her feet—she had stiffened into a pretzel sitting there—and Pete said, "Where're you off to?" but Rosie ignored him. She knelt next to her friend.

"Hey, Eryn. How's it going?"

No response.

"What's wrong, Eryn?" Rosie shook her shoulder when there was no response, looked at Dave and asked what Eryn had taken.

"Wha…?"

"You know. What's she had?"

"Nah! Eryn jus' likes…puts on an act. S'why she's fun."

"Well, she's not having fun now."

Eryn was groaning and muttering but saying nothing recognizable. She wasn't usually into trying *things*—said she could be high enough without chemicals—but she'd sure tried something this time.

"She needs to go home."

"Naaaah…be okay." Dave's eyes were closed.

"She needs to go home."

"Making…"—mumble, mumble—"…fuss."

How could he drive…? Oh, Rosie so wanted out of this. *No passengers!* Shit. Rosie stood watching sparks whirl out of the fire, dancing, riding the wind, and all those faces lit up by the fire, with dark hollows for eyes. She couldn't just leave Eryn. Carlie would understand.

"Will someone help me get Eryn up to my car?" She said at last. "Please?"

And at first there were murmurs of *leave her alone*, and *she'll be okay*. But then two of the guys who had helped start the fire came over, edging in on each side of Eryn. Dave did not seem to notice. They said *one, two, three,* hauled her up, and staggered off toward the parking lot. Rosie gathered up Eryn's backpack and her own stuff and followed them.

She said over her shoulder, "Nice meeting you all," then she wished she had skipped the farewells because Pete started growling about things just getting going and there were mutters about party poopers.

The two good guys took a long time manhandling Eryn over the rough, gravelly sand and up the steep bit with the rocks, slipping and staggering, with a couple of stops to change their hold. *Heavier than she looks,* said Lee. *More awkward than heavy*, said Jason as he hitched Eryn up a bit higher and tried to stop her arm from dangling. "Fold your arms, girl, so you don't bounce them off every rock." But Eryn was beyond being able to help and Rosie could not reach without getting in the way.

They had trouble bundling her into the car. They tried to stand her up by the door, but she was almost unconscious now. Her legs just crumpled, and the rest of her tumbled headfirst onto the back seat, limp and unresponsive. They lifted and pushed and shoved and cursed, Jason from the doorway, Lee hanging over the back of the front seat, shovelling her farther in. The front seat would have been easier, but Rosie was afraid that, in the passenger seat, Eryn might fall onto her while she was driving.

"Thank you, guys, both of you." Rosie was almost in tears by now. "I don't know what I'd have done without you. God, I hope she'll be alright."

"Sure she will," said Lee, walking away.

"Want me to drive behind you?" Jason's voice said it was the last thing he wanted to do, and Rosie said no, no, she would be fine now and thank you, thank you....

There was no movement, no sound from Eryn on the drive back to her house. *Eryn? You okay, Eryn? Talk to me.* Rosie took a curve too wide and slowed to a crawl. God, if a cop car stopped her now...she pulled off the road to check Eryn was still breathing, then she tried to get the seat belt around her but could not make it snap into the buckle. No response when Rosie shook her. Drunk or tripping? You talk to unconscious people, right? You keep trying to make them focus. *Wake up, Eryn....*

Mrs. Brown's car was missing from Eryn's driveway. Should she go straight to the emergency room? Not unless...*Eryn. We're at your house now, Eryn. Wake up.* Where were her keys? Rosie rummaged around in the backpack but there were no keys.

There was a little key pocket on the inside of Eryn's jacket, but she was lying on it. Maybe if Rosie sat her up... She leaned in and put her arms round Eryn's upper body and hauled her up to a sitting position. Eryn stirred, moaned, straightened up her head a little. At least she was still capable of moaning. Then she threw up all over the two of them. Gallons. Oceans. The smell made Rosie queasy, but at least it was just an ordinary barfy smell—no cinnamon hearts or fruit punch fumes—just alcohol. Rosie closed her eyes and wished she were anywhere but here, doing anything but this. The mess was all over Carlie's car too: the floor, the back of the front seat....

"What on earth is going on here?"

Oh, god, god, god. Eryn's mom.

CHAPTER THIRTY

2011

CARLIE

CARLIE CONSUMED MORE CHEAP WINE THAN USUAL BACKSTAGE because she was not driving, and they were all slightly euphoric after the play: *Mo, you were wonderful! Perfect. Didn't realize you had such a big part.* She finished off the red. Started on the white. It was almost midnight when Carlie was dropped off at her house and she vaguely registered that there were lights on inside. Rosie met her at the door. Her hair was wet and she was wearing that big ugly sweatshirt she had left at Carlie's house after the last power outage and pyjama bottoms and nothing on her feet.

"Rosie, what's going on?"

Rosie told her, shoulders hunched and arms folded, walking up and down the hallway in an agitated way, throwing sentence fragments over her shoulder: *She's going to kill me. Kill you too... stay in her room for a week.* Rosie had sent her mom a text saying she was safe and at Carlie's. Eve had texted back immediately: *Eryn's mom called. Talk about it tomorrow.*

"Rosie, you're making my head spin. Please stop pacing. If your mom's saying it can wait until tomorrow then she's not too concerned, so let's not get carried away." They moved upstairs, and Carlie made herself comfortable in her favourite corner where she could reach the coffee table, tend to the fire when needed, and see the sky through the window, all without having to move.

"It's being sneaky again, like breaking into her desk drawer," Rosie's voice was tragic.

Carlie was still in theatre mode and thought this particular production was overkill.

Then Rosie looked over at Carlie and brought her voice down a decibel. "And I made you go behind her back, too."

"Well, for what it's worth, you didn't *make me* do anything. I make my own decisions. It might have been your suggestion, but it was my choice to go along with it."

But in fact, Carlie had done the one thing she always swore she would never do: she had usurped Eve's role as mother. She knew Eve would never have allowed Rosie to drive at night on her own without a licence, especially to a party, and Carlie had ignored that and given her own permission behind Eve's back.

Rosie went on. "And I broke my promise to you, too, not to take any passengers."

A discussion followed about moral dilemmas, at the end of which Rosie agreed that yes, given the choice, she would do the same again. Carlie smiled.

Rosie said, "I'm sorry about the smell in your car. I was going to start cleaning it, but I had to change out of my slimy clothes first, and then you came..."

Carlie allowed herself a little rant about the bottled-up smell, fermenting overnight, and *don't think I'm driving you home*—and how she would have to wait until Monday now for one of those car-interior cleaning places....

Rosie was smiling by now, and it was Eve's impish smile. "Sorry, Aunty." At least Rosie had learned to tell a rant from a scold.

"Sorry, Eve." They were sitting at Eve's kitchen table with big mugs of coffee. Eve was still blowing on hers, but Carlie was halfway down already—that famous asbestos mouth. Rosie was back on Mulberry Street wrapped in an apron and rubber gloves, probably wearing a clothespin on her nose, attacking the car with a bucket of soapy water. "Part of me was saving you the mom-and-teenager argument. Part of me said a good driver like Rosie shouldn't have to wait all that time—she should be able to take the stupid test when she's ready." Carlie sighed. "But I went behind your back and as a result I encouraged Rosie to go behind your back, which is unforgivable." She looked across at Eve. "I hope you'll forgive me."

"Well, I felt a bit stupid when Mrs. Brown phoned me in near hysterics." Eve looked irritated rather than distressed. She'd had no idea what Eryn's mom was talking about—trying to piece things together through the flying sentences. At one point she thought they were heading for a lawsuit, only there were so many *thanks to Rosie* phrases thrown in that Eve realized it couldn't be that bad. But she wished Carlie had let her know. "And I wish you guys would stop protecting me. I want to know about anything related to Rosie. In fact, I demand to know. It's my job to take care of my daughter. If it's something awful, I'll just have to handle it." Eve was sitting very tall and straight now, her chin up.

Carlie smiled at her. "Point taken."

Eve shook her head in an exasperated way, said she appreciated all the care they had taken on her behalf, all of them, for years. She could not have managed without them. Eve smoothed out a placemat, one of those woven craft-fair types in shades of green, and she untangled the fringes at the two ends, thread by thread. She admitted she had a fright now and then—as when the waiter leaned over her the other day. He was just being solicitous, she knew, but he was tall and broad and blocked the light, and Eve was trapped in a corner. She tried to avoid corners. But then he left, and she took a few deep breaths, and everything went back to normal. Those little things still happened but she was coping with them. She pushed the placemat aside and looked straight at Carlie. "I can cope with problems around Rosie too."

Which was all very well, but Carlie wondered how Eve would deal with the likes of Joel Walsh. Eve's hands lay relaxed and motionless now, and she said, "And with regards to Rosie borrowing my car to go to Middle Cove, what made you think I'd have said no?"

Carlie's mouth dropped open. "You'd have let her?"

"Of course," Eve said. "Getting Mom into the car and taking her to pick Rosie up would have been far too slow, maybe an hour, and Rosie might have needed a faster getaway." Eve seemed surprised that Carlie was surprised. "If Rosie was determined to go, no matter what—and believe me I know how stubborn she can be—then a car would be the only way to give her a safe way out, and I would always put Rosie's safety first."

Then Eve smiled that little mischievous smile of hers. "But at least this way you ended up with the barfy car."

CHAPTER THIRTY-ONE

2011

ROSIE

ROSIE RAN ALONE BECAUSE THE RUNNERS SHE KNEW WERE faster, slower, too dedicated, too chatty.... It was just easier alone. She was erratic and liked it that way. So, it was ten days before she came across Kit. She woke with the sun calling her through a crack in the drapes and burst out of the house just before seven with that flame of enthusiasm that only flares up after a full week of the foggy wet dismals. She ran with her emotions rather than her head and was so out of breath by the time she reached the first intersection that she was delighted to come to a gasping standstill. She hoped the traffic would not come to an end before she was ready. And there was Kit. He was with a group doing an energetic run on the spot on the other side of the road.

The stream of cars passed, and the guys had crossed onto her side before Rosie even stepped off the curb. Kit slowed long enough to ask Rosie for her phone number then shot off after the others, and she heard *seven two* over his shoulder and hoped he'd get it right.

He texted that afternoon. His crowd was going to McDonald's for a burger later and would she like come? And yes, Rosie would. No one from her school was there, but she recognized two guys from Kit's running group and his two friends from the park and a girl from her last gymnastics camp, and they were all good company. Fun. "You'd like them, Mom," was her summary that evening. They did the same thing after school the following Friday, so Rosie did not hesitate when Kit invited her to go for a hike with them on the East Coast Trail.

So, Saturday morning, four guys and three girls squeezed into somebody's family SUV and drove to a boat launch out near Flatrock and hiked the Father Troy Trail—an easy walk about eighteen kilometres there and back, along the cliffs. Halfway through, they ate a picnic sitting in the sun, backs to warm rocks and watching for whales. The lack of whales was the only thing Rosie would have changed in the whole day.

The group was welcoming in a casual way, including her in conversations but without hammering her with questions. They were all a year ahead of her, having finished grade twelve at the school up the road from hers and now waiting to see if their marks were good enough for university. One guy, Nick, was thinking of political science and he was all worked up about the Arab Spring and worrying about what Assad would do about the protestors in Syria—fifty odd dead already over the last month or so. Nancy wanted to do an English degree so she and Rosie talked about books. Kit was planning on phys. ed. The others were probably doing sciences but were still undecided. It made Rosie think about her own plans. It made her pull out the summer reading list and go to the library to make a start. Growing up, she had dreamed of going to McGill like Mom, Michel, and Carlie, of reconnecting with Michel's parents. Well, that last part was out, but there were other places with charisma—a whole exciting world.

Kit worked at a twenty-four-hour gas station and never spent a cent if he could help it. The two of them walked everywhere—ran sometimes. A few times Rosie met him at the gas station after work. She waited outside the first time, watching through the window as he served people. He looked efficient, the way he reached for things with just a quick glance, knew where everything was, kept his eye and his smile on the customers, bagged things without fumbling. His height was an advantage when packing two-litre milk cartons into those tall vinyl supermarket bags—Rosie would have needed a ladder. Each customer gave him a second look, especially the women, and he had them laughing and smiling, even when they had to wait.

There was one woman, though, with sad shoulders and tired hair who held up the line buying scratch tickets, rubbing off the numbers then buying more with her winnings, on and on until she ran out of winnings. She turned away from the fidgety lineup when she left, and Kit just smiled slightly at the next guy, looking sympathetic.

There had been a holdup at Kit's store the previous Saturday—three in the morning, two young guys with a knife, and again a few weeks before that. But never when Kit was working. He thought maybe they didn't take him on because he was big. All the cashiers had had training for this: hit the button under the counter then just go along with what the thieves wanted; stay safe. He sounded so calm about it. It was not often Rosie regretted being small, but she would never want to work in a place like that. She was even glad about her mom insisting on karate lessons. Those guys were still out there somewhere.

Kit was into sports in a big way, said he hadn't had much time for dating. He took Rosie to watch his soccer and basketball games. The basketball was fun, and often there were kids she knew from school who she could watch the game with, but the soccer was boring. The action always seemed to be a confusing muddle at the corner of the field farthest away from Rosie, while the part she could see was a bunch of muddy knees running first one way and then the other. She was into her third game before anybody scored. Rosie started arriving twenty minutes before the end, but even that was a pain because of unpredictable overtime.

Kit was great to talk to, though, and argue with. He would discuss any topic under the sun, and she found their political ideas were much the same, although he wasn't keen on what he called *militant feminism*. He wasn't impressed by gymnastics or karate either. Said they were skills, not sports—skills that took a lot of practice and strength and control, all very admirable, but it was every man for himself. Woman. Herself. For him, sports had to involve a team because it was the give and take, the relying on and sharing with, that made them real sports—the setting up of other team members for the scoring, not just yourself, and the thinking of the group as a unit. That was what mattered about a team. Democracy.

So, what about his family? Mom and dad, one sister, one brother. Were they a team? There was the tiniest pause before he said, "Pretty much." When Rosie finally met them, they accepted her into the house like she was just another friend—one of the many. She was glad they were unaware of the pile of rejected outfits on her bed, after she waffled about what to wear for the occasion. In fact, it must have been much harder for Kit to come to Rosie's house, so quiet and with all the focus on him.

Kit walked home with her after their second date, even though it added an extra couple of kilometres. *Come in and meet my mom and grandma*, she'd said, and he walked in with such a beaming smile and his hand out. He told Mom all about the soccer game, maybe with too much enthusiastic detail but he was his own natural self. Kit was so comfortable with people. So open. Joel would never do this. Rosie wondered if that was shyness (no way), distrust of parental figures because his own family was so dysfunctional (probably), or just plain sneakiness. And yes, sneakiness was probably part of Joel's nature. Mom decided Kit was a Very Nice Young Man. Nana kept saying how big he was and looked a lot less certain. Paddles allowed him to scratch behind his ears and looked like he might purr.

CHAPTER THIRTY-TWO

2011

LIZ

WHO IS THAT HUGE YOUNG MAN WITH EVE? WHERE IS BEN? I hope nothing bad has happened between Eve and Ben because Ben Hutton is Mr. Right, no question. Still, this one—Tim, no, Kit—seems very nice. You can always tell something about a young person's upbringing by the way they treat old folks, even middle-aged folks. You can tell if someone has been close to a grandparent. They include you. Most Newfoundlanders are like that—accustomed to big families, big age ranges—but there are always a few....

Where did I see that sweet-faced boy? In a not-McDonald's hamburger place, where the servers all wore tall chefs' hats. You and I were having lunch on the mainland somewhere when we were visiting one of the girls. Dreadlocks, sooty rather than shiny, in front of me in the line. Hair and a sweatshirt, definitely a student. The server holds a plate bearing a single wiener in one hand, a king-sized ketchup bottle in the other, squeezes a squiggle of ketchup along the wiener, looks at Dreadlocks, squirts more. More. More. Long pause. Maybe two-squirts are the rule? More? The tall hat twitches. The plate changes hands but is still held out hopefully. Another squirt, server's face looking irritated—take your plate and go, why don't you. Dreadlocks holds the plate with the two hands underneath, thumbs just visible on the rim, almost touching the lake of ketchup. He nods and turns away, careful to keep the plate level. He flashes a smile back at me, apologetic, mischievous. Some teens never acknowledge the elderly, as if they are just taking up space. This boy is comfortable with seniors and his smile is conspiratorial and inclusive.

He's joining his friends at a table now, four of them, all Black and all wearing pink fluffy slippers. Gay and asserting themselves? Or just a spree for frosh week? I hope they give their studies as much concentration as they are giving to cleaning their plates.

I lie back in my recliner and smile. Eve is asking me something, but I don't answer because if I do, I'll lose my train of thought, and I'm enjoying the memory of that young Black man with dreadlocks and pink slippers and a charming smile.

CHAPTER THIRTY-THREE

2011

ROSIE

KIT'S CROWD HIKED PART OF THE EAST COAST TRAIL EVERY possible weekend from May to October, but the highlight was always the Spout Trail, which they had done once a year since grade nine, twice a year after grade eleven. It was twenty-two and a half kilometres from Shoal Bay Road to Bay Bulls and graded "strenuous to difficult." They liked to go early in the season because the trail's namesake geyser was more dramatic with the spring runoff, and the days were longer. So on the last Saturday in June, Nick's parents took eight of them to the start in two cars. They made a big fuss about Nick having the keys in a safe pocket, then drove off to leave their SUV for them at the other end.

The Shoal Bay track was always soggy—it was flat and sunless through scrappy trees—but it was more like a streambed that day after all the rain earlier in the week. They kept to the edges as much as they could. Rosie leaped from rock to rock, island to island, enjoying the freedom of it, the precision. Sometimes she missed gymnastics.

"Look like a gazelle," Kit said. "But you'll wear yourself out, doing that. It's a tough hike. Need to be a mountain goat farther in." Then he grinned. "My sister would take my head off if I said that to her."

"I'm thinking about it."

It was glorious when the trail opened out onto the cliffs, a glittering ocean, and a wide cloudless sky. The temperature was perfect for walking, and the wind played with your hair, cooled your face, but didn't push you around. They chatted when the path was wide enough to bunch up and every topic was interesting and the silliest joke was hilarious, the way even food you don't like tastes great out of doors.

They spent an hour fooling around at the Spout itself, eating sandwiches and watching the ocean force the freshwater stream up the blowhole with each wave, making it shoot high in the air, counting the spouts loudly to see if the seventh really would be the highest, trying to take pictures on their phones of rainbows in the spray. They were there longer than they intended, but it was the midpoint of the hike so there was no need to rush. They took the next stretch at a steady pace. The climbs were steeper here, the scrambles more difficult. Rosie even allowed Kit to pull her up one extra big boulder, muttering about guys with long legs having an unfair advantage. She was quite ready for another break at the Freshwater Bridge.

They stopped dead at the top of the last rise and just stood there, looking. *Oh my God. Holy shit.* The bridge was in decent shape, but it was an island in the middle of a torrent. The river had spread to twice its normal width, so the bridge was stranded in the middle with a stretch of six to eight feet of bouncing, rushing water on either end. Impassable. Even the bridge, normally high off the water, was awash now and then. The river was one long set of rapids, from the spray-filled horizon down to a greedy, snarling ocean. The slope next to it was steep, a brush-and-boulder wilderness all the way up and over the top.

"What's over the top?"

"How far before the river's narrow enough to cross?"

Yes, how far through that knee-deep shrubby undergrowth, where there was no path and you couldn't see your feet, or the waiting rocks and holes beneath? How far before you sprained an ankle, broke a leg?

They thought about it, tossed ideas about, but nobody insisted on trying it. They muttered and cursed for a bit then just turned around and started back, all of them, in silence for the most part, heads down, plodding. It was maybe seventeen kilometres back, so thirty-three or thirty-four kilometres of "strenuous to difficult" terrain altogether. At the top of the next rise, Kit walked closer to her.

"You okay, Rosie?"

"Sure. Goat steps."

Kit laughed and gave her a one-armed hug.

Gruelling was the word. It meant exhausting, wearying, and what on earth did it have to do with the gruel Oliver Twist had to eat? Maybe it just meant awful. And it grue more awful! She thought of telling that joke to the others, but it would take too much energy—more if they didn't get it and she had to explain. So she just kept on plodding.

She was glad of her new boots. Mostly she used her running shoes for hiking, but Mom had said, no, if she was going to do serious hiking with this crowd, she'd better have proper footwear. She had worn them in a bit on the last hike, so they had softened enough to be comfortable. Mom knew about boots—had done this trail too back in the day—and kept saying she would like to do it again. Carlie did part of it now and then with her walking buddies. Some of those photos of Michel were probably taken along here, one up by the Bay Bulls lighthouse certainly. Rosie had meant to have someone take a picture of her at that exact place, but they wouldn't be going past it now.

She tried to focus on making up a poem about boots but needed a pencil in her hand to think, and the second time she caught her toe on a rock and stumbled, she stopped trying. But by then they were back at the Spout so at least it had swallowed some distance. She did not remember much after that, just one foot in front of the other, uphill and down again, over and over. On the way out, the land had sloped down left to the ocean, so she'd felt pressure on her left-sided toes. On the way back, the slope was down to the right, so the pressure was on the other side, and it didn't matter how good your boots were. It was an offshore wind, so it blew into a different ear on the homeward trek and the sun shone on a different cheek. At least she'd have a more even tan.

This time, they all splodged, uncaring, through the pools on the Shoal Bay track. When effort was needed to lift a foot, minimum clearance was the rule, and the shortest distance between two points. The sun was sitting in the trees by then, and it was gloomy amongst the alders. Nick had phoned his parents from a high point on the trail with good reception, and his father was waiting when they finally clumped out of the woods at eight thirty. Conversation was sparse on the way home.

But there is something special about going through a trying time and getting through it as a group. It draws you together. Maybe that's what Kit meant about team sports, and Nana with her *trouble shared is trouble halved.* At the start of that day, Rosie thought of the others as casual guys—nice ones but just guys. By the end, they were friends.

CHAPTER THIRTY-FOUR

2011

CARLIE

GINNY HAD BEEN OFF FOR A FEW DAYS WITH THE FLU, SO Carlie took their mother for her appointment with the gerontologist. It took all afternoon between the physical tests and questionnaire and interviews and breaks to allow Liz to decompress.

Poor Mom. She had no idea of time or place for the Mini Mental State Test. Asked the time, she said it was almost lunchtime and she was hungry, when in fact they'd had lunch an hour before. She pushed her glasses up the bridge of her nose and leaned over the paper the psychometrist laid before her, staring at the two pentagrams she was asked to copy. *Whatever for?* Carlie thought she was going to refuse, but she frowned down at the paper and finally drew a few uncertain lines. They did not join or intersect, and she stopped at six lines instead of the total ten.

"Doesn't look right," she said, frowning at the psychometrist. She looked suspicious for a moment, then just plain wilted.

She looked that way so often these days. She could not work the new faucet in Ginny's bathroom, with one lever that needed pushing rather than the familiar two knobs that turned. She grumbled about *newfangled gadgets* and needed someone to do it for her; always as if it was the first time she had seen them. On feisty days Liz still wanted to assert her independence in the kitchen, resulting in spills and breakages, and she would still battle with the kettle. Once, she put the electric kettle on top of the stove and turned on the burner. The smell of melting plastic brought Mrs. Murphy in a rush. It was even more worrying when Liz tried to turn things on in the middle of the night. Eve took to turning off the relevant circuit breaker at bedtime. Caring for her was easier on her defeated days, when she didn't bother to try, but nobody wanted to acknowledge that.

The third time Liz asked if they could go home, after the final part of the assessment process, Carlie bowed and said, "Yes, Madame. Right now."

And perhaps it was the long, polished hospital hallway that triggered a memory, or the woman walking the other way in a neat navy suit, but Liz suddenly clutched Carlie's arm and leaned in, whispering, "Sister Severity kept telling me—" Sister Severity who had haunted Liz's school days, and whose real name was lost forever—"She kept telling me, *You forget yourself, Elizabeth.* And I have now, haven't I?"

❧

It was fortunate Carlie reached Liz in time when she was trying to take down Eve's precious Chagall. Liz had been dozing in her chair in the living room when Carlie went to the bathroom, but when she returned, there was her mother standing on the couch on those squashy unstable cushions, leaning back and swaying wildly. She was holding the sides of the picture, so the only thing stopping her from falling flat on her back was the picture hook and the wires from the back of the frame stretched out now at forty-five degrees. Carlie reached her just as a piece of the wall gave way and she seized her mother around the ribs as she fell, lowering her to the floor as the picture hook rattled down on the hardwood in a shower of plaster. *My god! Mom!*

There was a gunshot crack, and Liz still clutched the frame to her chest, but the glass stayed in place in its two pieces.

"Always hated that picture," Liz muttered. "Open my eyes and that man's staring at me. Ugly. Everything's closing in on me. Things on every wall. I need space."

George had willed that print to Eve in particular. The two of them had chosen it together after an exhibition in Paris during his sabbatical year. It was a good print of one of those fiddler paintings by Marc Chagall, which their father had confessed was really out of his price range but was special, both as a painting and as a memory of Paris. He had hung it in their living room and Mom had chosen a soft pastel of Monet's water lilies to oppose it on the facing wall. They both joked about how they'd each take *my painting* if they ever divorced. Eve had given the Chagall pride of place in her living room, until now. Now pictures came down off the walls in rooms Liz used, and ornaments were put away—not that there were many as Eve disliked clutter too, but the house did look a little stark after the purge.

Liz would often nap in her chair in the day and then be wide awake in the middle of the night, and Eve was feeling the effects more and more. Once, Liz set off down the street in her nightclothes while they were all in bed. On that occasion it was lucky Eve was a poor sleeper. There was Liz in the dark, bare feet inside her boots. Said she was going home and kept walking even when Eve caught up with her.

"But Mom, your house is sold, remember?"

Well, no, of course she didn't.

"To some people from Aberdeen."

Liz slowed down then, *Oh, yes,* but it was not until Eve told her the MacNeil family had been living in her old house for over a year that Liz finally allowed Eve to lead her home, shivering.

The temperature in the house was something else Liz complained about constantly. She spent much time and effort searching for *that thermathingy* and put it up on broil whenever she found it. Eve added a more complicated lock to the front door, so she did not have to sleep with one eye open.

All three sisters reluctantly agreed that Liz needed The Home. She had been on the waiting list since she moved in with Eve in preparation for this moment, but the administrator still said *possibly another year* when they inquired.

Carlie began sleeping there on Fridays while Eve stayed at Carlie's, and sometimes Rosie went too, just for a twenty-four-hour break. Liz no longer needed someone in the same house; she needed someone in the same room.

CHAPTER THIRTY-FIVE

2011

LIZ

I TRY TO WIND UP THAT THINGY ON THE WINDOW. THE BLIND. I have to reach over the bedside table and yank the cords and those prison bars go all sideways and bunch up at one end and the other end stays down, and now the string things are in a big aggravating knot and, really, I don't want anything at all over the glass. Eve—*It's Rosie, Nana*—comes when I call out and untangles everything and Eve's voice says *Not Again*, right outside the door. As if I'm in the habit of doing this. As if I'm deaf. My hearing is as good as the day I was born.

So Eve hangs curtains instead and yes, they are very pretty, but I just want to see through to the Outside, want some open space, want to see that hill over there...yes, Signal Hill, and that thing on the grass...yes, a maple...it's getting too big, I can't see round it. *Oh, nobody's looking at an old woman getting undressed, don't be ridiculous. Nobody is the least bit interested. What do you mean, inappropriate?* I know their windows overlook this room but they don't have to look in, and yes, it's at ground level, but there aren't many passersby, and it's a nice neighbourhood. *Complained? Why would anybody complain? Let me talk to them. Oh, alright. I'll leave them shut until I'm in bed.* Well, I can't get them open anyway when they're all pinned together like that. *As long as you come and open them when I'm in bed.*

I wake up and it's dark except for one of those little lights in the plug thing by the door, like the ones we used for the children...only theirs were fancier, like a Santa or a purple flower. This one's plain. There are strange clothes on the chair. Those are not my clothes, not my housecoat. I sit up and look around.

Where on earth am I? I'm wearing a nightdress I don't recognize, although I may have had this kind before, and it fits well. Nice colour. I'm shuffling a bit because my knees are stiff.

I wonder where the kitchen is in this place. I fancy a little snack. I turn right down the corridor because there's another of those little lights down that way, but I turn into a room before I reach it and almost fall over a chair. What a silly place to put a chair. I try to move it out of the way, but it tips over and clatters against the wall.

"Mom! What are you doing?"

Who is this? "I believe you have the wrong person. I'm… I'm…" Who am I? *My name is Jimmy Carter and I'm running for president.* Well, I'm not him.

"You're Liz Wallace, Mom," says the young woman. "You're my mother. I'm your daughter, Eve."

The woman has tears in her eyes. I pat her on the arm and say, "Come and have a cup of tea. You'll feel better."

CHAPTER THIRTY-SIX

2011

CARLIE

"WHEN WILL YOU SEE MR. BOSTON AGAIN?"

Eve was dropping Carlie off because Carlie's car was in the garage having new brake pads installed and something else technical—it all sounded essential, anyway. Rosie was with Liz. The sisters were sitting outside Carlie's house with the engine running, but Carlie made no move to open the passenger door. She had refrained from asking questions over the last weeks, other than asking once if Eve was still in contact with him, and Eve had said yes. That was all—*Yes.* This time Eve turned off the engine and said yes there was, in fact, a plan in the offing. Would Carlie be free to look after Mom in the second week of July? Eve had been invited to a wedding of a friend from her McGill days—a second marriage. It was in Newport, Vermont, and Eve would take Mr. Boston with her, and they would spend a whole week in New England.

This would be Eve's big test. What if the PTSD kicked in during an intimate moment? And there would definitely be an intimate moment unless the guy was made of granite. No good speculating....

Rosie was going to a four-day gymnastics camp at Gros Morne for her second year, and it coincided with the first half of the Vermont trip. Two of her gymnastics buddies were going and a chartered bus was arranged. It was all quite straightforward.

So, Eve went south while Rosie went west, and Carlie experienced the whole range of Liz's behaviour, including the everlasting snack at three in the morning and an attempted breakout early Sunday. They had to ration tea because Liz's sodium levels were too high and after a long discussion about her diet, Dr.

Fletcher said it was probably all the tea, a diuretic, making her pee out too much potassium and upsetting the balance. *Try water or juice or milk.* Well, Dr. Fletcher, you try persuading Mom that milk is better for her, at three in the morning.

During the day Liz was restless; "I have to go out. I feel trapped. I haven't been out of the house for a week."

"Let's go for a run round the Marine Drive then, Mom. We'll take a little picnic." And the ride was a great success, the picnic less so.

"I don't eat egg sandwiches…"

"…tomato sandwiches…"

"…ham sandwiches…"

"I don't eat cheese. You know it disagrees with me. I'd just like a little bowl of soup."

So back they came for a little bowl of soup, but by then Liz just wanted toast and tea. And as soon as she was finished—"I have to go out. I feel trapped. I haven't been out for a week."

When Eve returned, there was a glow about her. A little smile lingered when she was in repose and she responded to Liz with a more loving gentleness than the quiet resignation of the last few weeks, and with many more spontaneous hugs. There was no need for Carlie to ask how the trip went. She did ask when the next event would be, and Eve said she would like to go to the graduation of Mr. Boston's son when he received his master's degree. The whole family would be there: the two children (and current partners) and his mom and his younger brother and family. His wife had died years ago from cancer. Carlie was impressed; this was more information than she had ever received. To what did she owe the honour? Eve said she had not meant to exclude her, although yes, she was doing exactly that. A new place, perhaps a new time, a new beginning. It felt altogether separate from everything else. It was why Eve needed to be so careful introducing this new piece of herself to her old life.

"I'm still a bit afraid that it won't fit."

Eve was sitting in total stillness again. Carlie could see Oumar for a moment, motionless in those beautiful robes, with that same total concentration.

"Have you told him about Mexico?" Maybe she shouldn't have asked, but it was so very important, and when Eve said yes, Carlie relaxed against the back of the chair and let out all the compressed air accumulating inside her. "Well then, everything will be alright."

The Home contacted them a few weeks after Eve's Vermont trip, thankfully before the one-year forecast. There was an appropriate vacancy. So, it was with relief as well as sadness that they moved Liz into a bright single room on the second floor of Red Maples, with a view of said maples from her window, and with locks on the exits from her floor to prevent too much wandering. They moved her own recliner into the corner by the window with her favourite cushion and throw, bought her new bedding for the single bed, and laid the book she was currently reading on the bedside table. (Rereading, in fact, as Liz would forget she had finished a book and pick it up, saying, *this looks interesting*, then start at the beginning again.) It was the Home she herself had picked out years ago, she and George, but she still looked bewildered and panicked when they left her there. The admitting nurse hustled them out, saying this reaction was normal at the start, and their mom would settle better if they kept out of the way. So they huddled together in the parking lot in tears and a cloud of guilt.

Carlie and her sisters consoled themselves with an enormous lingering dinner at a new Thai restaurant the night their mom moved to Red Maples, with two bottles of wine for the drowning of emotions. They were well into their chosen entrées, Carlie and Eve being proficient with chopsticks, Ginny sticking to a fork and saying she was done with making an effort this day, when Eve dropped her bombshell: "I've met a guy. Thought you'd like to know."

A pile of sloppy vegetables fell off Ginny's fork and down out of sight and she said a whole row of *shits* as she mopped up. Eve asked Ginny in a concerned voice if the stain would come out of that fabric…

"Never mind that. What guy?"

"Someone I met at the conference in Boston—"

"And you never told us!"

Eve said she had been afraid to tell anyone until it was more certain, until things were more established, and she mentioned the week in Vermont and that now she was quite certain.

"Well! That's wonderful. Oh, Eve…" and Ginny reached across and gave her a hug so that the tablecloth rumpled up and tilted her wine glass and Carlie had to grab it. Ginny sat back down and straightened everything then stared hard at her other sister. "Carlie, you're not saying anything."

"I'm speechless."

"Hah!" Ginny was glaring at her now. "Did you *know*?" Voice full of suspicion, she was stretched up tall, almost lifting off her chair.

"Calm down. I don't know a thing more than you do and if you'd stop talking maybe Eve could give us more details."

Ginny still looked unconvinced but turned her eyes on Eve. "Well?"

Engineer. Widower with two children, a boy and a girl in their twenties. Lives in Springfield, Massachusetts—not that far from Boston. Eve thought she might go down to Boston in November to meet his family at the son's convocation. He was getting his masters from Boston College. Carlie sat back and let Ginny do the talking, and after a while Ginny demanded photographs. Eve said he was coming here at Christmas so they could see for themselves. Yes, but they still wanted to see photographs.

"I lost my phone, remember? With all the Vermont pictures."

"But you must have some from that first time, in Boston?"

It was all too tentative the first time. Eve hadn't taken pictures. Did he? Well, yes—Eve was the one with the doubts. So, could he send some? She could ask, but she thought his were all of Eve. They might actually have to wait until Christmas.

"Oh, come on, he can send his passport picture if nothing else." Ginny was levitating off her chair again, and Carlie's thumbs were flying over her phone, searching on social media.

"Nobody shows anyone their passport picture."

"You know what I mean. He can send *something*."

Then Eve smiled that tiny smile, saying surely they didn't think she would have gone all this time without a picture of him. She had some in her wallet.

"For god's sake!"

"Very funny…"

Ginny and Carlie leaned in towards each other to examine the photographs and there was a long silence, then frowns and mutters about the face being familiar and who does he remind you of…? Then a duet: loud, incredulous, delighted. "It is. It's Ben Hutton." And they both said he was the best of all Eve's boyfriends, and how upset Eve had been back in high school when the family moved down to the States.

Ginny was first on her feet, saying this was the best news she'd had in years, and she and Carlie were laughing and hugging Eve and throwing out comments about Eve being a dark horse as usual, and so sneaky. And nobody was overseeing the wrinkled-up cloth and tipped glasses. For the rest of the evening they went on exclaiming about how wonderful it was that they had met again and how delighted Mom would be, and Eve must take him to meet her at Christmas.

But when it came to Rosie, Eve was adamant that nothing be said to her about Ben Hutton. Rosie must meet him face-to-face as Eve's friend and make up her own mind. There must be no preconceived ideas in Rosie's head and no obligations, real or imagined.

"So where will he stay when he comes?"

"It will have to be the Newfoundland Hotel."

"Rosie will love him. Everyone loved Ben."

Later, Eve said Rosie was only slightly interested when she brought up the subject one suppertime. It was only some stray visitor coming, an old boyfriend of her mom's staying at a hotel—someone they'd have to look after for a few days around Christmas. No big deal.

The convocation visit lasted four days. Eve reported being accepted into the family with great kindness. Well of course she was. Eve would be welcomed anywhere with open arms.

"And did you like them?" Ginny asked.

Very much. Ben's mother was there and had remembered Eve and been very encouraging. She was still as sharp as a tack but used a wheelchair to get around now because of her arthritis. "She said she had her own wheels these days with her own driver, which made her feel very superior. She was always a darling."

Ben's flights were booked via Toronto. He arrived on Christmas Eve and departed nine days later. They prayed there would not be a blizzard, and for once the elements smiled.

CHAPTER THIRTY-SEVEN

2011

LIZ

THEY'RE TAKING ME OUT FOR CHRISTMAS DINNER. THAT'S what the woman just told me. Now the woman is trying to put this blue sweater on me. *That's not mine*, I say, but she keeps pushing my arm into the sleeve, saying, *yes, your daughter gave it to you for your birthday.* Somebody is going to be looking for that sweater. They're wheeling me down the corridor now and That Woman is waving. *Have a nice time, Liz.* Is this your sweater? *No, Liz. Eve gave you that for your birthday, remember?* Eve. Bundled into the car like a child. Can you turn up the heat, please? Bundled out again. What a fuss. Can I go home now? Taking off my coat again. I only just put it on. Is this your sweater?

Faces, voices, pats on the shoulder, kisses on the cheek. What a commotion. Where...? *You're at Ginny's house, Mom.* A face stops in front of me, says Merry Christmas. I know that voice. Maybe. *It's Ginny, Mom.* I keep looking at the woman because I know I've seen that face before. Ginny, you say? I shake my head a little. Maybe it will come to me. Someone says, *She's not having a good day. Maybe leave her in peace for a bit.* Yes, I want to go home. I close my eyes, lie back, and shut everything out, and I nod off in spite of the racket.

What a delicious smell! Turkey. Lovely. Hot. Gravy and dressing and turkey. Turkey the way I cook it. Used to cook it. But that's a nasty draft. *Close the door, you're heating the street.* More *Hello, Merry Christmas* noises and rustling and bustling. Yes, this does feel like Christmas. Turkey and bustle. I open my eyes.

There's a lovely tree in the corner, all shining and colourful. You always find a good tree. And that music: Oh, that takes me back. "Once in Royal David's City." Christmas, when the girls were growing up. I keep smiling. Another face is dangling. *Oooh, your hands are cold.* Carlie? Carlie—how nice. And Ginny. This is nice. Don't mind me if…I still love you. A hug from both sides at once. My girls. My heart feels full to bursting.

That draft again. Somebody else at the door. Well, come in, come in, and shut the door. I snuggle into the quilt on my knees, pull it higher. A big deep voice. Do I know that voice? It's saying everyone's name: Ginny, Anthony, Jeremy…mumble, mumble, big laugh. I know that laugh…. Then another laugh. Oh, that's Eve. Like a chime of bells. I would know that anywhere.

"Hello, Mom. It's Eve."

"Did you give me this sweater?"

"Yes, I did. For your birthday. It suits you. That shade of blue is good for us Wallace girls."

Us Wallace girls. Yes.

"Mom, there's someone I'd like you to meet." Eve moves aside and a big person folds himself down in front of my knees, so his face is level with mine. Nice not to have to keep looking up. Never seen him before but he has a nice face. The room has gone all quiet, even the music has stopped. Am I supposed to know this person?

"Hello, Mrs. Wallace. You probably won't remember me, but I remember you from years ago. I used to be around to your house all the time with Eve. Ben Hutton."

That name is familiar. I gaze into the face, trying to see something I know. The face starts to smile and the eyes twinkle as if this is all a big joke. I know that twinkle.

"Ben Hutton?" I'm not sure about this. "But you went away."

"Yes," he says. "I'm sorry. I'm back."

I keep studying the face a little longer. Oh, yes. Ben. Such a nice face. Then I hold out my hands and smile, beam. There is laughter all around now and clapping, and I beam so hard my face hurts.

CHAPTER THIRTY-EIGHT

2012

ROSIE

MOM WAS IN LOVE WITH THIS BEN PERSON. OH MY GOD. She hadn't been out on a date for decades. (Well, except with that loser guy with the hairy knuckles, and the tall one who kept calling Rosie *my dear girl.*) And now she was in love with this Ben. Well, she had known him since she was in high school, which made it a bit different. But still…it had all been behind Rosie's back. All that sneaking off to Boston was because of a man. Why didn't Mom tell her?

Why should she? A tiny voice nagged at her. *Did you tell your mother about Joel, Rosie Wallace?* Mom only met Kit because Kit wanted to meet her, and Ben would have been the same way about Rosie. Ben was definitely a Kit-person not a Joel-person. In fact, Ben was very nice. Really nice. And Mom deserved someone nice after all this time. And you were worried about her being lonely, Rosie Wallace, after you go off to university. So now she won't be lonely. Don't be a dog in the manger, as Nana would say. But she'll move down to the States. He'll be taking Mom away. Down to the States.

Rosie had been planning to apply to a university in British Columbia after Christmas but maybe she should be thinking more of eastern Canada, say McMaster or U of T—nearer to Springfield and St. John's. Everything was so uncertain…

Rosie had never really imagined her mother having *man-friends* like Eryn's mom. Now and then she had tried to picture her mother marrying again, of there being a father figure in the house, but it was beyond her. She could only visualize Michel. She had balked at the idea of some strange man walking into their house and disappearing into Mom's bedroom and being around at breakfast and maybe telling Rosie when to be home at night. No way. She probably would have been happy with anyone reasonable when she was little. She just wanted a daddy back then and did not consider the possibility of someone not being reasonable, but as a teenager she was more particular. It had to be Michel or nobody. Now, she thought maybe she could have tolerated having Ben around the last few years—enjoyed it even—if he had moved here to Newfoundland so the rest of her life would be undisturbed. But he would not have come here, would he? And now? Now it was too late. Now it was too late for him to be a father, and instead he was going to take Mom away and Rosie was going to lose her mother and her home as well.

She was sitting at the dining table, which used to be in Nana's old house and now looked perfectly comfortable in Carlie's dining room, looked as if it had grown there. That was alright if you were a table. Rosie was picking at a piece of lemon meringue pie and feeling sorry for herself. At least Carlie had just accused her of that, and Rosie thought maybe she was right. *You're seeing the glass half empty, Rosie.* Carlie said she had been mooching around with this hard-done-by face for long enough, and Rosie felt too blah to argue. Yes, she realized that Mom and Ben had not made any decisions yet, and that long-distance relationships were tricky, and they both wanted to be with their respective families in their own homes, and they both had jobs to consider. Give them time to work it out. Rosie could always apply to a university in Massachusetts if Eve did go down there. Rosie had wanted to go somewhere different, hadn't she? Now was her chance. And Eve would never give up her home here. She was too much a Newfoundlander, and everyone else was here. Just be glad they had found each other again. And Rosie was glad. Really, she was.

"And how did Paddles like Ben?"

Strange question. Carlie must have run out of sermons. Paddles had adored Ben. He was like his little shadow the whole time. Ben was practically wearing him by the end of his visit.

"And what about Joel?"

Joel? Why would Carlie ask about Joel? She hardly ever saw him these days. Only had one class together last semester. "We just say hello in passing, that's all." And to reassure Carlie, Rosie said she was totally over him and couldn't think why she had thought him so attractive. It was just his smile. "Anyway, I'm dating a new guy called Kit." And Rosie felt herself blushing and picked at her pie again. "Ben met him for two minutes on New Year's Eve and said he seemed nice. And Kit liked Ben."

"He must be the one Eve mentioned," Carlie said. "The one who's still taller than you when he's folded in half." And Rosie nodded and smiled round her pie.

CHAPTER THIRTY-NINE

2012

LIZ

THAT WOMAN OVER THE ROAD IS IN THIS PLACE TOO. OUT of all the people I know, she has to be the one staying just down the corridor. There is no avoiding her. Here I am, wondering if someone will bring me a cup of tea soon, when the door swings wide open, and That Woman walks right in. As if she owns the place. Doesn't even knock.

"Passion Flakie for you," the woman says. "Son brought me a box full." She hands me a little cellophane packet, and I lift the packet up close so I can see and I turn it over and over to read the labels.

"Thank you, Mrs.... Sorry, I forget."

"Helen. Helen Arbuthnot." Oh yes. "You're going to turn it all to crumbs doing that, Liz."

"Looks like a Dutch Cream to me," I say, looking at the woman over the top of my glasses. "George buys those for a treat: one Dutch Cream, a bottle of Spur, and a cigarette for fifteen cents at..." now what's the name of that place? "... Rosie's, on Hayward Avenue."

"I remember Rosie's. My goodness. That takes me back a bit."

"I have a daughter called Rosie."

The woman's voice drones on and on, but I'm trying to remember, puzzling over the name. There's Eve, but then there's Rosie....

"Have the Flakie with your cup of tea, Liz," says the woman as she leaves. "They'll be coming around soon."

I pick up the photo from the window ledge and study it—a whole lot of faces. One must be Eve and one must be Rosie, but I can't tell who is who. And there's something I should remember about Eve and Rosie…something important….

CHAPTER FORTY

2012

ROSIE

AT FIRST THE FAMILY BROUGHT NANA HOME FOR SUNDAY dinners every week, took her out to the Marine Drive on a nice day for a change of scene. She made a fuss about having to get dressed up for the weather and would forget she'd been out two minutes after she was back, but the staff said she was always more content for a couple of days afterwards. Mom said perhaps Nana's subconscious was aware of the outing and was comforted. After a while, though, even that deep-down memory seemed to be lost and there was no delayed contentment, only irritation at the change in routine. So, they stopped the outings except for special occasions. Instead, they took turns to visit every day, and only stayed to check on things and for as long as she seemed to be enjoying their company, which meant a maximum of half an hour and only a few minutes on bad days. Nana always mistook Rosie for Eve and sometimes didn't know Eve either. It seemed to agitate her when Eve and Rosie were there together, so the family decided Rosie didn't need to go anymore. In fact, her mom was quite insistent. She said the only plan for Nana these days was to keep her calm and happy.

It was amazing that Nana had remembered Ben at Christmastime. He had a very distinctive voice, and sometimes Rosie thought Nana recognized voices better than faces. Carlie said Nana had always loved Ben, probably more than Michel. He did seem nice, fun, and kind. Mom was so much happier and more alive, now that he was on the scene. It was just....

It was February, just after Rosie's eighteenth birthday. In creative writing class, they were given a final project before the run-up to exams. Mrs. Hammond asked for an essay about an older family member or family friend, showing some characteristic(s) particular to that person, with lots of sensory detail. Show, don't tell. Rosie thought of Nana and her Life Lessons. She started the essay but decided a visit to Nana was called for and it was a lovely crisp day for a walk—one of those false spring days between snowstorms, and she was given a ride halfway from school with Melanie's mom.

Rosie passed the tea trolley in the hallway out by the elevator. It gave a little clunk as it went over each join in the flooring, which made the cups clink on their saucers, and when the trolley picked up speed it sounded like that line of Irish dancers in *Riverdance*: a ripple of heel-clicks for the front wheels and another for the back: ripple-ripple, silence; ripple-ripple, silence. As the trolley rolled down the hall, dispensing its cups, the clinks grew fewer and fewer, and two doors past Nana's room they would stop altogether. So sad. Rosie should use that as a metaphor in her essay.

She knocked on Nana's door and walked in. Her grandmother was sitting in her recliner by the window with that gorgeous throw on her knees. Mom had found it at a craft fair: woven wool in green and cream and the blue of Nana's eyes. Wallace eyes. She looked like a china doll today with her pink-and-white complexion and the sun shining on her white fluff of hair. They must have just washed it. Rosie stood for a moment, fixing the picture in her mind for her essay.

Her grandmother was holding out both hands saying, "Eve," and Rosie did not bother to correct her this time. After the hugs, she moved to the second chair, lifted the magazines onto the bed out of the way, and prepared to ask Nana about her cooking and baking sayings. She avoided too much chat, just saying how pretty Nana looked and how the tea trolley was on its way. Nana smiled and nodded. She did not say anything but looked alert, as if she were taking things in.

"You know how when the potatoes boiled dry, you always said it was going to rain?" Rosie asked. It was all about humidity and atmospheric pressure, but she didn't go into that. Nana still looked alert, so Rosie kept going. "My friend Eryn thought that was silly, but then s*he* boiled some potatoes dry, and it started to pour down that very minute. She believed you then." Rosie beamed. Nana nodded slowly, but Rosie thought she'd better stop there. She did not go on to the actual Life Lesson where Nana said we had to control our own atmospheric pressure, so it did not upset everyone. *If someone's pressure is building up, don't add to it.* They sat in silence for a few minutes.

"Remember teaching me how to make pancakes, Nana?" *Be gentle stirring the liquid into the flour. Keep it light. Don't flatten the bubbles. We all need our bubbles.* Dumb word to use—*remember.*

Nana rested her head back against the chair. "Yes," she said, and smiled her soft familiar smile. "Yes, we all need our bubbles."

Good. She really was remembering things today. Some things. They stayed there in silence for a while, content.

Then Nana's head came up and she looked at Rosie with such a sad expression. "But you lost your bubbles in Mexico, didn't you?"

"What do you mean, Nana?"

"After the rape."

What?

Rosie stared at her grandmother with her mouth agape, not breathing, not consciously thinking of anything at all. An immeasurable space of blank nothing. She mouthed the word silently, *rape,* and little facts started clunking into place, slowly at first then gathering speed. Nana's voice goes on buzzing, her mouth bunching, relaxing, bunching again—soft lavender lips with their fan of well-worn grooves like runnels in the cliffs at Middle Cove. *It took the sea a thousand years…*

This cannot be true. Must not be true. Is not.

But Rosie knows it is. You could never *remember* an event like this if it hadn't happened. Mexico. Mom. It happened.

And that meant… *It took the sea an hour one night…* Nana's words slid down Rosie's throat, blocking her lungs, her stomach, leaning on her heart. Her whole body was being squeezed, crushed, no air left inside.

That meant...

It took the sea a thousand years,
A thousand years to trace
The granite features of this cliff,
In crag and scarp and base.

It took the sea an hour one night,
An hour of storm to place
The sculpture of these granite seams
Upon a woman's face.

Rosie must have walked home but she saw nothing, heard nothing, just felt—heavy. A thousand pounds of heavy. Now and then she stumbled and caught herself, unaware of what had tripped her, hardly aware of tripping. There was horror inside her bones, but she couldn't really feel it yet. Horror and shame. For ages she stood just inside the porch when she reached home, leaning against the door then sliding down to crouch on the floor, hardly noticing the dog whimpering, nudging and licking, wagging his whole rear end in his agitation. He put a paw on her foot and finally she picked him up and cuddled him, murmuring, *Paddles, Paddles.* Then he was struggling out of her arms and heading for the back door and stood making let-me-out noises. She opened it for him then rushed into the bathroom, tearing off her clothes, stood in the shower and scrubbed and scrubbed and half-scalded herself, steam so thick it felt hot in her lungs, only turning the water off when it ran cold. The water never ran cold.

She could not face her mother. Carlie did not answer the phone and Rosie didn't leave a message; she would walk over. She tried to focus on what to pack, throwing haphazard items into her gym bag. She didn't wait for her hair to dry, just towelled it and rammed a hat down over her ears and pulled up her hood.

Rosie reached her aunt's house and saw the car was missing, then remembered her key was back home in her backpack. She checked her phone. Almost six o'clock. Carlie would be home in a minute. She sent a text—*at ur house no key*—and sat on her bag on the top step. A girl with a bulging backpack and three supermarket bags walked by and went into a house a few doors down. A car was having trouble squeezing into its parking spot near the bottom of the hill. Rosie pulled herself into the corner of the door frame, behind the big pot of winter boughs, huddling into her clothes. Cold. Colder every minute. How did a person survive in a cardboard box on the street? The motion-sensor light had come on when she arrived, but once she had settled it faded again and the only light was from street lamps—one higher up the hill and one below. She tucked her head down and kept still, hiding, until she had to stand and slap at herself and go up and down on her toes a few times to warm up. Six thirty-five and the only messages were from Eryn and Kit and two of her gymnast friends. She ignored them. And a message from her mom, *Where are you?* Not answering. Where was Carlie? She curled into the corner again.

Feet. Stopping.

"Good Lord. It's Rosie, isn't it?" Mrs. Murphy next door. "It's Wednesday, child. Your aunt doesn't come home 'til after seven on Wednesdays. She has a class. Come into the house before you catch your death."

Rosie wanted to refuse, only she was so shivering cold that she followed Mrs. Murphy into her house, but turned and sat on the bottom stair inside, keeping her eyes averted, saying she was fine here and thank you and she'd just stay until seven. Mrs. Murphy argued and persuaded, but there were voices deeper in the house that Rosie did not want to meet, so she insisted she was fine right here. Thank you.

Kitchen noises: pots and dishes and cupboard doors. The smell of onions frying. Mrs. Murphy brought Rosie a mug of tea and her hands had warmed enough now for Rosie to tolerate the heat, so she could wrap them round the mug and absorb the comfort, sipping slowly, mapping the hot tea as it slid down into her chest.

Then the family was being summoned to come and eat and the voices were closing in, and Rosie called, *Thank you* and escaped before she was cornered. She sat by Carlie's door again, trying to be invisible. But soon she found herself looking across the road with that instinctive awareness that makes you look before you're even conscious of the act of looking, never mind being conscious of someone staring at you. And there was someone staring at her—a hoodie, at the end of that little alleyway between the houses opposite. It was turned away now, no face, just the glow of a cigarette, but he had been staring. Somehow, she knew it was a "he." He must have been there before she came out. Well, she was the only event going on down the whole street so of course he'd been looking. No harm in that. But she felt threatened, all the same. She shrank into herself, checked her cell—a text from Carlie said, *On my way*. Two minutes or fifteen? Rosie started to count up seconds in sixties.

Now and then she sneaked a look across the street, and that hood was always pointing her way, but pulled so far forward there was no face, just a Dementor. Now he was rubbing out his cigarette with a foot. Now he was crossing the road towards her, and Rosie prepared herself to run up Mrs. Murphy's steps and bang on the door, but headlights turned onto the street and blazed down the hill in two lines like cavalry. They slowed by the house and the guy veered off down the street as the motion-sensor light came on. Carlie slammed her car door.

"My god. What happened? No, come inside before you tell me. Does your mom know you're here?" Ushering her up to the living room.

"No. And I'm not going back. Don't let her come for me."

Carlie was staring at her. Rosie had never seen Carlie surprised like that. Shocked. She always said she was unshockable. "Are you hurt?"

Tears welled up.

"Rosie. Are you physically hurt? Tell me."

Rosie tried to say *no* but it stuck somewhere on the way out. She shook her head instead.

"So I'll just phone Eve to say you're safe. She'll be worried. Then you can stay here as long as you want."

Carlie made Rosie sit in the corner of the big chair and wrapped a blanket around her, the thick cream alpaca one with brown llamas round the bottom. *Warm you up*. Rosie wanted to shout out her questions, tell Carlie to stop fussing, but she couldn't get enough air behind the words to push them out and all the time tears were leaking, leaking. A thousand years of tears.

Then her aunt was sitting opposite, looking at her. "So. Tell me."

And the silence hurt Rosie's chest, everything—the pressure.

"I went to see Nana. She thought I was Mom." Long pause. Rosie squeezed her eyes shut and whispered it so low that if you didn't know what was coming you would never distinguish the word. "Rape."

Carlie moved to sit on the arm of the chair, half slid down next to her, and held her close.

"Is it true?" Rosie mumbled into Carlie's chest.

Silence.

"Carlie. Is it true?" Louder.

"It's true Eve was raped. Yes."

Rosie took a breath, made a little choked sound, took another breath.... "Is Michel my father?"

Carlie moved them over to the couch, saying she was getting cramps in her side, tried to tuck Rosie up again but Rosie pushed the blanket off, voice urgent, "Is he my father?"

"Probably not."

"But he might be?"

"They'd been trying for a baby for a long time and it hadn't happened. So, it's not impossible but—"

"What about DNA testing?"

"Not back then. Not for the general public. Maybe your mom's checked since—"

"Find out. Please. Phone Mom and ask. Now." Carlie said that was for Rosie to do, this should be between Rosie and Eve, but Rosie was growing more and more agitated so Carlie called, and Rosie could read the answer on her aunt's face. Eve had had tests done at a reputable laboratory as soon they became available. Rosie was definitely not related to Michel in any way.

So, who was her father? Did they try to find him? Did they catch him? Rosie put her head down in her hands, squeezed. The tears came again, not noisily but in a steady soaking downpour, and the mound of soggy tissues spread across her knees. This could not be true. When was the Mexico trip? But she already knew. Late April 1993. She'd always wondered if maybe she was conceived in Mexico. She had thought it kind of glamorous. Rosie did the calculations four times, five times, ten times. No way out. No way....

Carlie was back in front of Rosie with a ham and mushroom omelette, and toast the colour of the mushrooms, like Eryn's tan after her month down south with her father. Rosie didn't want to eat. Couldn't eat.

"You've said that three times now. Eat."

And once she started, Rosie ate and drank everything, nonstop. "You knew."

"Yes."

"Who else?"

"Ginny and Anthony. Mom. Dr. Clarke. Nobody else. Michel, of course. I don't know about Michel's family."

Carlie took the empty plate, laid it on the coffee table, sat next to Rosie, and tucked the blanket in again as if she wanted to keep things contained. The blanket pulled into folds: ridges and gullies. Granite seams.

"So, Mom told all of you, but she never told me."

"Eve would not have told anybody if she could have gotten away with it, Rosie, but we guessed and we confronted her."

"Why didn't you tell me? Mom should have told me." She wriggled, and Carlie loosened her grip.

"When?"

"Well. As soon as I was old enough to understand."

"Which was when?"

"Well. A teenager. When I hit puberty."

"So, you think you could have handled all the mood swings and the boy thing and periods and hormones and more hormones—*and* finding out your mom was raped?" Rosie was thrashing around now so Carlie sat back, let go of the blanket altogether.

"She should at least have told me Michel wasn't…isn't… my father."

"And what would have been your first question?"

"She still should have told me." This was at the top of her voice.

Carlie's voice was low and controlled. "How could she tell you about Michel without telling you the rest? Difficult enough being an innocent victim without you thinking she'd been messing around with some other man."

Oh, god. How could it happen? How could it? "Where was Michel?"

"You'll have to ask your mom that."

"Why didn't Mom have an abortion?" *I'd have had an abortion.* How could she not know she was pregnant all those months? Stupid. Adoption? So why didn't they?

Carlie's face softened and she smiled. "As soon as Eve saw you, she loved you. Bonded with you. She wouldn't let you go then. You could have been bounced from foster home to foster home all this time, you know. You've been lucky, growing up with—"

"Lucky!" It was a shriek. "Lucky." Rosie pushed herself to her feet, elbowing Carlie in the chest in her effort to pry herself free, charging around the room. Then it was back to how her mother should have told her. Should have, should have, on and on.

She stopped and looked her aunt full in the face and said, "Even my *grandmother* knew. You told her even though—"

Carlie interrupted, saying Liz was the first person to know, way before the rest of the family. Don't forget, she did not have dementia back then.

"Yes, and *you* knew, too." Rosie spat it out. "My own aunt. I *trusted* you! You went behind my back. It's a fucking conspiracy. You all knew and not one of you fucking told me. How could you look me in the face all these years and keep it from me? How could you?"

Carlie stayed calm. "I couldn't tell you if Eve didn't," she said. "But I wouldn't have told you anyway until you were old enough. Mature enough. And you're not being very mature right now."

"Great. Now it's my fault."

"Don't be ridiculous. This is nobody's *fault* except tho…that awful man."

Rosie paced, stopped, paced, all the time hugging herself and looking at the floor. She swung round with her arms out and flung her head back with an *aaah* sound then went back to hugging herself and circling, head down. Murmurs in the next room—Carlie phoning Mom. Rosie wanted to yell obscenities or rush in and throw the phone at the wall, but she just kept pacing and finally, finally, she wilted down into the armchair and just lay there, where she landed.

CHAPTER FORTY-ONE

2012

LIZ

I KEEP LOOKING AT EVE'S FACE. SOMETHING HAS HAPPENED. Whatever is the matter? She looks as if she's seen a ghost… or worse. "Eve," I say again. "What is it, Eve?" But she doesn't answer, just stares straight ahead, eyes ghastly and face deathly pale, as if she might faint. I try to get that blanket off my knees and stand up and go to her, but the movement seems to break the spell, and Eve jumps to her feet and turns and runs out of the room. "Eve! Come back, Eve."

I collapse back into the chair, all snarled up in the blanket. Did I say something silly? What we were talking about? Pancakes? The lady with the tea trolley is putting a cup on my side table, saying something in a cheery voice, and I ask her to run after Eve and bring her back, but the woman says it's too late, she just heard the elevator doors close. She could be halfway across the parking lot… *But you must stop her. Stop…* I try to stand and I'm breathless suddenly and dizzy and I reach for the woman's arm to steady myself. The woman is pushing me back into the chair instead of helping me up and I don't have the strength to stop her. I try to say please, but my mouth won't work and my tongue feels huge. I try to reach for the aide's arm but my own arm flops down, dangling outside the chair, and the aide lifts my wrist and tucks my hand inside the blanket on my knee so it's trapped. *There you are, my love.*

No, no…come back….

The woman is still talking in her chirpy voice, not listening, and then she's gone. I can see the buzzer pinned to the blanket and try to press it, but I can't get my hand out so I have to bring my other hand across and I'm not sure if my thumb actually made the thing buzz, so I keep on pressing. I'm struggling and struggling and realize I'm tipped over sideways somehow but don't know how it happened. Maybe I fell asleep. Now there are voices and rustles around the chair, and I'm being lifted, and the blood pressure thingy is being tightened on my arm and someone is saying, *It's alright, Liz,* but it isn't all right. It's all wrong and I need to talk to Eve, and they won't listen, and I'm being lifted and where are they taking me? And the air on my face is freezing cold suddenly and the wheel-rumbles turn into gravel noises and there are male voices and metal noises and my mouth feels as if I've been dribbling and I try to wipe it but can't untangle my hand from the straps round me and I can feel tears running sideways across my face and someone wipes at them and says something about going to the hospital to check me out, but it's not me who needs checking out, it's Eve....

CHAPTER FORTY-TWO

2012

ROSIE

AFTER A WHILE, ROSIE BECAME AWARE OF HER AUNT SITTING nearby and she started another round of questions. Did they ever catch him? Canadian police, if the Mexican ones couldn't? Trace him themselves: flights to Europe, the groups, the resorts? Only flights to German-sounding places? Michel could have... This guy should be in prison. Getting away with it. And how, on a beach full of people and where was Michel and why didn't... why did...how could...?

Somehow Rosie wound down and eventually got herself into bed and lay looking at the ceiling, expecting to be awake all night but falling asleep, still looking. She awoke at ten in the morning feeling like a plant after a long drought—flaccid, cell linings all shrivelled. How could she not have guessed Michel was not her father? All the signs she had missed. How could she have been so obtuse? She lay motionless until she absolutely had to go to the bathroom. Breakfast noises floated up from the kitchen, the smell of coffee and toast, her favourite raisin bread toast. Who cared? She dragged herself through the bathroom routines, stopping now and then to stare at nothing bleakly, blankly.

Carlie called, "Rosie! Come and eat."

Rosie appeared at the top of the stairs and peered suspiciously at her aunt. "Why aren't you at work?"

"You're more important."

Rosie snorted, scuffed into the kitchen, scowling as Carlie put toast and juice in front of her. She had juiced some of those big navel oranges with the extra-thick skins—Rosie used to call them snowsuit oranges, suits like the traffic-control people wore on the highways. Her aunt was trying to wheedle her way back into Rosie's good books, but she wouldn't succeed. Ever. Rosie finished her breakfast in silence and sat for a while.

Then: "Why did Michel leave?"

"You'll have to ask your mom that."

"He didn't want me, did he?"

Carlie paused for a long time then said, "No." She brought over some small yogurt containers to choose from, and Rosie picked the nearest one without really looking, then sat staring at it.

"So they got divorced because of me."

"I wouldn't say that. It probably would have happened anyway. Things were never right between them after Mexico."

"What was he like? Nobody ever talks about him. What did *you* see when you looked at Michel?"

Carlie leaned against the fridge and stared across the room and said Michel was grey. He was probably a mixture of all the usual colours—he was human after all—but mix a lot of colours together and they come out grey. Somehow there was always something equal and opposite in Michel. He was a diplomat by upbringing, able to converse with anyone, get someone talking without giving away anything of himself. Always presented both sides, so that what he said seemed like a balanced observation, not a personal belief. "We're all a mixture of biases and certainly we need to control them, but put him on any scale and he'd be right slap in the middle."

"You didn't like him."

"I did like him, actually. He was charming and funny and he was always friendly, treated everyone the same. But there was nothing to get hold of. After six years of knowing him, I still didn't *know* him. Until you were born. Then he couldn't maintain that balance. It struck at something he wasn't trained for, prepared for.

"I did that?"

"You didn't create it. But you seemed to bring something out in him that he couldn't control. A phobia maybe, or some deep-rooted belief. Like my friend, Tom."

Tom had been an archaeologist on one of Carlie's expeditions who had picked up some tropical disease and had to have a leg amputated. Used a prosthetic limb when she knew him. But he was someone who just couldn't look at such an injury. "Lots of sickness and amputations in impoverished places and he hated seeing it. He empathized, donated money for people's care—was extremely generous, in fact—but he couldn't look at them."

Carlie had thought it was a phobia, although she was not trained to diagnose that kind of thing. He hated his own physical state, did not take care of the residual limb because he hated looking at it, so it became infected. Then his doctor told him that he needed the other foot amputated. Tom started drinking. Well, he always did drink, but it started to be a real problem. Went back to the States and died a few months later.

"So now I'm a deformity."

"God, Rosie. Look at yourself in the mirror! You're more like a tropical disease that every young man *wants* to catch."

Rosie's phone kept buzzing. There was a string of texts. Shit, it was a school day, and she hadn't let them know she wasn't coming. She couldn't face seeing anybody or even texting anybody now. What was she going to do? Carlie said Mom had phoned the school, said Rosie would be off sick the rest of the week. That gave her two school days and the weekend. Then what?

"Are you ready for your mom?"

"No. God, no."

Would she ever be ready for her mom? Rosie walked over to the window. The sun was weak and wintery, but it streamed in as if this was any old day.

"Mom getting all distant, ending up in that clinic...is that because of Mexico?"

"Yes. Growing up, your mother had the most even keel of us all. I was always blowing up, ranting about the unfairness of life. Ginny was always trying to change people to fit her idea of how they should be." Carlie was gazing over Rosie's head in that unsighted, elsewhere way. "Eve was so peaceful. She could be in the middle of a racket and yet stay outside of it. Nothing got to her. Unflappable. They say she's an excellent counsellor. But after Mexico, she couldn't handle working with victims of rape or family violence, which was what she had been doing. Left work altogether for a while."

Carlie's voice came back to Earth and her eyes to Rosie's face. She said lately Eve had taken on a private patient or two with those abuse histories. Trying again, to see how it went. She was utilizing her experience and getting some good out of it after all. That felt right to Rosie. Go Mom. Even through all the hopeless black turmoil inside her, this felt like a little ray of retaliation. She so wanted to nail that man, but at least this would be a small way of saying, *Can't stop me.*

"God. Finding out she was pregnant must have been…I can't imagine."

"Your mom would say you were the silver lining. Worth all the rest."

They sat in silence for a while, and Rosie asked in a calmer voice what set off the PTSD episodes.

"Hard to know." Carlie listed some of the triggers they had noticed over the years and told Rosie about George's uncle—Rosie's great-great-uncle—who had spent years in a Japanese prisoner-of-war camp during the Second World War. Sometimes he screamed in his sleep. Mom did not do that—at least, Rosie had never heard her. George said his uncle started to shake right in the middle of Christmas dinner once. They thought maybe it was the sound the knife made when he leaned on it and it slipped and made a screech on the plate. Not something you would think of—so specific, so individual.

Half of Rosie came from a Bad Man. Was her mother afraid Rosie would do something bad? Rosie would never hurt anybody.

Would she? Her mother was afraid she would. Look at how upset she got when they dressed up Paddles, the way she withdrew when Rosie broke into that drawer, and every time she threw a hissy fit. Her mother was wondering: would Rosie be a bully? Take advantage of people? Abuse power? Tag along with bullies and be sucked into their nasty ways without having the courage to argue or walk away? Was Eryn turning into a bully? When did loyalty to a long-term friend become *tagging along*? Did Mom still wonder if Rosie was acting like her rapist-father's daughter? Were there nasty genes lurking under the surface, waiting to make Rosie do evil things? Was she going to have to think about every single move she made before she made it, like that nice psychopath on CBC? She felt like her head was about to explode.

❧

"Ready for your mom yet?" It was almost noon and Rosie was still sitting at the kitchen table.

"I suppose I'd better get it over with."

When her mom walked in, her eyes had a wild, big-pupil look rather than the frozen face of her Bad Times. There were dark shadows under them, and her cheeks were all drawn in. She looked old. It was the first time Rosie had thought of Mom as getting old. She came up the stairs and stopped still just inside the living room door, and Carlie said in a matter-of-fact voice, "Eve, I told Rosie what I know when she asked me. I'm going up to mark some papers in my office now. Let me know when you're ready for a coffee or something to eat."

After she left, Mom came into the middle of the room and opened her arms. "I love you, Rosie. You don't know how much. I'll always love you, whatever happens."

Rosie stood still for a moment. Sorrow and sympathy, resentment and blame, *how could you?* and *how could he?* all fought for space in her head. She took a step forward and stopped, and her mom came the rest of the way and wrapped her arms round Rosie, enclosing her in that way that says *you're safe, I'm here.* "You're still the same," she whispered. "Still my Rosie," and their hug grew more definite, the primal hug of two living creatures comforting each other. Then they stood a little apart, just looking.

"God, Mom." She touched her mother's arm again with one hand then let it drop in a slow, down-through-water way, and her mom nodded a slow nod back. They went on looking at each other, sending feelings and messages: horror, sympathy, *I'm trying to understand.* "But when were you going to tell me?" The question broke the spell and they sat down opposite each other, never losing eye contact.

"I didn't want you to know, planned never to tell you. I thought you would be happier not knowing. But now and then, when you were upset with me, you would talk about finding Michel, how you would track him down and fly to Qatar and meet him face to face." And Mom knew Rosie had been saving up for the flight for years. Rosie hadn't realized that. Her mother straightened her shoulders, lifted her chin, and for a moment she looked just like Carlie.

"You'd find out. So I decided to tell you after grade ten, during the holidays, maybe take you on a little trip to Toronto or New York afterwards. I wish I had." Only that was when Michel got married and Rosie had been so angry with him, stopped talking about wanting to meet him. Then there was the gymnastics camp in the middle of the vacation, so no recovery time. Mom shook her head and sagged back against the chair. "Oh, I had endless reasons to put it off, Rosie."

Carlie and Ginny had kept warning her not to delay, Ginny especially; they said Rosie could find out from DNA tests. But Rosie wouldn't have access to Michel's DNA (or that's what she told herself), and Rosie's DNA would only tell her there were some foreign bits in there, which could be from decades ago and would just be interesting, not horrifying. Mom closed her eyes for a moment and took a few breaths, then sat up tall, and her chin came up again.

"So, why didn't I tell you? The real answer is that I was afraid, Rosie. Afraid for you, afraid for me. Afraid about how we might feel about each other." She sagged again but her voice stayed firm. "Rape does that to a person because of how the world looks at them afterwards. I know it from studying psychology, from talking to victims, from hearing about court cases where the victim has to answer questions and, despite legislation to prevent her name being publicized, it leaks out and ends up on social media, and she's vilified. Mocked. Despised." Her voice was getting husky now and she swallowed and cleared her throat. "But most of all I know it from being a victim myself."

All this time, tears were pouring and pouring down Rosie's face. Her mother was looking down at her knees, but she glanced up with a self-mocking smile. "You'd think a psychologist would handle this better. And at a conscious level I know I'm blameless, that all the blame belongs to those men and only them, but…"

"Them. *Them*?" Rosie's voice squealed up and up to the heights and disappeared. Her mom's face turned white and her eyes screwed up tight and her mouth, her hands—everything, and she whispered something Rosie couldn't catch. Then she said it clearly: "Three."

Rosie had her hands over her face, digging her fingers in, crouched down, wanting to hide—to dig a hole and hide in it. Three. Finally, she sat up again, and said in a flat, bitter voice that she supposed it didn't matter how many. There'd just be one sperm that did the deed. And her mother's face twisted into something even more agonized and Rosie was down on her knees trying to hug her. "I don't mean that. I'm sorry. Way worse for you. God, Mom, *three*?! You would never be able to fight off three of them."

Mom kept swallowing, and something under the corner of her eye was twitching. Her voice scraped and she tried to clear her throat but couldn't get a straight run at it.

"I've never been able to say it out loud. I've answered people's questions—yes or no, sometimes just a nod or a shake of the head. It's incredibly hard to say it. But I promised myself…" She sat straighter, looked right at Rosie, and said, "I was raped. By three men."

Rosie was afraid to do anything, say anything, to make things worse. "Thank you, Mom," she said at last. "Hard. Yes. To say it." There was no need to say anything else. Her mom's face did not have that frozen faraway look now, just the ordinary, bleary, wrung-out look that anyone has after a big emotional upheaval. She even smiled. It was tiny and quivery, but it was a smile and full of love.

Mom called up the stairs to Carlie to say they were going home, and Carlie came down and hugged them goodbye without a word.

They were almost home when Mom said Rosie would need to be very careful around Paddles. He was still in some pain. He'd got a touch of frostbite in his paws and tail and scrotum—

"Paddles! Oh my god, Paddles. I left him out."

Mom said the vet gave him a warm water enema to raise his body temperature, told Eve what to do. She'd had him wrapped up in blankets, given him warm compresses—

"When did you come home, Mom? When did you find him?"

They estimated he'd been outside in the snow an hour or more, and he was such a little dog, so close to the icy ground, not built for such conditions. And she hadn't put on his booties. Rosie rushed into the living room with her jacket still on.

"Calmly, Rosie. He might still be in shock."

She slowed down and knelt beside his cushion and stroked him ever so carefully. *Paddles, Paddles. How could I forget about you? I'm so, so, so sorry.* He was all tail and feet and undercarriage. It was hard to avoid touching them. She wanted to pick him up and hug him, but Mom said best to leave him. He licked her hand a couple of times but nothing else moved. Rosie kept saying *Oh my god* over and over. How could she have done this?

"It was an accident, Rosie. Extreme circumstances. Keep it in proportion."

Proportion! Paddles could lose a foot because Rosie had been so careless. She had thought she couldn't feel any worse, but she could.

Sunday night. Days had passed in a blur of wandering round the house, being gentle with Paddles, staring into space, ignoring her phone, of sprawling anywhere she happened to be when she ran out of steam, of lying awake in her bed and falling asleep in a chair, of eating whatever was put in front of her and not noticing, of rushing off to hug her mom, saying how much she loved her. She had to go to school tomorrow. How was she going to survive? How could she look anybody in the eye? What could she tell them about being off sick? She was never off sick. *You're as good as any of them. Stand tall and look the world in the face.* Carlie's war cry.

Aunt Ginny stopped by twice that Sunday and said, "Tell them you had a vicious headache and it's gone now, but you still feel a bit delicate." That would explain her ignoring the phone and looking washed out and being less bouncy than usual. She could skip all the after-school things for that reason too. "And if anybody asks," said her aunt, "tell them it was one of those girl things, although they probably won't ask."

Rosie sent one text to everyone to explain the headache and how reading had made it worse, so no texts. Sorry. Mom said when she was face to face with someone, just ask them about their weekend and the latest gossip and about what she'd missed in school. *Let them do the talking.*

Mom dropped her off in the morning, but Rosie said she wouldn't need to be picked up—she'd manage. *That's my girl.* And Rosie *was* her girl. Nothing could change that. She wasn't sure why, because they'd all been harping on that theme ever since it happened, but those few words, said by her mom in that way at that moment, made a difference.

Rosie made it through the day without any fuss after the first flurry of questions, and nobody made a big deal out of it because to them, it wasn't. But the world was standing a few steps away from where it usually stood, leaving a gap between Rosie and the rest of the planet. She could feel her two feet on the ground, but they felt disconnected somehow. Even when Eryn linked arms with her, the arm felt distant.

Kit would be the worst of all. He would dig and dig until he found out what was wrong, so she would have to tell him straight out that she was not going to tell him. And then what would happen? Besides that, his was such a perfect family. Nothing simmered under the surface. How could someone like Rosie... She felt tainted.

"There are always things below the surface," Mom said. "Kit's family just manage them well. At least, when things are going smoothly they manage them well. You don't know how they'll behave if things go wrong—but it seems they have good habits to fall back on."

"So, what if they knew my father was a rapist?"

"They'd be horrified, I'm sure. They'd be sorry for you, for me. They'd probably absorb it after a while, then business as usual." But people could always surprise you. They might start thinking of Rosie in a category, like a minority group—like having a mental health problem—which was quite right. This did affect her mental health.

They were sitting at the kitchen table, Rosie not quite looking her mom in the eye. Then Rosie turned away completely and looked out of the window. A guy would never want to marry someone like her, would he? Start a family? Not with those genes. Not that Rosie was thinking of marrying anybody for years and years, but still. It was a thought she could not voice, would never voice. It was a thought she did not want to think.

"I keep picturing people's faces if they found out."

"But how would they find out? Why would you tell them?" Would anyone tell someone if their ancestor stole a loaf of bread in the Depression, ran off with someone's husband, fought on the other side in a war? Would they even know? There was probably something embarrassing in everyone's ancestry. Did it matter today? "It's none of their business, anyway. It's our secret and it's something we just have to live with."

Still, despite what anybody else thought, Rosie felt dirty. She had cells that came from a dirty person. Some phrase from the Bible floated by—about being unclean. Mom was watching her face... *Oh god, wipe those thoughts away. Quick.*

"If you have inherited a nasty personality trait, you can control it," Mom said. "And you've grown up with people who've tried not to nurture nasty tendencies."

Psychology talk. That's all that was. "Not that you've shown any bad tendencies—just the usual teenage testing of wings. You are a good person, Rosie. You have no reason to feel ashamed of anything. It's the rapists who own the shame. Not you."

Yes.

Yes.

But Rosie couldn't sleep. She came down and curled up next to the dog's cushion and whispered, *My father's a rapist, Paddles.* Did those men make a habit of raping people? Were they serial rapists? Or maybe just one of them was, and the other two just followed? Was it a one-off and did they, or some of them, feel guilty afterwards and swear they would never do it again?

I'm a wild oat, Paddles. Somebody's wild oat. I'm a left-handed maybe-Dutch wild oat who can't sing.

CHAPTER FORTY-THREE

2012

LIZ

I'M LYING FLAT ON MY BACK AND ALL I CAN SEE IS THE CEILING. No, not quite flat. I'm tilted a bit—comfortable though. No spiderweb up there. Why would I expect...? There was some ceiling with a spider thing...a tightrope...stretching from an ordinary light. Not these awful tube things, so harsh. That other light was round and soft. Comforting. Like home. Makes me think of you, George. I need you, George.

A face hangs over me, blocking those lights. *Hello, Mom.*

Mom? This is nobody I know, this middle-aged woman.

"It's Eve, Mom."

No.

Is it?

Maybe.

The hair's right. The voice.

There's something I had to say to Eve. "I think I did something silly," I say. "I was talking to the other Eve, the young one, and she got upset. Tell her I'm sorry. Didn't mean to upset her. I forget what I said but..."

The woman is looking down at me, frowning as if she doesn't understand, and I suddenly hear myself: *Mmmmmmmmmbbbbbph.* I try to sit up, pulling hard on the blanket, but I can't. I try to speak again, but no proper words come out. Have to tell her...have to. How can I tell her if...have to tell her. I try to lift myself up again. The woman shakes her head at me, takes hold of my hand, but I need to...

"It's alright, Mom. Rosie understands. My daughter. Your granddaughter, Rosie. The one who looks like me when I was young."

Oh. Yes.

"You told her about Mexico. She needed to know. I was going to tell her myself. Maybe. Should have told her myself. So there's no harm done. She's upset now, but she'll be alright. Don't worry."

Always telling me not to worry. So annoying. But still. Maybe it *is* alright. No harm done, she says. Mexico. I told her about Mexico? What did I say? There was something bad…but it's gone. Important though. But this woman keeps saying there's no harm done. Too hard to talk…to move. I take a deep breath and close my eyes against those lights.

CHAPTER FORTY-FOUR

2012

ROSIE

ROSIE TOOK TO WALKING DOWN TO CARLIE'S SOMETIMES after school to avoid all the girl talk. In public, she claimed Carlie's was a good place to study. Eryn looked sceptical but they were all aware of exams looming so she didn't say much—just something sarcastic about aiming for Harvard. And she and Mark were a couple now, so Eryn was around less at weekends. She and Eryn still texted, but less often, and Rosie could dodge things in texts. They had not done anything together, just the two of them, since before…Before.

Rosie would sit at Carlie's dining table after school with her schoolbooks open in front of her, seeing nothing, then walk back home up the hill in time for supper. Sometimes she cooked supper for her mom and herself. One day, on the way down, Joel was suddenly there, walking beside her. He had this way of appearing out of nowhere, like a cobra rearing up in front of her face. The Cobra of Carbury Street. She said hi but couldn't manage a smile and afterwards she was glad she had not smiled.

"I see you're going to your aunt's more often these days," he said. "Had a fight with your mom?"

Was he spying on her? "No. Oh, no." Her reasons wouldn't sound too convincing but who cared. "Just seeing if I can study better at my aunt's house. Fewer distractions."

His eyebrows lifted like he didn't really believe her, and there was a lingering smirk as he spoke. "Yeah, mothers can be a problem. I keep out of the way of mine as much as I can—stay at my father's all the time these days."

Silence.

"I guess your mother and your aunt don't get along either, if you run off to your aunt's every time you're upset with your mom? Must keep them on their toes."

My god. What a creep! And what sort of relatives did he think she had? This was her family he was talking about. Something must have shown on her face because next thing Joel was saying *see you around*, pulling up his hood, and turning away. She was reminded of the hoodie across the street when she was waiting on the step that night. No! Yes. No. The walk was similar, the build. Coincidence. Pure coincidence. Anyway, it didn't matter. If it had really been Joel—how different he was from Kit. Kit would have bounced right across the road, asking what was wrong, asking if he could help before he'd come to a halt.

It was Kit who was worrying her now. Kit would want to know what the matter was, would dig until he found out, and she could not put him off anymore. She was going to a post-game party with him tomorrow night because he'd threatened to come round when she said she was not up to going out. Well, he meant it kindly, but it felt like a threat. She did not want to be alone with him, argue with him. And if he kissed her…? She didn't know what she would do if he kissed her. And of course he would. But she didn't think she could kiss him back. Those men were coming between her and everybody. Every Body. And if she felt this way, what must it have been like for her mother?

Her mother said Kit was maybe one person she could actually tell one day, when she was ready, which was an amazing vote of confidence. Mom had asked Rosie to let her know beforehand if she planned to tell anyone, because it was Mom's secret too. Well, no way was she ready. Right now, she thought she would never be ready. Mom said in that case, she just had to plead headaches to excuse past behaviour, and apologize, then behave as she always did. Be her normal self. *I wish.*

If she had to face Kit, Rosie wanted it to be in a crowd. Rosie could not handle being alone with him, looking him in the eye while she…while she lied to his face. You could not lie to Kit. He was too open, and anyway he would just know. But she couldn't tell him the truth.

So when she heard the guys were planning a party at Monty's after this last game on Friday, she said she would go.

Mom dropped her off and agreed to pick her up at eleven thirty. Rosie would text if she wanted to change anything. Two minutes later, she heard Kit was planning to take her home. He had the car.

"Watch out for him, Rosie," one of his buddies said, straight-faced. "First time he's driven since he passed his test."

"Careful when you shift gears, b'y. R doesn't stand for Rosie. Car goes backwards."

Ribald laughter. That's what it would say in a book. What was she going to do? She couldn't insist she went with her mom—couldn't do that to Kit. Here he was, drinking cola all night, and he'd probably had to fight for the car on a Friday. She must have shown the worry on her face. Kit put an arm around her.

"Don't believe that bunch, Rosie. Sure, I drove them out to the game in CBS just last week. No complaints. And Amy got a ride easy enough. Said she hoped you were feeling better."

They were all euphoric, and the room sizzled with excitement. They were jubilant because they had trounced the team that had played so dirty at their last game. They had qualified for the Next Level and were off to Somewhere New in two weeks for the first game. *Cheers.* The noise went on and on, up and up. She liked that usually; it meant Friday night. It meant being in the middle of things, having fun. Now her head was pounding and she wanted to scream. She had ordered a plate of fries but couldn't eat them. And what did it matter if the stupid ball went through a stupid hoop or who put it there or who stopped it? It was all so frigging trivial. And Kit was planning to spend his whole life on this kind of garbage. They'd been congratulating him about getting some volunteer coaching job in Toronto with inner city kids. In the summer. Too bad it wasn't next week—take the pressure off Rosie. She wanted to get out of there. Right that minute. She phoned her mother. *Come and get me. Now. Please. I'll be outside.* She waited five minutes before she did anything. Kit was listening to some boring sports rant from one of the guys and she waited for the burst of laughter at the end before tugging on his arm and saying, "Sorry, Kit. Gotta go. Not feeling—"

"I'll take you."

"No. Mom's on her way. Thanks. Sorry."

She was doing up her jacket and moving away but was still looking at him, and there was an expression on his face that... well, it was grim. Icy. He turned his back on her before she turned away herself. She'd hurt his feelings, should have let him take her home, should have explained as much as she could—that she'd had really bad news—but it was too late now. This was running away. Pure cowardice. She turned back to say something, but he'd started talking to one of the guys.

In the car, the only thought in her head was, *What should I do now?* She'd have to make the first move and she wasn't ready. She couldn't tell him, but she couldn't put on a good enough show to carry on as normal. The only other option was to break up and she didn't want to do that either. If only she could put life on hold for a few weeks until she was normal again. Mom must have felt like this, only way worse. No wonder her father... No wonder Michel left.

When Mom asked if everything was okay, Rosie just mumbled and shook her head. She went straight to Paddles when they were home, still with her jacket on. The dog stayed on his cushion although he gave a few sleepy wags and lifted his head for a moment. Mom stood looking at her and said, "Why so glum?"

"I think...I might have broken up with Kit. Kind of."

Mom sat on the floor by Paddles and stroked his back: stroke, pause, stroke, pause. "Don't let everything fall apart because of what happened. That's letting the bad guys win. Don't let them choose your friends eighteen years after the fact."

"He's going to Toronto to coach inner city kids."

Long silence.

"Kit's an idealist," her mom said. "He wants to put the world right. He doesn't care about doing the prestigious thing."

"What makes you think I care about prestige?" How could her mother think that? She did *not* care about that.

More silence.

"You need to be careful with people's dreams." *Watch out for those bubbles.* Her mom was scratching Paddles on that sweet spot behind his ears now and he lay back with his eyes closed and an ecstatic expression on his face.

Rosie said, "Well, anyway," and stood up. Paddles's head shot up and his eyes flew open and his whole body said, *You just ruined everything.*

That was Friday night. Rosie stayed home all Saturday and tried to concentrate on schoolwork, told Eryn and the girls she would not be on her phone all weekend. She wrote a bunch of emails to Kit and deleted all but one.

> *Sorry I was such bad company last night. Things on my mind—bad news but I can't explain more than that. And I never congratulated you on your coaching gig. I know you'll make a wonderful coach and will inspire the kids who sign up. (I hope there'll be some girls amongst them!!) Will you be coaching soccer or basketball or both? I'd like to know all about it, please.*
>
> *xx Rosie*

By Thursday, there was still no reply. For two hours Rosie struggled to keep her mind first on French verbs, then on chemistry, then she closed up her books and curled up on the loveseat next to Paddles, leaning down to smooth the safe part on the top of his head. His tail thumps were more vigorous now and he moved around enough to make his collar jingle. They still had to carry him into the kitchen to eat, and outside to use the bathroom, but at least he was standing these days, three legs only then switching legs. Now he perked up his ears and panted at her with his damp pink smile, wafting up the faint smell of warm dog.

Mom came and sat by Rosie, laid one hand on her back. It was comforting. But then Mom said she had been to see Nana, and Rosie shrank away, digging further into the back of the seat and turning her face into it, ignoring the tweedy scratchiness on her cheek. Not now. Please.

"Nana had a stroke after she saw you last week. They admitted her to hospital."

Oh god. No. "Hospital?"

"She's paralyzed on one side and her speech is affected."

Rosie could not put her thoughts together for a moment. She pulled her face out of the seat, and the air was cool on her cheek. "Is she going to get better?"

She had improved a little already. She was stable, and they said she was responding well. Her leg was moving more, and she might be able to walk again but, so far, she could not move her arm and could not speak. They sat in silence, then Mom said in her look-on-the-bright-side voice that there might be further improvement. These things took time. The medical people would send her back to Red Maples as soon as they could.

It took a while for the facts to sink in, then Rosie said, "I wonder what she remembers."

Nana had been very agitated when Mom visited, apparently. She had tried to tell Mom something, but it was just a big mumble. "I said it was good that she told you about Mexico and that you needed to be told. I said you were upset at the moment, but you would be fine." Mom thought Nana had seemed calmer after that. Maybe she had understood.

"I'm not up to visiting, Mom. Not yet."

"No. But soon."

Mexico, Paddles, Kit, and now Nana. What else could go wrong?

Life went on, school went on. Exams were still coming and coming. Ben came for a long weekend, but Rosie was hardly aware of him. Well yes, he was a big guy, he took up a lot of space, but Rosie did not have to make polite conversation or tiptoe around him this time. Ben just fitted in around them, behaved like part of the family. He went with her mom to visit Nana, and the whole family went to Aunt Ginny's for Sunday dinner. He was coming again at Easter. There was no talk about the future. Even Aunt Ginny, who was a great one for questions, didn't ask anything about the future.

There was still the constant girl talk about graduation: dresses, hair, who to take—Sean said if Rosie wasn't seeing Kit anymore, maybe she would go with him, and Rosie said yes. She didn't care whether she went or not. She felt drained, wrung out. But even during all the earlier tears and commotion, the awareness of Mexico stayed centre stage. She went to sleep thinking about it and if it was not in the foreground when she awoke, it was there by the time she brushed her teeth. And like a dark shadow, trailing behind, was the problem of Michel.

"Carlie, do you think Michel saw a rapist when he looked at me?"

Rosie had been waiting to ask this question, and it was definitely not something she could ask her mother. Carlie was silent for a while, motionless in her chair. "I think maybe he never got past finding your mom in the dunes, and maybe that's what he saw when he looked at you. I don't think he saw you as a person at all. He tried, but in the end, months later, he just said, *I can't do this.* And left."

"What would he see now?"

"Rosie, I'm going to show you some statistics about rape, the children of rape. It's not easy reading, and I have been wondering about showing you, but I think they may answer your question better than I can."

Rosie was thinking no, no I don't want to see this, but not saying anything out loud, and all the while Carlie was setting up her laptop on the coffee table in front of her.

"Bear in mind your mother loved you from the word go, and Michel never really accepted you." Rosie's shoulders stiffened, she couldn't help it, but Carlie kept right on talking. "Bear in mind you have always looked like your mother and behaved like her, right from the start." She swivelled her laptop round for Rosie to see, pressed the link, and said, "I'll be in the kitchen."

The Rwanda Genocide, April to July 1994.

The year Rosie was born.

Eight hundred thousand minority Tutsi were murdered by Hutu. Hutu nationalists encouraged the use of rape as a weapon, a demonstration of power, and a method of diluting the next generation of Tutsi. Between two thousand and five thousand babies were born to raped Tutsi women…

Rosie stopped reading. She could not do this. But the photographs below caught her eye. The pictures were of mothers with the children of their rape, taken ten years or so later. The first mother stood with an arm round her little girl, holding her close and smiling, and the girl was wearing a neat sundress in bright orange and yellow, and had a huge gap-toothed smile. The commentary read, *She's my daughter and I love her. That's all that matters.*

The second was a picture of a mother and son with a noticeable space between them, turned away from each other. The woman's face was set in bitter lines, her mouth tight and unsmiling. The boy was hunched over, looking angry and sullen. The commentary read, *Every time I look at him I see that Hutu soldier.*

Imagine…no, don't imagine. Rosie went over and over that article until her aunt called her for lunch, then dragged herself down to the kitchen and scuffed over to the table.

"You're making that sandwich curl up at the edges, staring at it like that."

How could she eat anything?

"D'you think, if Michel saw me now, he would think the same way?"

Carlie stood with both hands on the table and leaned on them, bending toward Rosie.

"I've no idea, Rosie, but why would you care?" She sounded angry, exasperated.

"Because—" She could not form the words, could not explain to herself, certainly not to anyone else.

"Rosie." Still angry. "What is it you really want? From Michel?"

She'd wanted him to come home, to be her father, to be a family. But now? She looked away and after a minute she said, "I want him to be sorry he left."

⁂

She had to see him. Maybe it was stupid, but it was the only way to put her mind at rest once and for all. She imagined scenarios with Michel alone and others with his new wife present. Rosie would be articulate and logical and utterly in control each time. The wife of course would be a bitch—beautiful, probably, and elegant, but dismissive and arrogant. Rosie would sail in and sail out victorious, having put Michel in his place and ignored the wife and made them both realize Rose Wallace was a force to be reckoned with. But wouldn't that make him even more glad that he had left? This thought edged its way in whenever Rosie paused for breath. Did she want to convince him of her worth instead? Her niceness? Did she need a testimonial to say she had never pulled the wings off of butterflies?

His wife wouldn't know anything about her. Wait, yes, of course she would. Will his wife speak English? She will probably speak a dozen languages fluently. Too bad Rosie can't dazzle them with her French. Will Michel have to stop and translate as they go along? That would mess up the flow. She'd never get on a roll then.

Rosie told her mother she was going to Paris at Easter, no matter what. Easter Sunday would be on April 8 this year. She had almost enough money saved for a return flight, but she would need to borrow the rest. Please? She did not want to sit in the airport all night but… She'd get a job in the summer and pay her back.

Everyone argued with her and said she might feel even worse afterwards, especially Aunt Ginny. She would not be able to concentrate on exams, they said. But Rosie insisted she had not been able to do a stitch of studying since the day she had heard the news, and she'd have four weeks after Easter until exams started when she could really concentrate. Mom said she was glad she was at least considering her future. "Will it put your mind at rest enough to start studying right now, if I book tickets?"

So, Mom would go too, but not to the meeting with Michel, and no, Mom would not interfere in any way.

"Carlie?" Winning smile. Rosie's most persuasive voice.

"Cut the crap, Rosie. Just say what you want to say."

Carlie made you grind your teeth sometimes. "Would you look after Paddles while Mom and I go to Paris, please?"

"Of course I will. Your mom asked me the other day." Oh. Well, good. Kind of. Only this was Mom interfering already.

She had to let Eryn know. Eryn was always more easygoing when she was with Mark, but still. Rosie deliberately waited until the last minute. Then she sent a whole email about going to meet her father. In Paris. And Eryn texted back, *Wow!!! Tell me everything when you're home.* Then there was Kit. Rosie had written again—three times in all. No response. Absolutely nothing.

As for studying: she had to get into a university away from here, but maybe not too far. She'd sent off applications, all to universities in eastern Canada. So now she really had to study—study and Catch Up. After Paris.

Reservations had been made. Mom received a "communication" through Mr. Wojcik: M. Michel Simard would be at the Café Such-and-Such at three o'clock, et cetera et cetera, with his wife, who spoke excellent English. Well, that cut the possibilities down some. The remaining unknowns were his new wife's attitude and Michel's own.

Remember Nana's rule: if you don't have all the ingredients, improvise. Rosie would have to line up all the points she wanted to get across and reduce them to their briefest, punchiest form, then play it by ear.

CHAPTER FORTY-FIVE

2012

ROSIE

HER MOTHER ASKED TWICE WHAT ROSIE PLANNED TO SAY to Michel. Twice, from Mom, was almost nagging. Rosie did not wish to discuss it with her mother, did not wish to hear reasons for not saying, not asking, not feeling…no censoring.

"I'm working on it," she said each time.

"Remember, he allowed his name to be used on your birth certificate. Not every man would have done that." On the plane, Mom said Michel was expert at hiding his feelings. Rosie must not expect to read his face or his body language—there would be nothing to read.

Her whole attention was on her meeting with Michel, so Rosie hardly noticed stopping over in Toronto, hardly noticed Paris. Yes, she saw the Eiffel Tower in the distance and heard all the French voices—Parisian French not Québécois—but they were hardly real. Mom stopped pointing out things when Rosie didn't respond, said they would sightsee tomorrow instead.

A waiter showed her to their table when she arrived at the café a careful four minutes late. The place was all wrought iron and flowers, low murmurs and the clinking of glasses, but Rosie was too focused on Michel and his wife to notice more than that. It was their elegance that caught her eye: simple but perfect, both of them. That was Mom's philosophy too.

Michel looked older than his photographs, but the same—thinner in the face, maybe. His hands were tanned, darker than his face. He must wear a hat a lot. He was still tall and slim and classy in the way he dressed, the way he held himself. It was his mouth that looked different. He wasn't smiling. All his photos showed a gorgeous wide smile with just a glimpse of neat bottom teeth. Now, Michel's mouth looked narrow and straight with disappointingly thin lips.

He stood as Rosie approached, introduced Justine, his wife, then indicated the chair opposite and they all sat down. Nobody shook hands. Michel offered coffee, which Rosie declined, and he asked about the flight. Then, as soon as she was settled and the waiter had disappeared, he said in a brisk, let's-get-this-over-with voice, all business, "So, Rose. What can I do for you?"

Her spine stiffened. She was conscious of her back coming away from her chair, of her weight shifting forward onto her feet. If she were a cat, her claws would be out. That's not the way a father should greet a long-lost daughter—an almost-father. Frig, this was not how she'd planned to start. Breathe. Think karate. She let down her shoulders and her rib cage.

"I had all kinds of reasons for coming, things to say, things to ask, but now they've all flown out of my head."

She'd rehearsed an impish Carlie-grin to go with this sentence but now it felt inappropriate, so she kept her face blank. Michel just sat there. At the edge of Rosie's vision, the wife gave her an encouraging smile. Justine. Her head had come forward and tilted as if she were listening carefully, and that was definitely an encouraging smile, not a sneer. Afterwards Rosie would never be able to recall exactly what Michel's wife looked like—she had the same overall effect of a well-tended garden: beauty with a soft blend of textures, shapes, and colours. And perfume. But no details. It was Michel she remembered.

A different waiter appeared at her elbow asking if mademoiselle had decided yet. Yes, mademoiselle had decided. She didn't want a frigging thing paid for by Michel thank you, or anything she might spill, either. *Rien pour moi, merci.* She glared at the guy but his eyes slithered past, settling on Michel, and Michel sighed and said he could bring some pastries. The waiter gave a creepy little smile and nodded a knowing us-men-together nod and oozed away and Rosie glared at Michel instead.

"I wanted to meet you. I've always wanted to meet you. I wish you had come to see how I turned out."

No reaction.

"I haven't done too badly. Not that I brought my report card or anything…" Rosie allowed the tiniest smile but got no reaction to that either. "…Or my brown belt in karate. Mom wanted me to learn to defend myself. She says you're always alone when it comes to the crunch." Yes, she wanted to get that comment in. She was looking directly at Michel as she said this, and his face didn't alter by a millimetre, but out of the corner of her eye Rosie saw his wife's hands twitch.

The waiter was back with a frilly dish full of mille-feuilles and other luscious-looking cookies she would normally drool over, and he laid it down with a toreador flourish. Rosie waited until he was gone. Breathe.

"Growing up, I always wanted you to come home and be a father. I guess that's a normal wish for any child with a single parent. Then, when I found out the truth, I wanted to come and beat you to a pulp for leaving my mother to face everything by herself."

Now there was a look of pain in his eyes and a tightening of his lips. So, he wasn't total marble.

"But I do have to thank you for putting your name on my birth certificate. That must have gone against all your instincts, and I take it as a measure of how much you loved Mom." She said thank you on her own behalf too. It had been a generous thing to do. Rosie would hate someone behind a desk at the passport office to read *father unknown* along with the application. They would probably turn out to be somebody's cousin, knowing St. John's, the City of Wagging Tongues. Nobody moved, but there was a sense of softening around the table, the slightest easing of diplomatic tensions.

"Did you…" said Michel. "Do you think it carries… responsibilities?"

"What? I'm sorry. I don't understand."

Michel gave a little dismissive wave of his hand and said to carry on. Well, she was trying to, if he'd stop interrupting.

"Of course, later I realized it was not my mother you couldn't face, it was me." She paused here to gather her strength. This was the hard part. His wife, Justine, reached a hand an inch toward Rosie then withdrew it. "It was Carlie who made me look *that* little fact in the face, not Mom."

A tiny nod from Michel.

"Carlie showed me statistics about rape victims in Rwanda: how mothers sometimes took the daughters to their hearts but hated the sons because they reminded them of the soldier-rapist-fathers. And I've come to realize that the same kind of thing might have happened to you, in reverse. I can't forgive you. I don't think I can ever forgive you. But I understand." But she had to be honest here. "Or I'm trying to understand. That's the best I can do."

Rosie sat back. For all the speechifying she had practiced, there was really nothing else she wanted to say. This was the part that showed her maturity and benevolence, so now he could say something about being glad she came or whatever.

Justine stood, leaned over, and rested her hands on Rosie's shoulders, kissed her on both cheeks, said how brave she was and what a lovely person she has turned out to be. Rosie felt tears come into her eyes. She was not going to cry. No way. But the tears kept coming. And Michel's face was a blur just when she wanted to see. *Sorry. Tired...Nana's stroke...exams...jet lag.*

Michel was saying something about Nana having a stroke, sounding surprised, saying how sorry he was.

Rosie just nodded. Yes.

She gritted her teeth, dug in her pocket for a tissue and there wasn't one so she had to squeeze her hand down past her wallet and phone in her tiny Fossil purse and by the time she'd teased out one tissue, her nose had dripped onto the back of her hand and she had to wipe her hand and blow and...how humiliating. She glared at the two of them and saw Justine was holding out one of her tissues. Well, she might have said! Michel wasn't noticing at all. He was saying how Rosie was very like her Aunt Caroline.

"Like Eve too. You're all Wallace, anyway, and I can't give you a greater compliment." There was a trace of a smile and then it was gone. "I'm sorry, Rose. For everything. You don't know how often I've regretted taking that swim. But apart from that, given my time back, there is nothing else I could have done differently."

Nothing. What does he mean, Nothing? She stared at him and realized her mouth was open and closed it, and he was looking a bit surprised, looking as if he'd expected her, Rosie, to say something. Breathe. But…nothing?

"I did what I could, did my duty—a lot more than my duty, in fact. Helped Eve with…" His lips were still moving, those skimpy lips, but Rosie didn't hear anything else. His wife leaned over and put a hand on his knee, and he stopped talking, looked at Justine with his eyebrows up.

Duty. His *Duty.* That's all Rosie was. Ever. She was some bill to pay every month like oil and electricity. Somebody else's bill that he was noble enough to pay. Not done for her sake, Rosie's. He'd paid *Eve's* mortgage. He didn't care whether Rosie lived or died. He'd forgotten…no, not forgotten, because she, Rosie, was never in his head to forget. He really had been indifferent all along. Frankly, my dear…

"You did your duty." Her voice wobbled a bit, and she swallowed and sat tall to give her throat some space. "How very *gracious* of you."

He was looking puzzled. She had to get out of there, fast, before she did something. She stood and the two of them stood too, but she was turning to leave before they were fully on their feet, turning so fast she caught the strap of her purse on the back of the chair and the chair bounced after her then fell with a clang.

Rosie walked as quickly as those stupid shoes would allow. Stupid, stupid shoes, meant to wow an almost-father with their high-heeled elegance, legs arranged just so, at a table—the way her Aunt Caroline arranged her gorgeous long legs when she was out to impress. Those shoes were not designed for almost running, sweating like a horse, along a sidewalk. *Bastard, bastard, bastard.* She could feel the strain on the heels, hear the creaks—only meant to take weight when they were vertical, not at however many degrees they were angled right now—at the end of her longest stride. She shortened her step so they wouldn't skid. *Bastard.* But bastard was not the right word, was it? It was Rosie…she was not slowing down, not for him, not for anybody. Duty. He'd done his duty. Blind, holier-than-thou frigging duty. Not in the least sorry he left. Never would be sorry he left. *Bastard.*

She marched. She slammed her heels down and charged along with her arms pumping and her purse bouncing, tipped forward because of those shoes, weight forced onto the toes, bunching them up, squeezing them, and Rosie ignored everything in favour of turning the hurt and anger into movement, something blindly physical. Dust blew into her eyes, flicked up by passing cars, and she rubbed at them, which was a mistake because she was probably smearing mascara all over her face.

She checked her purse, hoping that tissue was still tucked into the top, just as her so-elegant left heel jammed in a crevice. Her foot was held back in a vice while her body kept going, swivelling a little around that fixed point, and there was a snap as the heel cracked off. Then she was trying to get her feet under her to keep from falling, but she went down so fast—down on her knees and falling hardest on her right hand and it *hurt*—that crunch down onto unyielding concrete and that burning sharp pain. It jarred everything right up to her head, which stopped just short of smashing into the sidewalk. And there in front of her nose was a glob of something slimy, like someone had coughed up a lung and it hadn't dried out yet, and her hair swept through it. She could picture her hair all slimed together and felt a shuddering disgust and an urgent need to wash it off—more urgent than all the rest.

It took a while for Rosie to stand up because everything hurt more when she used it for leverage. Finally she stood, leaning against a wall and nursing her right arm, tilting her head to keep her hair away from her skin, keening with the pain then hearing herself and trying to stifle the sound, although there was nobody around to hear anyway. Then she noticed the chorus of smaller pains and stings and burns—from her knees and feet, the other palm, her shoulder, the metallic smell of blood. *Mom. I'm hurt, Mom.* Oh, god, her mother didn't know where she was. She would be worried. Must phone.

But then, Rosie didn't know where she was either.

There were no signs anywhere. She looked up and down the street, and there was a man in the distance walking away from her, but nobody behind, nobody heading her way. She could hardly see anything on the other side of the road through the cars parked nose to tail on both sides; a man's bald head sailed by over distant car roofs, oblivious. Dusty warmth puffed through gaps between vehicles parked on her side with every swish of traffic. The sidewalks were reasonably clean, as sidewalks went, but there were still grit and dust and cigarette ends—so many more smokers here than at home—and shiny fragments that might be glass. They were all things she didn't want stuck in her feet, but she was going to have to walk, to find out where she was. She tried to pick out the largest piece of grit embedded in her knee but it just sank in further and the blood welled out faster so she left it there.

Buildings stretched endlessly in both directions without a break, and she could not remember crossing any roads or even driveways although, surely, she must have done. Stone buildings rose above her four, no five storeys high, leaning, swaying dizzily. She closed her eyes. She had passed shop doorways as she walked along but now she was by a blank wall, not a door in sight. This was not the road Rosie had taken to go to meet Michel. The café was on a corner so she must have taken the road at right angles to it.

She hobbled along in her stocking feet—not that there was much stocking left—picking her way around the miniature flotsam and jetsam of Paris now looming larger on the not-so-clean sidewalk. She held her arm across her chest in the position Aunt Ginny had strapped Nana's arm when she broke it that time. Steps for Survival: find out where you are, Rosie Wallace, and then phone Mom. After an age, she came to a little store smelling of curry, then tried to dredge up the French for *Where am I?* Later she might enjoy remembering the farcical mixture of Newfoundland French and Punjabi French in that excitable, top-of-the-voice exchange, but Rosie was too distraught at that moment. She managed to extract a street name, definitely different from the one first taken, and a street number. The lady helped pull out Rosie's phone which was jammed so tightly in that infuriating purse (to be thrown in the garbage as soon as she was home, although she would have preferred to throw it out the plane window over the Atlantic.) Then she had to extricate herself from those sweet, concerned people who sounded ready to phone ambulances and police and a choir of angels on her behalf.

She made it out of the store and limped up the street a safe distance, saying, *non merci, non merci*. Then she leaned against a wall and phoned Mom. Poor Mom. She was so worried, panicked, kept saying, *Where are you?* And the phone kept fading and Rosie was shouting the address over and over in case it died altogether, drowning out Mom's questions: *Are you alright? Are you safe?* Then the phone gave out as Mom was saying something about a cab…

And while she waited, Rosie leaned and closed her eyes and tried not to think about all the bits that hurt. She thought of Nana's warm hugs and gingerbread cookies, of how they always phoned Aunt Ginny if they were in trouble, of Carlie's stories of coping with problems in foreign places. And most of all, she thought of her mother, overpowered by three disgusting perverts, overpowered by the memories of it ever since, but always loving and protecting Rosie in every possible way.

She kept shifting her weight from foot to foot like a tired horse. Had to get off her feet. She slid down the wall with difficulty, making her knees scream and setting one of them off bleeding again. But now she could rest both feet and sit with her back to the wall. She'd get up again in a minute so her mom could see her. She started counting seconds, just as she had when she was waiting for Carlie the night she found out.

And that scumbag, Joel…had that hoodie been Joel? How could she possibly have compared her family with his? She must have been out of her mind. Her family was highly functional, giving her everything she'd ever needed. When Mom was out of sorts, another family member filled in until she was better. Teamwork. What Kit so admired. Kit. And she had been so, so mean to Kit. She had to talk to him, somehow. Oh, Kit, take care of yourself in those rough places. I know you're big, but you'll be all alone and you're so trusting. Please. Please. Come home safe.

She heard Mom's voice calling, frantic, but didn't know how to stand up. Everything felt frozen as if it had set in protective mode—splinted itself. She tried to call out, but her throat felt splinted too, and her voice hardly reached the end of her nose. Then her mom was dropping down in front of her on her knees with her arms out, tears streaming, eyes terrified.

"I'm fine, Mom. I'm fine. Just fell in those stupid shoes. Must look a mess. Got my hair in some pukey stuff on the sidewalk." She let go of the other arm to point at her hair and winced. "Think I broke my arm."

Mom was wiping her face and said, "We'll get you to a hospital." Then Rosie became aware of scuffed suede-looking brown shoes next to her mother and a pair of jeans rising to a green checked shirt and a scruffy chin. "Bonjour," said Rosie. It was painful getting into the cab. The driver rushed to help her up off the ground but he yanked on Rosie's shoulder and made her squawk, and when he tried to help her into the cab he didn't understand Rosie's French and wasn't listening to Mom on her other side, so he did his own thing and kept rushing her. She was slow placing her foot carefully on the floor of the cab, and he pushed her in on top of it before she was organized and... Well, you could tell he was more used to heaving suitcases.

It took ages to reach l'Urgence, though the driver insisted this hospital was the closest. Then Mom was ages at the registration desk, first with one woman asking questions, then a second, then a man joined them. And there was Mom's fluent-sounding French weaving through it all, with the word *Assurance* for punctuation. Then she was showing them something on her phone. But Rosie had total confidence her mother would sort it out. This was Competent Mom, In-Charge Mom. Rosie did not have to hover around her, wondering if she might freeze or collapse or go off in a daze. This was a lady with a mission. It must be how she was at work, focused on someone else's problems. How she must have been Before.

There was another woman at the desk now. Well, a couple really, only it was the woman doing all the talking, in Spanish-flavoured French. There seemed to be some confusion over her name, and she had a whole string of them: Castel-something and Echeverria and Garcia and something with Nuovo in the middle. Some of Rosie's classmates had two parental surnames, but this woman must have names back to the great-grandparents on both sides—what a weight of ancestry to carry around. In that culture would Rosie have to have *Nada* in her name? No thank you. She was plain Rosie Wallace and liked it that way.

Mom wheeled her into a more select waiting room, and after a while Rosie was siphoned off into a cubicle and given pain medications and then brought back again. She could still hear the Spanish lady's voice along the corridor, faster and louder now. It was full of those throat-scraping j sounds, the jota, and her Spanish rrrs rattling right over the softer French ones, flattening, dominating. Mom in the dunes. Rosie's head was floating, and she wasn't in charge of her lips or tongue any more, or her thoughts. All the aching, throbbing, burning pieces of her blurred into one fuzzy soreness, and after a while all she could differentiate clearly was the forearm. She was aware of herself mumbling and rambling so she stopped, but her thoughts kept on rambling.

She had been so mean to Mom. Every time she whined about her missing father it must have implied her mother was not adequate, which was so not true. Poor Mom. What she had gone through for Rosie's sake… She had taken so much garbage from Rosie and had hardly ever fought back. And maybe she, Rosie, had triggered flashbacks and horror-memories in Michel too. Not going to think about that. But really, what could Michel have done for her that the rest of the family hadn't? Why had she thought she needed him in the first place? Better to have no father than one who rejected her, and he must have realized that. He *had* given her a legal identity, given her a home and stability through that mortgage. And he'd always been honest with her—she had never thought of that before, never given him credit. Look at that last letter—it had been kind and thoughtful really. Rosie had toasted it because she couldn't face the unpalatable truth. How childish! Really, her whole behaviour had been childish, including coming here to Paris.

Realization flooded her. *Rosie Wallace, you have been a fucking idiot.*

She thumped her hand down on her thigh and the pain brought back her awareness. My god, all this extra trouble for a silly pair of shoes. Where were they? Still on the sidewalk, probably in a worse state than she was. Thoughts glided and circled like vultures around carrion. The dead dreams of having a father. No—poetic, but no. It was Rosie they were flapping over, ready to tear her apart. Who am I? *I'm Nobody! Who are you? Are you - Nobody - too?*

That was one of Emily Dickinson's poems with all the dashes and dots. Kit's friend Nancy was a big fan. Was Rosie Nobody? She was always saying to herself, *What would Carlie do now? What would Nana say?* Or she would think of how Eryn might act and do the opposite—not copying but still being influenced. Or she would be halfway to saying something, then stop because it might upset her mom.

Why did she always have to have a role model or a precedent or permission, for god's sake, before she could make a move? Was she a gutless shadow with no voice of her own? *Collect the data first.* Shut up! The only times she'd really insisted on her own way, like this trip, she'd been wrong. But at least she now knew she did not need a father. At least there was so much here-and-now family presence that there was no room… And yes, Dutch Dude; try squeezing your rotten Nature in amongst all this Nurture.

There were x-rays of her arm and right foot, glass and gravel removed from everything, and that never-ending cleansing with stinging solutions of Javex or its medical knock-off: battalions of molecules with pointy purposeful teeth, hunting for germs. Then they gave her a back slab for the broken left arm—not a cast because of the swelling, just something to protect it until she could see an orthopaedic person at home. Steri-strips and needles and a pressure bandage for her knee and a cushion thing for her right foot. And thank heavens Mom was there to take over with the listening and explaining because it would have been beyond Rosie. It seemed a long time before her head stopped free floating and began to feel synchronized with the rest of her. And intermittently, around and through all the interventions and the waiting, they talked.

"I didn't lose it, Mom."

"Of course you didn't. You never do."

"Got tears in my eyes though—kind of mad about that at the time."

"But are you glad you came?"

Rosie reached over and took her mom's hand with her free one and held it tight. "I'm sorry I put you through all this. I know it was ridiculous but… Yes, Mom, I am." She sat back again. "You know when you stand up at the end of an exam and all the information drains down to your toes and out through the soles of your feet?" She looked down at her pink, sterilized feet. "There goes Michel."

CHAPTER FORTY-SIX

2012

ROSIE

BEFORE THE TRIP TO PARIS, MOM KEPT ASKING ROSIE TO go see Nana—and Rosie kept procrastinating. Nana was back at Red Maples and they all said she was improving, was sitting up well and walking to the bathroom with a tripod cane in her good hand and one person on her other side. That meant no urgency, right? Mom kept saying, *go and make your peace,* but her mom had explained to Nana already and said it had calmed her down, and Nana could never tell the difference between the two of them anyway. It was not as if Rosie had had a fight with her or anything, so what did Mom mean, *make your peace?*

But she had gone in the end. They had stopped in on their way to the airport and Mom had waited outside. The day before yesterday. Was that really only two days ago?

Nana had been sitting in a chair with her arm on a pillow, but it was as if half of her had slid downhill—just a centimetre or so, but...and when she smiled only half her mouth turned up and her lips twisted in a non-Nana way and her nose was pulled a tiny bit off centre and...it just wasn't Nana. Rosie wanted to grab the droopy side and push it back up. Her eyes blurred and she dived at her grandmother, burying her face in the blanket over her knees, in horror and remorse and a desperate wish not to let Nana see her thoughts. Nana might have trouble understanding words, but sometimes she seemed to know what you didn't say. They stayed like that for ages, then Rosie lifted her head.

"Nana. I'm so sorry. Sorry I ran out like that. Sorry I didn't come and see you sooner." She sat back on her heels, and Nana was patting her shoulder with her good hand and trying to say something that sounded like *Boned* and shaking her head. Was that *Don't*?

"Okay, I won't." Rosie wiped her eyes and blew her nose and smiled. "I won't." And Nana was smiling too, and nodding, so it had been a good guess. "I'm glad you told me about Mexico, Nana. I needed to hear that. I didn't want to hear it, didn't want to believe it, but I needed to know. You can't build your life on a lie."

Nana was frowning a bit, her eyebrows still trying to move together in the old way. She was not disagreeing, just concentrating. Rosie knew that look. *Speak slowly, Rosie Wallace, so she can take it in. Say it again, to make sure.* "I'm so, so glad you told me about Mexico."

Pause.

The nurse said Nana fatigued quickly, so just say the rest clearly and leave.

"I'm going to see Michel tomorrow, Nana." She waited a minute, but Nana was still frowning and concentrating, staring at her. "I'm going to see Michel tomorrow," she said, more slowly. "I want him to see that I've turned out okay. Show him what he's missed." She pulled herself up tall, there on her knees. She said that last bit again and waited a moment then nodded and stood up. "I'll tell you all about it when we come back." She gave her grandmother another hug and a kiss on the cheek, waved from the doorway, and left.

LIZ

Oh dear. Mexico. Michel…But my girl was smiling. A real all-the-way-through smile, so she must feel confident inside. That feels—right. That's what we wanted, George, isn't it? Remind me. We wanted her to be confident after she found out…

whatever it was. Right? Good. I can close my eyes at last and let everything go. I'm glad you're driving. I hate driving in the rain. But it's brighter up ahead, George—I think we're driving out of it.

ACKNOWLEDGEMENTS AND THANKS

TO WHITNEY MORAN, MANAGING EDITOR OF VAGRANT PRESS (Nimbus Publishing) for the suggested restructuring of an early draft that gave this novel its shape, and to all the people who have since helped put meat on its bones.

For background information on various topics, thanks to Alison Drover, Jon Drover, Diana Gustafson, Rebecca Horsman, Mary Lawlor, Andrea MacDonald, John R., John K., and Kate Sinnott. Any errors are my own. Amongst the written research, the Pelican book *How to Think like an Anthropologist* by Matthew Engelke was especially helpful.

For ongoing learning of the art and craft of writing, there are too many people to mention in this writing-rich province: Michael Crummy, Ed Kavanagh, Robert Finley, Don Mackay, Lisa Moore, Anne Simpson—to name just a few. Also, for the stimulation of the annual literary awards and festivals, with all the extra effort involved in these trying Covid times.

To members of the Newfoundland Writers Guild, for all their thoughtful comments.

To the Port Authority writing group, which grew out of Lisa Moore's wonderful creative fiction course, for ten years of challenging and nurturing: Sharon Bala, Melissa Barbeau, Jamie Fitzpatrick, Carrie Ivardi, Morgan Murray, and those who have moved on.

To Vagrant editors Emily MacKinnon and Claire Bennet, for all their care and patience.

To the city of St. John's, Newfoundland and Labrador, for providing the setting (although the story could have taken place in any small city anywhere), with apologies for the fictional additions.

Most of all, to my lovely family. This book would not exist without the inspiration, support, and encouragement from my family, past and present. Thank you for Being There.

Photo by Rhonda Hayward Photography

SUSAN SINNOTT is a Newfoundland writer who grew up in the UK and now lives in St. John's. Her first novel, *Catching the Light* (2018), won the 2019 Ann Connor Brimer Award and was long- and short-listed for several awards, including the 2020 International Dublin Literary Award. *The Remembering* is her second novel.